Agatha Christie

AGATHA CHRISTIE

MURDER IN MESOPOTAMIA

Complete and Unabridged

ULVERSCROFT
Leicester

First published in Great Britain in 1936 by
Collins
London

First Large Print Edition
published 2010
by arrangement with
HarperCollins*Publishers* Limited
London

British Library CIP Data

Christie, Agatha, *1890 – 1976.*
  Murder in Mesopotamia.
  1. Poirot, Hercule (Fictitious character)- -Fiction.
  2. Private investigators- -Belgium- -Fiction.
  3. Excavations (Archaeology)- -Iraq- -Fiction.
  4. Detective and mystery stories. 5. Large type books.
  I. Title
  823.9'12–dc22

  ISBN 978–1–44480–254–2

Published by
F. A. Thorpe (Publishing)
Anstey, Leicestershire

Set by Words & Graphics Ltd.
Anstey, Leicestershire
Printed and bound in Great Britain by
T. J. International Ltd., Padstow, Cornwall

This book is printed on acid-free paper

46 841 383 X

Agatha Christie is known throughout the world as the Queen of Crime. She is the most widely published author of all time and in any language, outsold only by the Bible and Shakespeare. She is the author of 80 crime novels and short story collections, 19 plays, and six novels written under the name of Mary Westmacott.

Agatha Christie's first novel, *The Mysterious Affair at Styles*, was written towards the end of the First World War, in which she served as a VAD. In it she created Hercule Poirot, the little Belgian detective who was destined to become the most popular detective in crime fiction since Sherlock Holmes.

Agatha Christie was made a Dame in 1971. She died in 1976.

MURDER IN MESOPOTAMIA

It is clear to Amy Leatheran that something sinister is going on at the Hassanieh
dig in Iraq; something associated with the
presence of 'Lovely Louise', wife of cel-
ebrated archaeologist Dr Leidner. In a few
days' time Hercule Poirot is due to drop in
at the excavation site. But with Louise
suffering from terrifying hallucinations, and
tension within the group becoming almost
unbearable, Poirot might just be too late . . .

Dedicated to
My many archaeological friends
in Iraq and Syria

Contents

Foreword
by Giles Reilly, MD

The events chronicled in this narrative took place some four years ago. Circumstances have rendered it necessary, in my opinion, that a straightforward account of them should be given to the public. There have been the wildest and most ridiculous rumours suggesting that important evidence was suppressed and other nonsense of that kind. Those misconstructions have appeared more especially in the American Press.

For obvious reasons it was desirable that the account should not come from the pen of one of the expedition staff, who might reasonably be supposed to be prejudiced.

I therefore suggested to Miss Amy Leatheran that she should undertake the task. She is obviously the person to do it. She had a professional character of the highest, she is not biased by having any previous connection with the University of Pittstown Expedition to Iraq and she was an observant and intellectual eye-witness.

It was not very easy to persuade Miss Leatheran to undertake this task — in fact, persuading her was one of the hardest jobs of my professional career — and even after it was completed she displayed a curious reluctance to let me see the manuscript. I discovered that this was partly due to some critical remarks she had made concerning my daughter Sheila. I soon disposed of that, assuring her that as children criticize their parents freely in print nowadays, parents are only too delighted when their offspring come in for their share of abuse! Her other objection was extreme modesty about her literary style. She hoped I would 'put the grammar right and all that.' I have, on the contrary, refused to alter so much as a single word. Miss Leatheran's style in my opinion is vigorous, individual and entirely apposite. If she calls Hercule Poirot 'Poirot' in one paragraph and 'Mr Poirot' in the next, such a variation is both interesting and suggestive. At one moment she is, so to speak, 'remembering her manners' (and hospital nurses are great sticklers for etiquette) and at the next her interest in what she is telling is that of a pure human being — cap and cuffs forgotten!

The only thing I have done is to take the liberty of writing a first chapter — aided by a letter kindly supplied by one of Miss Leatheran's friends. It is intended to be in the nature of a frontispiece — that is, it gives a rough sketch of the narrator.

1

Frontispiece

In the hall of the Tigris Palace Hotel in Baghdad a hospital nurse was finishing a letter. Her fountain-pen drove briskly over the paper.

. . . Well, dear, I think that's really all my news. I must say it's been nice to see a bit of the world — though England for me every time, thank you. The *dirt* and the *mess* in Baghdad you wouldn't believe — and not romantic at all like you'd think from the *Arabian Nights*! Of course, it's pretty just on the river, but the town itself is just awful — and no proper shops at all. Major Kelsey took me through the bazaars, and of course there's no denying they're *quaint* — but just a lot of rubbish and hammering away at copper pans till they make your head ache — and not what I'd like to use myself unless I was sure about the cleaning. You've got to be so careful of verdigris with copper pans.

I'll write and let you know if anything comes of the job that Dr Reilly spoke about. He said this American gentleman was in Baghdad now and might come and see me this afternoon. It's for his wife — she has 'fancies', so Dr Reilly said. He didn't say any more than that, and of course, dear, one knows what that *usually means* (but I hope not actually D.T.s!). Of course, Dr Reilly didn't *say* anything — but he had a look — if you know what I mean. This Dr Leidner is an archaeologist and is digging up a mound out in the desert somewhere for some American museum.

Well, dear, I will close now. I thought what you told me about little Stubbins was simply *killing*! Whatever did Matron say?

No more now.

Yours ever,

Amy Leatheran

Enclosing the letter in an envelope, she addressed it to Sister Curshaw, St Christopher's Hospital, London.

As she put the cap on her fountain-pen, one of the native boys approached her.

'A gentleman come to see you. Dr Leidner.'

Nurse Leatheran turned. She saw a man of middle height with slightly stooping shoulders, a brown beard and gentle, tired eyes.

Dr Leidner saw a woman of thirty-five or thereabouts, of erect, confident bearing. He saw a good-humoured face with slightly prominent blue eyes and glossy brown hair. She looked, he thought, just what a hospital nurse for a nervous case ought to look. Cheerful, robust, shrewd and matter-of-fact.

Nurse Leatheran, he thought, would do.

2

Introducing Amy Leatheran

I don't pretend to be an author or to know anything about writing. I'm doing this simply because Dr Reilly asked me to, and somehow when Dr Reilly asks you to do a thing you don't like to refuse.

'Oh, but, doctor,' I said, 'I'm not literary — not literary at all.'

'Nonsense!' he said. 'Treat it as case notes, if you like.'

Well, of course, you *can* look at it that way.

Dr Reilly went on. He said that an unvarnished plain account of the Tell Yarimjah business was badly needed.

'If one of the interested parties writes it, it won't carry conviction. They'll say it's biased one way or another.'

And of course that was true, too. I was in it all and yet an outsider, so to speak.

'Why don't you write it yourself, doctor?' I asked.

'I wasn't on the spot — you were. Besides,' he added with a sigh, 'my daughter won't let me.'

The way he knuckles under to that chit of a girl of his is downright disgraceful. I had half a mind to say so, when I saw that his eyes were twinkling. That was the worst of Dr Reilly. You never knew whether he was joking or not. He always said things in the same slow melancholy way — but half the time there was a twinkle underneath it.

'Well,' I said doubtfully, 'I suppose I *could*.'

'Of course you could.'

'Only I don't quite know how to set about it.'

'There's a good precedent for that. Begin at the beginning, go on to the end and then leave off.'

'I don't even know quite where and what the beginning was,' I said doubtfully.

'Believe me, nurse, the difficulty of beginning will be nothing to the difficulty of knowing how to stop. At least that's the way it is with me when I have to make a speech. Someone's got to catch hold of my coat-tails and pull me down by main force.'

'Oh, you're joking, doctor.'

'It's profoundly serious I am. Now what about it?'

Another thing was worrying me. After hesitating a moment or two I said: 'You know, doctor, I'm afraid I might tend to be — well, a little *personal* sometimes.'

'God bless my soul, woman, the more personal you are the better! This is a story of human beings — not dummies! Be personal — be prejudiced — be catty — be anything you please! Write the thing your own way. We can always prune out the bits that are libellous afterwards! You go ahead. You're a sensible woman, and you'll give a sensible common-sense account of the business.'

So that was that, and I promised to do my best.

And here I am beginning, but as I said to the doctor, it's difficult to know just where to start.

I suppose I ought to say a word or two about myself. I'm thirty-two and my name is Amy Leatheran. I took my training at St Christopher's and after that did two years maternity. I did a certain amount of private work and I was for four years at Miss Bendix's Nursing Home in Devonshire Place. I came out to Iraq with a Mrs Kelsey. I'd attended her when her baby was born. She was coming out to Baghdad with her husband and had already got a children's nurse booked who had been for some years with friends of hers out there. Their children were coming home and going to school, and the nurse had agreed to go to Mrs Kelsey when they left. Mrs Kelsey was delicate and nervous about the journey out with so young a child, so Major Kelsey arranged that I should come out with her and look after her and the baby. They would pay my passage home unless we found someone needing a nurse for the return journey.

Well, there is no need to describe the Kelseys — the baby was a little love and Mrs Kelsey quite nice, though rather the fretting kind. I enjoyed the voyage very much. I'd never been a long trip on the sea before.

Dr Reilly was on board the boat. He was a black-haired, long-faced man who said all sorts of funny things in a low, sad voice. I think he enjoyed pulling my leg and used to make the most extraordinary statements to see if I would swallow them. He was the civil surgeon at a place called Hassanieh — a day and a half's journey from Baghdad.

I had been about a week in Baghdad when I ran across him and he asked when I was leaving the Kelseys. I said that it was funny his asking that because as a matter of fact the Wrights (the other people I mentioned) were going home earlier than they had meant to and their nurse was free to come straight-away.

He said that he had heard about the Wrights and that that was why he had asked me.

'As a matter of fact, nurse, I've got a possible job for you.'

'A case?'

He screwed his face up as though considering.

'You could hardly call it a case. It's just a lady who has — shall we say — fancies?'

'Oh!' I said.

(One usually knows what *that* means — drink or drugs!)

Dr Reilly didn't explain further. He was very discreet. 'Yes,' he said. 'A Mrs Leidner. Husband's an American — an American Swede to be exact. He's the head of a large American dig.'

And he explained how this expedition was excavating the site of a big Assyrian city something like Nineveh. The expedition house was not actually very far from Hassanieh, but it was a lonely spot and Dr Leidner had been worried for some time about his wife's health.

'He's not been very explicit about it, but it seems she has these fits of recurring nervous terrors.'

'Is she left alone all day amongst natives?' I asked.

'Oh, no, there's quite a crowd — seven or eight. I don't fancy she's ever been alone in the house. But there seems to be no doubt

11

that she's worked herself up into a queer state. Leidner has any amount of work on his shoulders, but he's crazy about his wife and it worries him to know she's in this state. He felt he'd be happier if he knew that some responsible person with expert knowledge was keeping an eye on her.'

'And what does Mrs Leidner herself think about it?'

Dr Reilly answered gravely:

'Mrs Leidner is a very lovely lady. She's seldom of the same mind about anything two days on end. But on the whole she favours the idea.' He added, 'She's an odd woman. A mass of affection and, I should fancy, a champion liar — but Leidner seems honestly to believe that she is scared out of her life by something or other.'

'What did she herself say to you, doctor?'

'Oh, she hasn't consulted me! She doesn't like me anyway — for several reasons. It was Leidner who came to me and propounded this plan. Well, nurse, what do you think of the idea? You'd see something of the country before you go home — they'll be digging for another two months. And excavation is quite interesting work.'

After a moment's hesitation while I turned the matter over in my mind: 'Well,' I said, 'I really think I might try it.'

'Splendid,' said Dr Reilly, rising. 'Leidner's in Baghdad now. I'll tell him to come round and see if he can fix things up with you.'

Dr Leidner came to the hotel that afternoon. He was a middle-aged man with a rather nervous, hesitating manner. There was something gentle and kindly and rather helpless about him.

He sounded very devoted to his wife, but he was very vague about what was the matter with her.

'You see,' he said, tugging at his beard in a rather perplexed manner that I later came to know to be characteristic of him, 'my wife is really in a very nervous state. I — I'm quite worried about her.'

'She is in good physical health?' I asked.

'Yes — oh, yes, I think so. No, I should not think there was anything the matter with her physically. But she — well — imagines things, you know.'

'What kind of things?' I asked.

But he shied off from the point, merely murmuring perplexedly: 'She works herself up over nothing at all . . . I really can see no foundations for these fears.'

'Fears of what, Dr Leidner?'

He said vaguely, 'Oh, just — nervous terrors, you know.'

Ten to one, I thought to myself, it's drugs.

And he doesn't realize it! Lots of men don't. Just wonder why their wives are so jumpy and have such extraordinary changes of mood.

I asked whether Mrs Leidner herself approved of the idea of my coming.

His face lighted up.

'Yes. I was surprised. Most pleasurably surprised. She said it was a very good idea. She said she would feel very much safer.'

The word struck me oddly. *Safer*. A very queer word to use. I began to surmise that Mrs Leidner might be a mental case.

He went on with a kind of boyish eagerness.

'I'm sure you'll get on very well with her. She's really a very charming woman.' He smiled disarmingly. 'She feels you'll be the greatest comfort to her. I felt the same as soon as I saw you. You look, if you will allow me to say so, so splendidly healthy and full of common sense. I'm sure you're just the person for Louise.'

'Well, we can but try, Dr Leidner,' I said cheerfully. 'I'm sure I hope I can be of use to your wife. Perhaps she's nervous of natives and coloured people?'

'Oh, dear me no.' He shook his head, amused at the idea. 'My wife likes Arabs very much — she appreciates their simplicity and their sense of humour. This is only her second season — we have been married less than two years — but she already speaks quite a fair amount of Arabic.'

I was silent for a moment or two, then I had one more try.

'Can't you tell me at all what it is your wife is afraid of, Dr Leidner?' I asked.

He hesitated. Then he said slowly, 'I hope — I believe — that she will tell you that herself.'

And that's all I could get out of him.

3

Gossip

It was arranged that I should go to Tell Yarimjah the following week.

Mrs Kelsey was settling into her house at Alwiyah, and I was glad to be able to take a few things off her shoulders.

During that time I heard one or two allusions to the Leidner expedition. A friend of Mrs Kelsey's, a young squadron-leader, pursed his lips in surprise as he exclaimed: 'Lovely Louise. So that's her latest!' He turned to me. 'That's our nickname for her, nurse. She's always known as Lovely Louise.'

'Is she so very handsome then?' I asked.

'It's taking her at her own valuation. *She* thinks she is!'

'Now don't be spiteful, John,' said Mrs Kelsey. 'You know it's not only she who thinks so! Lots of people have been very smitten by her.'

'Perhaps you're right. She's a bit long in the tooth, but she has a certain attraction.'

'You were completely bowled over your-self,' said Mrs Kelsey, laughing.

The squadron-leader blushed and admitted rather shamefacedly: 'Well, she has a way with her. As for Leidner himself, he worships the ground she walks on — and all the rest of the expedition has to worship too! It's expected of them!'

'How many are there altogether?' I asked.

'All sorts and nationalities, nurse,' said the squadron-leader cheerfully. 'An English architect, a French Father from Carthage — he does the inscriptions — tablets and things, you know. And then there's Miss Johnson. She's English too — sort of general bottle-washer. And a little plump man who does the photography — he's an American. And the Mercados. Heaven knows what nationality they are — Dagos of some kind! She's quite young — a snaky-looking creature — and oh! doesn't she hate Lovely Louise! And there are a couple of youngsters and that's the lot. A few odd fish, but nice on the whole — don't you agree, Pennyman?'

He was appealing to an elderly man who was sitting thoughtfully twirling a pair of pince-nez.

The latter started and looked up.

'Yes — yes — very nice indeed. Taken individually, that is. Of course, Mercado is rather a queer fish — '

'He has such a very *odd* beard,' put in Mrs

Kelsey. 'A queer limp kind.'

Major Pennyman went on without noticing her interruption.

'The young 'uns are both nice. The American's rather silent, and the English boy talks a bit too much. Funny, it's usually the other way round. Leidner himself is a delightful fellow — so modest and unassuming. Yes, individually they are all pleasant people. But somehow or other, I may have been fanciful, but the last time I went to see them I got a queer impression of something being wrong. I don't know what it was exactly . . . Nobody seemed quite natural. There was a queer atmosphere of tension. I can explain best what I mean by saying that they all passed the butter to each other too politely.'

Blushing a little, because I don't like airing my own opinions too much, I said: 'If people are too much cooped up together it's got a way of getting on their nerves. I know that myself from experience in hospital.'

'That's true,' said Major Kelsey, 'but it's early in the season, hardly time for that particular irritation to have set in.'

'An expedition is probably like our life here in miniature,' said Major Pennyman. 'It has its cliques and rivalries and jealousies.'

'It sounds as though they'd got a good

many newcomers this year,' said Major Kelsey.

'Let me see.' The squadron-leader counted them off on his fingers. 'Young Coleman is new, so is Reiter. Emmott was out last year and so were the Mercados. Father Lavigny is a newcomer. He's come in place of Dr Byrd, who was ill this year and couldn't come out. Carey, of course, is an old hand. He's been out ever since the beginning, five years ago. Miss Johnson's been out nearly as many years as Carey.'

'I always thought they got on so well together at Tell Yarimjah,' remarked Major Kelsey. 'They seemed like a happy family — which is really surprising when one considers what human nature is! I'm sure Nurse Leatheran agrees with me.'

'Well,' I said, 'I don't know that you're not right! The rows I've known in hospital, and starting often from nothing more than a dispute about a pot of tea.'

'Yes, one tends to get petty in close communities,' said Major Pennyman. 'All the same I feel there must be something more to it in this case. Leidner is such a gentle, unassuming man, with really a remarkable amount of tact. He's always managed to keep his expedition happy and on good terms with each other. And yet I *did* notice that feeling of tension the other day.'

Mrs Kelsey laughed.

'And you don't see the explanation? Why, it leaps to the eye!'

'What do you mean?'

'*Mrs* Leidner, of course.'

'Oh come, Mary,' said her husband, 'she's a charming woman — not at all the quarrelsome kind.'

'I didn't say she was quarrelsome. She *causes* quarrels!'

'In what way? And why should she?'

'Why? Why? Because she's bored. She's not an archaeologist, only the wife of one. She's bored shut away from any excitements and so she provides her own drama. She amuses herself by setting other people by the ears.'

'Mary, you don't know in the least. You're merely imagining.'

'Of course I'm imagining! But you'll find I'm right. Lovely Louise doesn't look like the Mona Lisa for nothing! She mayn't mean any harm, but she likes to see what will happen.'

'She's devoted to Leidner.'

'Oh! I dare say, I'm not suggesting vulgar intrigues. But she's an *allumeuse*, that woman.'

'Women are so sweet to each other,' said Major Kelsey.

'I know. Cat, cat, cat, that's what you men

say. But we're usually right about our own sex.'

'All the same,' said Major Pennyman thoughtfully, 'assuming all Mrs Kelsey's uncharitable surmises to be true, I don't think it would quite account for that curious sense of tension — rather like the feeling there is before a thunderstorm. I had the impression very strongly that the storm might break any minute.'

'Now don't frighten nurse,' said Mrs Kelsey. 'She's going there in three days' time and you'll put her right off.'

'Oh, you won't frighten me,' I said, laughing.

All the same I thought a good deal about what had been said. Dr Leidner's curious use of the word 'safer' recurred to me. Was it his wife's secret fear, unacknowledged or expressed perhaps, that was reacting on the rest of the party? Or was it the actual tension (or perhaps the unknown cause of it) that was reacting on *her* nerves?

I looked up the word *allumeuse* that Mrs Kelsey had used in a dictionary, but couldn't get any sense out of it.

'Well,' I thought to myself, 'I must wait and see.'

4

I Arrive in Hassanieh

Three days later I left Baghdad.

I was sorry to leave Mrs Kelsey and the baby, who was a little love and was thriving splendidly, gaining her proper number of ounces every week. Major Kelsey took me to the station and saw me off. I should arrive at Kirkuk the following morning, and there someone was to meet me.

I slept badly, I never sleep very well in a train and I was troubled by dreams. The next morning, however, when I looked out of the window it was a lovely day and I felt interested and curious about the people I was going to see.

As I stood on the platform hesitating and looking about me I saw a young man coming towards me. He had a round pink face, and really, in all my life, I have never seen anyone who seemed so exactly like a young man out of one of Mr P. G. Wodehouse's books.

'Hallo, 'allo, 'allo,' he said. 'Are you Nurse Leatheran? Well, I mean you must be — I can see that. Ha ha! My name's Coleman. Dr

Leidner sent me along. How are you feeling? Beastly journey and all that? Don't I know these trains! Well, here we are — had any breakfast? This your kit? I say, awfully modest, aren't you? Mrs Leidner has four suitcases and a trunk — to say nothing of a hat-box and a patent pillow, and this, that and the other. Am I talking too much? Come along to the old bus.'

There was what I heard called later a station wagon waiting outside. It was a little like a wagonette, a little like a lorry and a little like a car. Mr Coleman helped me in, explaining that I had better sit next to the driver so as to get less jolting.

Jolting! I wonder the whole contraption didn't fall to pieces! And nothing like a road — just a sort of track all ruts and holes. Glorious East indeed! When I thought of our splendid arterial roads in England it made me quite homesick.

Mr Coleman leaned forward from his seat behind me and yelled in my ear a good deal.

'Track's in pretty good condition,' he shouted just after we had been thrown up in our seats till we nearly touched the roof.

And apparently he was speaking quite seriously.

'Very good for you — jogs the liver,' he said. 'You ought to know that, nurse.'

'A stimulated liver won't be much good to me if my head's split open,' I observed tartly.

'You should come along here after it's rained! The skids are glorious. Most of the time one's going sideways.'

To this I did not respond.

Presently we had to cross the river, which we did on the craziest ferry-boat you can imagine. It was a mercy we ever got across, but everyone seemed to think it was quite usual.

It took us about four hours to get to Hassanieh, which, to my surprise, was quite a big place. Very pretty it looked, too, before we got there from the other side of the river — standing up quite white and fairy-like with minarets. It was a bit different, though, when one had crossed the bridge and come right into it. Such a smell and everything ramshackle and tumble-down, and mud and mess everywhere.

Mr Coleman took me to Dr Reilly's house, where, he said, the doctor was expecting me to lunch.

Dr Reilly was just as nice as ever, and his house was nice too, with a bathroom and everything spick and span. I had a nice bath, and by the time I got back into my uniform and came down I was feeling fine.

Lunch was just ready and we went in, the

24

doctor apologizing for his daughter, who he said was always late. We'd just had a very good dish of eggs in sauce when she came in and Dr Reilly said, 'Nurse, this is my daughter Sheila.'

She shook hands, hoped I'd had a good journey, tossed off her hat, gave a cool nod to Mr Coleman and sat down.

'Well, Bill,' she said. 'How's everything?'

He began to talk to her about some party or other that was to come off at the club, and I took stock of her.

I can't say I took to her much. A thought too cool for my liking. An off-hand sort of girl, though good-looking. Black hair and blue eyes — a pale sort of face and the usual lipsticked mouth. She'd a cool, sarcastic way of talking that rather annoyed me. I had a probationer like her under me once — a girl who worked well, I'll admit, but whose manner always riled me.

It looked to me rather as though Mr Coleman was gone on her. He stammered a bit, and his conversation became slightly more idiotic than it was before, if that was possible! He reminded me of a large stupid dog wagging its tail and trying to please.

After lunch Dr Reilly went off to the hospital, and Mr Coleman had some things to get in the town, and Miss Reilly asked me whether I'd like to see round the town a bit or whether I'd rather stop in the house. Mr Coleman, she said, would be back to fetch me in about an hour.

'Is there anything to see?' I asked.

'There are some picturesque corners,' said Miss Reilly. 'But I don't know that you'd care for them. They're extremely dirty.'

The way she said it rather nettled me. I've never been able to see that picturesqueness excuses dirt.

In the end she took me to the club, which was pleasant enough, overlooking the river, and there were English papers and magazines there.

When we got back to the house Mr Coleman wasn't there yet, so we sat down and talked a bit. It wasn't easy somehow.

She asked me if I'd met Mrs Leidner yet.

'No,' I said. 'Only her husband.'

'Oh,' she said. 'I wonder what you'll think of her?'

I didn't say anything to that. And she went on: 'I like Dr Leidner very much. Everybody likes him.'

That's as good as saying, I thought, that you don't like his wife.

I still didn't say anything and presently she asked abruptly: 'What's the matter with her? Did Dr Leidner tell you?'

I wasn't going to start gossiping about a

patient before I got there even, so I said evasively: 'I understand she's a bit run-down and wants looking after.'

She laughed — a nasty sort of laugh — hard and abrupt.

'Good God,' she said. 'Aren't nine people looking after her already enough?'

'I suppose they've all got their work to do,' I said.

'Work to do? Of course they've got work to do. But Louise comes first — she sees to that all right.'

'No,' I said to myself. 'You *don't* like her.'

'All the same,' went on Miss Reilly, 'I don't see what she wants with a professional hospital nurse. I should have thought amateur assistance was more in her line; not someone who'll jam a thermometer in her mouth, and count her pulse and bring everything down to hard facts.'

Well, I must admit it, I was curious.

'You think there's nothing the matter with her?' I asked.

'Of course there's nothing the matter with her! The woman's as strong as an ox. 'Dear Louise hasn't slept.' 'She's got black circles under her eyes.' Yes — put there with a blue pencil! Anything to get attention, to have everybody hovering round her, making a fuss of her!'

There was something in that, of course. I had (what nurse hasn't?) come across many cases of hypochondriacs whose delight it is to keep a whole household dancing attendance. And if a doctor or a nurse were to say to them: 'There's nothing on earth the matter with you!' Well, to begin with they wouldn't believe it, and their indignation would be as genuine as indignation can be.

Of course it was quite possible that Mrs Leidner might be a case of this kind. The husband, naturally, would be the first to be deceived. Husbands, I've found, are a credulous lot where illness is concerned. But all the same, it didn't quite square with what I'd heard. It didn't, for instance, fit in with that word 'safer'.

Funny how that word had got kind of stuck in my mind.

Reflecting on it, I asked: 'Is Mrs Leidner a nervous woman? Is she nervous, for instance, of living out far from anywhere?'

'What is there to be nervous of? Good heavens, there are ten of them! And they've got guards too — because of the antiquities. Oh, no, she's not nervous — at least — '

She seemed struck by some thought and stopped — going on slowly after a minute or two.

'It's odd your saying that.'

28

'Why?'

'Flight-Lieutenant Jervis and I rode over the other day. It was in the morning. Most of them were up on the dig. She was sitting writing a letter and I suppose she didn't hear us coming. The boy who brings you in wasn't about for once, and we came straight up on to the verandah. Apparently she saw Flight-Lieutenant Jervis's shadow thrown on the wall — and she fairly screamed! Apologized, of course. Said she thought it was a strange man. A bit odd, that. I mean, even if it was a strange man, why get the wind up?'

I nodded thoughtfully.

Miss Reilly was silent, then burst out suddenly:

'I don't know what's the matter with them this year. They've all got the jumps. Johnson goes about so glum she can't open her mouth. David never speaks if he can help it. Bill, of course, never stops, and somehow his chatter seems to make the others worse. Carey goes about looking as though something would snap any minute. And they all watch each other as though — as though — Oh, I don't know, but it's *queer*.'

It was odd, I thought, that two such dissimilar people as Miss Reilly and Major Pennyman should have been struck in the same manner.

Just then Mr Coleman came bustling in. Bustling was just the word for it. If his tongue had hung out and he had suddenly produced a tail to wag you wouldn't have been surprised.

'Hallo, 'allo, 'allo,' he said. 'Absolutely the world's best shopper — that's me. Have you shown nurse all the beauties of the town?'

'She wasn't impressed,' said Miss Reilly dryly.

'I don't blame her,' said Mr Coleman heartily. 'Of all the one-horse tumble-down places!'

'Not a lover of the picturesque or the antique, are you, Bill? I can't think why you are an archaeologist.'

'Don't blame me for that. Blame my guardian. He's a learned bird — fellow of his college — browses among books in bedroom slippers — that kind of man. Bit of a shock for him to have a ward like me.'

'I think it's frightfully stupid of you to be forced into a profession you don't care for,' said the girl sharply.

'Not forced, Sheila, old girl, not forced. The old man asked if I had any special profession in mind, and I said I hadn't, and so he wangled a season out here for me.'

'But haven't you any idea really what you'd *like* to do? You *must* have!'

'Of course I have. My idea would be to give work a miss altogether. What I'd like to do is to have plenty of money and go in for motor-racing.'

'You're absurd!' said Miss Reilly.

She sounded quite angry.

'Oh, I realize that it's quite out of the question,' said Mr Coleman cheerfully. 'So, if I've got to do something, I don't much care what it is so long as it isn't mugging in an office all day long. I was quite agreeable to seeing a bit of the world. Here goes, I said, and along I came.'

'And a fat lot of use you must be, I expect!'

'There you're wrong. I can stand up on the dig and shout '*Y'Allah*' with anybody! And as a matter of fact I'm not so dusty at drawing. Imitating handwriting used to be my speciality at school. I'd have made a first-class forger. Oh, well, I may come to that yet. If my Rolls-Royce splashes you with mud as you're waiting for a bus, you'll know that I've taken to crime.'

Miss Reilly said coldly: 'Don't you think it's about time you started instead of talking so much?'

'Hospitable, aren't we, nurse?'

'I'm sure Nurse Leatheran is anxious to get settled in.'

'You're always sure of everything,' retorted

Mr Coleman with a grin.

That was true enough, I thought. Cocksure little minx.

I said dryly: 'Perhaps we'd better start, Mr Coleman.'

'Right you are, nurse.'

I shook hands with Miss Reilly and thanked her, and we set off.

'Damned attractive girl, Sheila,' said Mr Coleman. 'But always ticking a fellow off.'

We drove out of the town and presently took a kind of track between green crops. It was very bumpy and full of ruts.

After about half an hour Mr Coleman pointed to a big mound by the river bank ahead of us and said: 'Tell Yarimjah.'

I could see little black figures moving about it like ants.

As I was looking they suddenly began to run all together down the side of the mound.

'Fidos,' said Mr Coleman. 'Knocking-off time. We knock off an hour before sunset.'

The expedition house lay a little way back from the river.

The driver rounded a corner, bumped through an extremely narrow arch and there we were.

The house was built round a courtyard. Originally it had occupied only the south side of the courtyard with a few unimportant out-buildings on the east. The expedition had continued the building on the other two sides. As the plan of the house was to prove of special interest later, I append a rough sketch of it here.

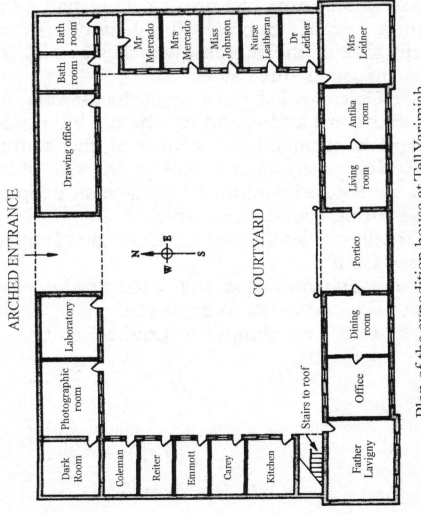

Plan of the expedition house at Tell Yarimjah

ARCHED ENTRANCE

Bath room
Bath room
Drawing office
Laboratory
Photographic room
Dark Room
Coleman
Reiter
Emmott
Carey
Kitchen
Stairs to roof

Mr Mercado
Mrs Mercado
Miss Johnson
Nurse Leatheran
Dr Leidner
Mrs Leidner
Antika room
Living room
Portico
Dining room
Office
Father Lavigny

COURTYARD

N W E S

All the rooms opened on to the courtyard, and most of the windows — the exception being in the original south building where there were windows giving on the outside country as well. These windows, however, were barred on the outside. In the south-west corner a staircase ran up to a long flat roof with a parapet running the length of the south side of the building which was higher than the other three sides.

Mr Coleman led me along the east side of the courtyard and round to where a big open verandah occupied the centre of the south side. He pushed open a door at one side of it and we entered a room where several people were sitting round a tea-table.

'Toodle-oodle-oo!' said Mr Coleman. 'Here's Sairey Gamp.'

The lady who was sitting at the head of the table rose and came to greet me.

I had my first glimpse of Louise Leidner.

5

Tell Yarimjah

I don't mind admitting that my first impression on seeing Mrs Leidner was one of downright surprise. One gets into the way of imagining a person when one hears them talked about. I'd got it firmly into my head that Mrs Leidner was a dark, discontented kind of woman. The nervy kind, all on edge. And then, too, I'd expected her to be — well, to put it frankly — a bit vulgar.

She wasn't a bit like what I'd imagined her! To begin with, she was very fair. She wasn't a Swede, like her husband, but she might have been as far as looks went. She had that blonde Scandinavian fairness that you don't very often see. She wasn't a young woman. Midway between thirty and forty, I should say. Her face was rather haggard, and there was some grey hair mingled with the fairness. Her eyes, though, were lovely. They were the only eyes I've ever come across that you might truly describe as violet. They were very large, and there were faint shadows underneath them. She was very thin and fragile-looking, and if I say that she had an air of intense weariness and was at the same time very much alive, it sounds like nonsense — but that's the feeling I got. I felt, too, that she was a lady through and through. And that means something — even nowadays.

She put out her hand and smiled. Her voice was low and soft with an American drawl in it.

'I'm so glad you've come, nurse. Will you have some tea? Or would you like to go to your room first?'

I said I'd have tea, and she introduced me to the people sitting round the table.

'This is Miss Johnson — and Mr Reiter. Mrs Mercado. Mr Emmott. Father Lavigny. My husband will be in presently. Sit down here between Father Lavigny and Miss Johnson.'

I did as I was bid and Miss Johnson began talking to me, asking about my journey and so on.

I liked her. She reminded me of a matron I'd had in my probationer days whom we had all admired and worked hard for.

She was getting on for fifty, I should judge, and rather mannish in appearance, with iron-grey hair cropped short. She had an abrupt, pleasant voice, rather deep in tone. She had an ugly rugged face with an almost laughably turned-up nose which she was in the habit of rubbing irritably when anything troubled or perplexed her. She wore a tweed coat and skirt made rather like a man's. She told me presently that she was a native of Yorkshire.

Father Lavigny I found just a bit alarming. He was a tall man with a great black beard and pince-nez. I had heard Mrs Kelsey say that there was a French monk there, and I now saw that Father Lavigny was wearing a monk's robe of some white woollen material. It surprised me rather, because I always understood that monks went into monasteries and didn't come out again.

Mrs Leidner talked to him mostly in French, but he spoke to me in quite fair English. I noticed that he had shrewd, observant eyes which darted about from face to face.

Opposite me were the other three. Mr Reiter was a stout, fair young man with glasses. His hair was rather long and curly, and he had very round blue eyes. I should think he must have been a lovely baby, but he wasn't much to look at now! In fact he was just a little like a pig. The other young man had very short hair cropped close to his head. He had a long, rather humorous face and very good teeth, and he looked very attractive when he smiled. He said very little, though, just nodded if spoken to or answered in monosyllables. He, like Mr Reiter, was an American. The last person was Mrs Mercado, and I couldn't have a good look at her because whenever I glanced in her direction I always found her staring at me with a kind of hungry stare that was a bit disconcerting to say the least of it. You might have thought a hospital nurse was a strange animal the way she was looking at me. No manners at all!

She was quite young — not more than about twenty-five — and sort of dark and slinky-looking, if you know what I mean. Quite nice-looking in a kind of way, but rather as though she might have what my mother used to call 'a touch of the tar-brush'. She had on a very vivid pullover and her nails matched it in colour. She had a thin bird-like eager face with big eyes and rather a tight, suspicious mouth.

The tea was very good — a nice strong blend — not like the weak China stuff that Mrs Kelsey always had and that had been a sore trial to me.

There was toast and jam and a plate of rock buns and a cutting cake. Mr Emmott was very polite passing me things. Quiet as he was he always seemed to notice when my plate was empty.

Presently Mr Coleman bustled in and took the place beyond Miss Johnson. There didn't seem to be anything the matter with *his* nerves. He talked away nineteen to the dozen.

Mrs Leidner sighed once and cast a wearied look in his direction but it didn't have any effect. Nor did the fact that Mrs Mercado, to whom he was addressing most of his conversation, was far too busy watching me to do more than make perfunctory replies.

Just as we were finishing, Dr Leidner and Mr Mercado came in from the dig.

Dr Leidner greeted me in his nice kind manner. I saw his eyes go quickly and anxiously to his wife's face and he seemed to be relieved by what he saw there. Then he sat down at the other end of the table, and Mr Mercado sat down in the vacant place by Mrs Leidner. He was a tall, thin, melancholy man, a good deal older than his wife, with a sallow complexion and a queer, soft, shapeless-looking beard. I was glad when he came in, for his wife stopped staring at me and transferred her attention to him, watching him with a kind of anxious impatience that I found rather odd. He himself stirred his tea dreamily and said nothing at all. A piece of cake lay untasted on his plate.

There was still one vacant place, and

presently the door opened and a man came in.

The moment I saw Richard Carey I felt he was one of the handsomest men I'd seen for a long time — and yet I doubt if that were really so. To say a man is handsome and at the same time to say he looks like a death's head sounds a rank contradiction, and yet it was true. His head gave the effect of having the skin stretched unusually tight over the bones — but they were beautiful bones. The lean line of jaw and temple and forehead was so sharply outlined that he reminded me of a bronze statue. Out of this lean brown face looked two of the brightest and most intensely blue eyes I have ever seen. He stood about six foot and was, I should imagine, a little under forty years of age.

Dr Leidner said: 'This is Mr Carey, our architect, nurse.'

He murmured something in a pleasant, inaudible English voice and sat down by Mrs Mercado.

Mrs Leidner said: 'I'm afraid the tea is a little cold, Mr Carey.'

He said: 'Oh, that's quite all right, Mrs Leidner. My fault for being late. I wanted to finish plotting those walls.'

Mrs Mercado said, 'Jam, Mr Carey?'

Mr Reiter pushed forward the toast.

And I remembered Major Pennyman saying: '*I can explain best what I mean by saying that they all passed the butter to each other a shade too politely.*'

Yes, there was something a little odd about it . . .

A shade formal . . .

You'd have said it was a party of strangers — not people who had known each other — some of them — for quite a number of years.

6

First Evening

After tea Mrs Leidner took me to show me my room.

Perhaps here I had better give a short description of the arrangement of the rooms. This was very simple and can easily be understood by a reference to the plan.

On either side of the big open porch were doors leading into the two principal rooms. That on the right led into the dining-room, where we had tea. The one on the other side led into an exactly similar room (I have called it the living-room) which was used as a sitting-room and kind of informal work-room — that is, a certain amount of drawing (other than the strictly architectural) was done there, and the more delicate pieces of pottery were brought there to be pieced together. Through the living-room one passed into the antiquities-room where all the finds from the dig were brought in and stored on shelves and in pigeon-holes, and also laid out on big benches and tables. From the antika-room there was no exit save through the living-room.

Beyond the antika-room, but reached through a door which gave on the courtyard, was Mrs Leidner's bedroom. This, like the other rooms on that side of the house, had a couple of barred windows looking out over the ploughed countryside. Round the corner next to Mrs Leidner's room, but with no actual communicating door, was Dr Leidner's room. This was the first of the rooms on the east side of the building. Next to it was the room that was to be mine. Next to me was Miss Johnson's, with Mr and Mrs Mercado's beyond. After that came two so-called bathrooms.

(When I once used that last term in the hearing of Dr Reilly he laughed at me and said a bathroom was either a bathroom or not a bathroom! All the same, when you've got used to taps and proper plumbing, it seems strange to call a couple of mud-rooms with a tin hip-bath in each of them, and muddy water brought in kerosene tins, *bathrooms*!)

All this side of the building had been added by Dr Leidner to the original Arab house. The bedrooms were all the same, each with a window and a door giving on to the courtyard. Along the north side were the drawing-office, the laboratory and the photographic rooms.

To return to the verandah, the arrangement

of rooms was much the same on the other side. There was the dining-room leading into the office where the files were kept and the cataloguing and typing was done. Corresponding to Mrs Leidner's room was that of Father Lavigny, who was given the largest bedroom; he used it also for the decoding — or whatever you call it — of tablets.

In the south-west corner was the staircase running up to the roof. On the west side were first the kitchen quarters and then four small bedrooms used by the young men — Carey, Emmott, Reiter and Coleman.

At the north-west corner was the photographic-room with the dark-room leading out of it. Next to that the laboratory. Then came the only entrance — the big arched doorway through which we had entered. Outside were sleeping quarters for the native servants, the guard-house for the soldiers, and stables, etc., for the water horses. The drawing-office was to the right of the archway occupying the rest of the north side.

I have gone into the arrangements of the house rather fully here because I don't want to have to go over them again later.

As I say, Mrs Leidner herself took me round the building and finally established me in my bedroom, hoping that I should be comfortable and have everything I wanted.

The room was nicely though plainly furnished — a bed, a chest of drawers, a washstand and a chair.

'The boys will bring you hot water before lunch and dinner — and in the morning, of course. If you want it any other time, go outside and clap your hands, and when the boy comes say, *jib mai' har*. Do you think you can remember that?'

I said I thought so and repeated it a little haltingly.

'That's right. And be sure and shout it. Arabs don't understand anything said in an ordinary 'English' voice.'

'Languages are funny things,' I said. 'It seems odd there should be such a lot of different ones.'

Mrs Leidner smiled.

'There is a church in Palestine in which the Lord's Prayer is written up in — ninety, I think it is — different languages.'

'Well!' I said. 'I must write and tell my old aunt that. She *will* be interested.'

Mrs Leidner fingered the jug and basin absently and shifted the soap-dish an inch or two.

'I do hope you'll be happy here,' she said, 'and not get too bored.'

'I'm not often bored,' I assured her. 'Life's

not long enough for that.'

She did not answer. She continued to toy with the washstand as though abstractedly.

Suddenly she fixed her dark violet eyes on my face.

'What exactly did my husband tell you, nurse?'

Well, one usually says the same thing to a question of that kind.

'I gathered you were a bit run-down and all that, Mrs Leidner,' I said glibly. 'And that you just wanted someone to look after you and take any worries off your hands.'

She bent her head slowly and thoughtfully.

'Yes,' she said. 'Yes — that will do very well.'

That was just a little bit enigmatic, but I wasn't going to question it. Instead I said: 'I hope you'll let me help you with anything there is to do in the house. You mustn't let me be idle.'

She smiled a little.

'Thank you, nurse.'

Then she sat down on the bed and, rather to my surprise, began to cross-question me rather closely. I say rather to my surprise because, from the moment I set eyes on her, I felt sure that Mrs Leidner was a lady. And a lady, in my experience, very seldom displays curiosity about one's private affairs.

But Mrs Leidner seemed anxious to know everything there was to know about me. Where I'd trained and how long ago. What had brought me out to the East. How it had come about that Dr Reilly had recommended me. She even asked me if I had ever been in America or had any relations in America. One or two other questions she asked me that seemed quite purposeless at the time, but of which I saw the significance later.

Then, suddenly, her manner changed. She smiled — a warm sunny smile — and she said, very sweetly, that she was very glad I had come and that she was sure I was going to be a comfort to her.

She got up from the bed and said: 'Would you like to come up to the roof and see the sunset? It's usually very lovely about this time.'

I agreed willingly.

As we went out of the room she asked: 'Were there many other people on the train from Baghdad? Any men?'

I said that I hadn't noticed anybody in particular. There had been two Frenchmen in the restaurant-car the night before. And a party of three men whom I gathered from their conversation had to do with the Pipe line.

She nodded and a faint sound escaped her.

It sounded like a small sigh of relief.

We went up to the roof together.

Mrs Mercado was there, sitting on the parapet, and Dr Leidner was bending over looking at a lot of stones and broken pottery that were laid in rows. There were big things he called querns, and pestles and celts and stone axes, and more broken bits of pottery with queer patterns on them than I've ever seen all at once.

'Come over here,' called out Mrs Mercado. 'Isn't it *too* too beautiful?'

It certainly was a beautiful sunset. Hassanieh in the distance looked quite fairy-like with the setting sun behind it, and the River Tigris flowing between its wide banks looked like a dream river rather than a real one.

'Isn't it lovely, Eric?' said Mrs Leidner.

The doctor looked up with abstracted eyes, murmured, 'Lovely, lovely,' perfunctorily and went on sorting potsherds.

Mrs Leidner smiled and said: 'Archaeologists only look at what lies beneath their feet. The sky and the heavens don't exist for them.'

Mrs Mercado giggled.

'Oh, they're very queer people — you'll soon find *that* out, nurse,' she said.

She paused and then added: 'We are all *so*

glad you've come. We've been so very worried about dear Mrs Leidner, haven't we, Louise?'

'Have you?'

Her voice was not encouraging.

'Oh, yes. She really has been *very* bad, nurse. All sorts of alarms and excursions. You know when anybody says to me of someone, 'It's just nerves,' I always say: but what could be *worse*? Nerves are the core and centre of one's being, aren't they?'

'Puss, puss,' I thought to myself.

Mrs Leidner said dryly: 'Well, you needn't be worried about me any more, Marie. Nurse is going to look after me.'

'Certainly I am,' I said cheerfully.

'I'm sure that will make all the difference,' said Mrs Mercado. 'We've all felt that she ought to see a doctor or do *something*. Her nerves have really been all to pieces, haven't they, Louise dear?'

'So much so that I seem to have got on *your* nerves with them,' said Mrs Leidner. 'Shall we talk about something more interesting than my wretched ailments?'

I understood then that Mrs Leidner was the sort of woman who could easily make enemies. There was a cool rudeness in her tone (not that I blamed her for it) which brought a flush to Mrs Mercado's rather sallow cheeks. She stammered out something,

49

but Mrs Leidner had risen and had joined her husband at the other end of the roof. I doubt if he heard her coming till she laid her hand on his shoulder, then he looked up quickly. There was affection and a kind of eager questioning in his face.

Mrs Leidner nodded her head gently. Presently, her arm through his, they wandered to the far parapet and finally down the steps together.

'He's devoted to her, isn't he?' said Mrs Mercado.

'Yes,' I said. 'It's very nice to see.'

She was looking at me with a queer, rather eager sidelong glance.

'What do you think is really the matter with her, nurse?' she asked, lowering her voice a little.

'Oh, I don't suppose it's much,' I said cheerfully. 'Just a bit run-down, I expect.'

Her eyes still bored into me as they had done at tea. She said abruptly: 'Are you a mental nurse?'

'Oh, dear, no!' I said. 'What made you think that?'

She was silent for a moment, then she said: 'Do you know how queer she's been? Did Dr Leidner tell you?'

I don't hold with gossiping about my cases. On the other hand, it's my experience that it's often very hard to get the truth out of relatives, and until you know the truth you're often working in the dark and doing no good. Of course, when there's a doctor in charge, it's different. He tells you what it's necessary for you to know. But in this case there wasn't a doctor in charge. Dr Reilly had never been called in professionally. And in my own mind I wasn't at all sure that Dr Leidner had told me all he could have done. It's often the husband's instinct to be reticent — and more honour to him, I must say. But all the same, the more I knew the better I could tell which line to take. Mrs Mercado (whom I put down in my own mind as a thoroughly spiteful little cat) was clearly dying to talk. And frankly, on the human side as well as the professional, I wanted to hear what she had to say. You can put it that I was just everyday curious if you like.

I said, 'I gather Mrs Leidner's not been quite her normal self lately?'

Mrs Mercado laughed disagreeably.

'Normal? I should say not. Frightening us to death. One night it was fingers tapping on her window. And then it was a hand without an arm attached. But when it came to a yellow face pressed against the window — and when she rushed to the window there was nothing there — well, I ask you, it *is* a bit creepy for all of us.'

'Perhaps somebody was playing a trick on her,' I suggested.

'Oh, no, she fancied it all. And only three days ago at dinner they were firing shots in the village — nearly a mile away — and she jumped up and screamed out — it scared us all to death. As for Dr Leidner, he rushed to her and behaved in the most ridiculous way. 'It's nothing, darling, it's nothing at all,' he kept saying. I think, you know, nurse, men sometimes *encourage* women in these hysterical fancies. It's a pity because it's a bad thing. Delusions shouldn't be encouraged.'

'Not if they *are* delusions,' I said dryly.

'What else could they be?'

I didn't answer because I didn't know what to say. It was a funny business. The shots and the screaming were natural enough — for anyone in a nervous condition, that is. But this queer story of a spectral face and hand was different. It looked to me like one of two things — either Mrs Leidner had made the story up (exactly as a child shows off by telling lies about something that never happened in order to make herself the centre of attraction) or else it was, as I had suggested, a deliberate practical joke. It was the sort of thing, I reflected, that an unimaginative hearty sort of young fellow like

Mr Coleman might think very funny. I decided to keep a close watch on him. Nervous patients can be scared nearly out of their minds by a silly joke.

Mrs Mercado said with a sideways glance at me:

'She's very romantic-looking, nurse, don't you think so? The sort of woman things *happen* to.'

'Have many things happened to her?' I asked.

'Well, her first husband was killed in the war when she was only twenty. I think that's very pathetic and romantic, don't you?'

'It's one way of calling a goose a swan,' I said dryly.

'Oh, nurse! What an extraordinary remark!'

It was really a very true one. The amount of women you hear say, 'If Donald — or Arthur — or whatever his name was — had *only* lived.' And I sometimes think but if he had, he'd have been a stout, unromantic, short-tempered, middle-aged husband as likely as not.

It was getting dark and I suggested that we should go down. Mrs Mercado agreed and asked if I would like to see the laboratory. 'My husband will be there — working.'

I said I would like to very much and we made our way there. The place was lighted by a lamp, but it was empty. Mrs Mercado showed me some of the apparatus and some copper ornaments that were being treated, and also some bones coated with wax.

'Where can Joseph be?' said Mrs Mercado.

She looked into the drawing-office, where Carey was at work. He hardly looked up as we entered, and I was struck by the extraordinary look of strain on his face. It came to me suddenly: 'This man is at the end of his tether. Very soon, something will snap.' And I remembered somebody else had noticed that same tenseness about him.

As we went out again I turned my head for one last look at him. He was bent over his paper, his lips pressed very closely together, and that 'death's head' suggestion of his bones very strongly marked. Perhaps it was fanciful, but I thought that he looked like a knight of old who was going into battle and knew he was going to be killed.

And again I felt what an extraordinary and quite unconscious power of attraction he had.

We found Mr Mercado in the living-room. He was explaining the idea of some new process to Mrs Leidner. She was sitting on a straight wooden chair, embroidering flowers in fine silks, and I was struck anew by her strange, fragile, unearthly appearance. She looked a fairy creature more than flesh and blood.

Mrs Mercado said, her voice high and shrill: 'Oh, *there* you are, Joseph. We thought we'd find you in the lab.'

He jumped up looking startled and confused, as though her entrance had broken a spell. He said stammeringly: 'I — I must go now. I'm in the middle of — the middle of — '

He didn't complete the sentence but turned towards the door.

Mrs Leidner said in her soft, drawling voice: 'You must finish telling me some other time. It was very interesting.'

She looked up at us, smiled rather sweetly but in a far-away manner, and bent over her embroidery again.

In a minute or two she said: 'There are some books over there, nurse. We've got quite a good selection. Choose one and sit down.'

I went over to the bookshelf. Mrs Mercado stayed for a minute or two, then, turning abruptly, she went out. As she passed me I saw her face and I didn't like the look of it. She looked wild with fury.

In spite of myself I remembered some of the things Mrs Kelsey had said and hinted about Mrs Leidner. I didn't like to think they were true because I liked Mrs Leidner, but I wondered, nevertheless, if there mightn't perhaps be a grain of truth behind them.

I didn't think it was all her fault, but the fact remained that dear ugly Miss Johnson, and that common little spitfire Mrs Mercado, couldn't hold a candle to her in looks or in attraction. And after all, men are men all over the world. You soon see a lot of that in my profession.

Mercado was a poor fish, and I don't suppose Mrs Leidner really cared two hoots for his admiration — but his wife cared. If I wasn't mistaken, she minded badly and would be quite willing to do Mrs Leidner a bad turn if she could.

I looked at Mrs Leidner sitting there and sewing at her pretty flowers, so remote and far away and aloof. I felt somehow I ought to warn her. I felt that perhaps she didn't know how stupid and unreasoning and violent jealousy and hate can be — and how little it takes to set them smouldering.

And then I said to myself, 'Amy Leatheran, you're a fool. Mrs Leidner's no chicken. She's close on forty if she's a day, and she must know all about life there is to know.'

But I felt that all the same perhaps she didn't.

She had such a queer untouched look.

I began to wonder what her life had been. I

56

knew she'd only married Dr Leidner two years ago. And according to Mrs Mercado her first husband had died about fifteen years ago.

I came and sat down near her with a book, and presently I went and washed my hands for supper. It was a good meal — some really excellent curry. They all went to bed early and I was glad, for I was tired.

Dr Leidner came with me to my room to see I had all I wanted.

He gave me a warm handclasp and said eagerly:

'She likes you, nurse. She's taken to you at once. I'm so glad. I feel everything's going to be all right now.'

His eagerness was almost boyish.

I felt, too, that Mrs Leidner had taken a liking to me, and I was pleased it should be so.

But I didn't quite share his confidence. I felt, somehow, that there was more to it all than he himself might know.

There was *something* — something I couldn't get at. But I felt it in the air.

My bed was comfortable, but I didn't sleep well for all that. I dreamt too much.

The words of a poem by Keats, that I'd had to learn as a child, kept running through my head. I kept getting them wrong and it worried me. It was a poem I'd always hated — I suppose because I'd had to learn it whether I wanted to or not. But somehow when I woke up in the dark I saw a sort of beauty in it for the first time.

'*Oh say what ails thee, knight at arms, alone — and* (what was it?) — *palely loitering . . .* ? I saw the knight's face in my mind for the first time — it was Mr Carey's face — a grim, tense, bronzed face like some of those poor young men I remembered as a girl during the war . . . and I felt sorry for him — and then I fell off to sleep again and I saw that the Belle Dame sans Merci was Mrs Leidner and she was leaning sideways on a horse with an embroidery of flowers in her hands — and then the horse stumbled and everywhere there were bones coated in wax, and I woke up all goose-flesh and shivering, and told myself that curry never *had* agreed with me at night.

7

The Man at the Window

I think I'd better make it clear right away that there isn't going to be any local colour in this story. I don't know anything about archaeology and I don't know that I very much want to. Messing about with people and places that are buried and done with doesn't make sense to me. Mr Carey used to tell me that I hadn't got the archaeological temperament and I've no doubt he was quite right.

The very first morning after my arrival Mr Carey asked if I'd like to come and see the palace he was — *planning* I think he called it. Though how you can plan for a thing that's happened long ago I'm sure I don't know! Well, I said I'd like to, and to tell the truth, I was a bit excited about it. Nearly three thousand years old that palace was, it appeared. I wondered what sort of palaces they had in those days, and if it would be like the pictures I'd seen of Tutankahmen's tomb furniture. But would you believe it, there was nothing to see but *mud*! Dirty mud walls about two feet high — and that's all there was to it. Mr Carey took me here and there telling me things — how this was the great court, and there were some chambers here and an upper storey and various other rooms that opened off the central court. And all I thought was, 'But how does he *know*?' though, of course, I was too polite to say so. I can tell you it *was* a disappointment! The whole excavation looked like nothing but mud to me — no marble or gold or anything handsome — my aunt's house in Cricklewood would have made a much more imposing ruin! And those old Assyrians, or whatever they were, called themselves *kings*. When Mr Carey had shown me his old 'palaces', he handed me over to Father Lavigny, who showed me the rest of the mound. I was a little afraid of Father Lavigny, being a monk and a foreigner and having such a deep voice and all that, but he was very kind — though rather vague. Sometimes I felt it wasn't much more real to him than it was to me.

Mrs Leidner explained that later. She said that Father Lavigny was only interested in 'written documents' — as she called them. They wrote everything on clay, these people, queer, heathenish-looking marks too, but quite sensible. There were even school tablets — the teacher's lesson on one side and the pupil's effort on the back of it. I confess that that did interest me rather — it seemed so human, if you know what I mean.

Father Lavigny walked round the work with me and showed me what were temples or palaces and what were private houses, and also a place which he said was an early Akkadian cemetery. He spoke in a funny jerky way, just throwing in a scrap of information and then reverting to other subjects.

He said: 'It is strange that you have come here. Is Mrs Leidner really ill, then?'

'Not exactly ill,' I said cautiously.

He said: 'She is an odd woman. A dangerous woman, I think.'

'Now what do you mean by that?' I said. 'Dangerous? How dangerous?'

He shook his head thoughtfully.

'I think she is ruthless,' he said. 'Yes, I think she could be absolutely ruthless.'

'If you'll excuse me,' I said, 'I think you're talking nonsense.'

He shook his head.

'You do not know women as I do,' he said.

And that was a funny thing, I thought, for a monk to say. But of course I suppose he might have heard a lot of things in confession. But that rather puzzled me, because I wasn't sure if monks heard confessions or if it was only priests. I supposed he *was* a monk with that long woollen robe — all sweeping up the dirt — and the rosary and all!

'Yes, she could be ruthless,' he said musingly. 'I am quite sure of that. And yet — though she is so hard — like stone, like marble — yet she is afraid. What is she afraid of?'

That, I thought, is what we should all like to know!

At least it was possible that her husband did know, but I didn't think anyone else did.

He fixed me with a sudden bright, dark eye.

'It is odd here? You find it odd? Or quite natural?'

'Not quite natural,' I said, considering. 'It's comfortable enough as far as the arrangements go — but there isn't quite a comfortable feeling.'

'It makes *me* uncomfortable. I have the idea' — he became suddenly a little more foreign — 'that something prepares itself. Dr Leidner, too, he is not quite himself. Something is worrying him also.'

'His wife's health?'

'That perhaps. But there is more. There is — how shall I say it — an uneasiness.'

And that was just it, there was an uneasiness.

We didn't say any more just then, for Dr

Leidner came towards us. He showed me a child's grave that had just been uncovered. Rather pathetic it was — the little bones — and a pot or two and some little specks that Dr Leidner told me were a bead necklace.

It was the workmen that made me laugh. You never saw such a lot of scarecrows — all in long petticoats and rags, and their heads tied up as though they had toothache. And every now and then, as they went to and fro carrying away baskets of earth, they began to sing — at least I suppose it was meant to be singing — a queer sort of monotonous chant that went on and on over and over again. I noticed that most of their eyes were terrible — all covered with discharge, and one or two looked half blind. I was just thinking what a miserable lot they were when Dr Leidner said, 'Rather a fine-looking lot of men, aren't they?' and I thought what a queer world it was and how two different people could see the same thing each of them the other way round. I haven't put that very well, but you can guess what I mean.

After a bit Dr Leidner said he was going back to the house for a mid-morning cup of tea. So he and I walked back together and he told me things. When *he* explained, it was all quite different. I sort of *saw* it all — how it used to be — the streets and the houses, and he showed me ovens where they baked bread and said the Arabs used much the same kind of ovens nowadays.

We got back to the house and found Mrs Leidner had got up. She was looking better today, not so thin and worn. Tea came in almost at once and Dr Leidner told her what had turned up during the morning on the dig. Then he went back to work and Mrs Leidner asked me if I would like to see some of the finds they had made up to date. Of course I said 'Yes,' so she took me through into the antika-room. There was a lot of stuff lying about — mostly broken pots it seemed to me — or else ones that were all mended and stuck together. The whole lot might have been thrown away, I thought.

'Dear, dear,' I said, 'it's a pity they're all so broken, isn't it? Are they really worth keeping?'

Mrs Leidner smiled a little and she said: 'You mustn't let Eric hear you. Pots interest him more than anything else, and some of these are the oldest things we have — perhaps as much as seven thousand years old.' And she explained how some of them came from a very deep cut on the mound down towards the bottom, and how, thousands of years ago, they had been broken and mended with bitumen, showing people prized their things just as much then as they do nowadays.

'And now,' she said, 'we'll show you something more exciting.'

And she took down a box from the shelf and showed me a beautiful gold dagger with dark-blue stones in the handle.

I exclaimed with pleasure.

Mrs Leidner laughed.

'Yes, everybody likes gold! Except my husband.'

'Why doesn't Dr Leidner like it?'

'Well, for one thing it comes expensive. You have to pay the workmen who find it the weight of the object in gold.'

'Good gracious!' I exclaimed. 'But why?'

'Oh, it's a custom. For one thing it prevents them from stealing. You see, if they *did* steal, it wouldn't be for the archaeological value but for the intrinsic value. They could melt it down. So we make it easy for them to be honest.'

She took down another tray and showed me a really beautiful gold drinking-cup with a design of rams' heads on it.

Again I exclaimed.

'Yes, it is beautiful, isn't it? These came from a prince's grave. We found other royal graves but most of them had been plundered. This cup is our best find. It is one of the most lovely ever found anywhere. Early Akkadian. Unique.'

Suddenly, with a frown, Mrs Leidner brought the cup up close to her eyes and scratched at it delicately with her nail.

'How extraordinary! There's actually wax on it. Someone must have been in here with a candle.' She detached the little flake and replaced the cup in its place.

After that she showed me some queer little terracotta figurines — but most of them were just rude. Nasty minds those old people had, I say.

When we went back to the porch Mrs Mercado was sitting polishing her nails. She was holding them out in front of her admiring the effect. I thought myself that anything more hideous than that orange red could hardly have been imagined.

Mrs Leidner had brought with her from the antika-room a very delicate little saucer broken in several pieces, and this she now proceeded to join together. I watched her for a minute or two and then asked if I could help.

'Oh, yes, there are plenty more.' She fetched quite a supply of broken pottery and we set to work. I soon got into the hang of it and she praised my ability. I suppose most nurses are handy with their fingers.

'How busy everybody is!' said Mrs Mercado. 'It makes me feel dreadfully idle. Of course I *am* idle.'

'Why shouldn't you be if you like?' said Mrs Leidner.

Her voice was quite uninterested.

At twelve we had lunch. Afterwards Dr Leidner and Mr Mercado cleaned some pottery, pouring a solution of hydrochloric acid over it. One pot went a lovely plum colour and a pattern of bulls' horns came out on another one. It was really quite magical. All the dried mud that no washing would remove sort of foamed and boiled away.

Mr Carey and Mr Coleman went out on the dig and Mr Reiter went off to the photographic-room.

'What will you do, Louise?' Dr Leidner asked his wife. 'I suppose you'll rest for a bit?'

I gathered that Mrs Leidner usually lay down every afternoon.

'I'll rest for about an hour. Then perhaps I'll go out for a short stroll.'

'Good. Nurse will go with you, won't you?'

'Of course,' I said.

'No, no,' said Mrs Leidner, 'I like going alone. Nurse isn't to feel so much on duty that I'm not allowed out of her sight.'

'Oh, but I'd like to come,' I said.

'No, really, I'd rather you didn't.' She was

quite firm — almost peremptory. 'I must be by myself every now and then. It's necessary to me.'

I didn't insist, of course. But as I went off for a short sleep myself it struck me as odd that Mrs Leidner, with her nervous terrors, should be quite content to walk by herself without any kind of protection.

When I came out of my room at half-past three the courtyard was deserted save for a little boy with a large copper bath who was washing pottery, and Mr Emmott, who was sorting and arranging it. As I went towards them Mrs Leidner came in through the archway. She looked more alive than I had seen her yet. Her eyes shone and she looked uplifted and almost gay.

Dr Leidner came out from the laboratory and joined her. He was showing her a big dish with bulls' horns on it.

'The prehistoric levels are being extraordinarily productive,' he said. 'It's been a good season so far. Finding that tomb right at the beginning was a real piece of luck. The only person who might complain is Father Lavigny. We've had hardly any tablets so far.'

'He doesn't seem to have done very much with the few we have had,' said Mrs Leidner dryly. 'He may be a very fine epigraphist but he's a remarkably lazy one. He spends all his afternoons sleeping.'

'We miss Byrd,' said Dr Leidner. 'This man strikes me as slightly unorthodox — though, of course, I'm not competent to judge. But one or two of his translations have been surprising, to say the least of it. I can hardly believe, for instance, that he's right about that inscribed brick, and yet he must know.'

After tea Mrs Leidner asked me if I would like to stroll down to the river. I thought that perhaps she feared that her refusal to let me accompany her earlier in the afternoon might have hurt my feelings.

I wanted her to know that I wasn't the touchy kind, so I accepted at once.

It was a lovely evening. A path led between barley fields and then through some flowering fruit trees. Finally we came to the edge of the Tigris. Immediately on our left was the Tell with the workmen singing in their queer monotonous chant. A little to our right was a big water-wheel which made a queer groaning noise. It used to set my teeth on edge at first. But in the end I got fond of it and it had a queer soothing effect on me. Beyond the water-wheel was the village from which most of the workmen came.

'It's rather beautiful, isn't it?' said Mrs Leidner.

'It's very peaceful,' I said. 'It seems funny

to me to be so far away from everywhere.'

'Far from everywhere,' repeated Mrs Leidner. 'Yes. Here at least one might expect to be safe.'

I glanced at her sharply, but I think she was speaking more to herself than to me, and I don't think she realized that her words had been revealing.

We began to walk back to the house.

Suddenly Mrs Leidner clutched my arm so violently that I nearly cried out.

'Who's that, nurse? What's he doing?'

Some distance ahead of us, just where the path ran near the expedition house, a man was standing. He wore European clothes and he seemed to be standing on tiptoe and trying to look in at one of the windows.

As we watched he glanced round, caught sight of us, and immediately continued on the path towards us. I felt Mrs Leidner's clutch tighten.

'Nurse,' she whispered. 'Nurse . . . '

'It's all right, my dear, it's all right,' I said reassuringly.

The man came along and passed us. He was an Iraqi, and as soon as she saw him near to, Mrs Leidner relaxed with a sigh.

'He's only an Iraqi after all,' she said.

We went on our way. I glanced up at the windows as I passed. Not only were they barred, but they were too high from the ground to permit of anyone seeing in, for the level of the ground was lower here than on the inside of the courtyard.

'It must have been just curiosity,' I said.

Mrs Leidner nodded.

'That's all. But just for a minute I thought — '

She broke off.

I thought to myself. 'You thought *what*? That's what I'd like to know. *What* did you think?'

But I knew one thing now — that Mrs Leidner was afraid of a definite flesh-and-blood person.

8

Night Alarm

It's a little difficult to know exactly what to note in the week that followed my arrival at Tell Yarimjah.

Looking back as I do from my present standpoint of knowledge I can see a good many little signs and indications that I was quite blind to at the time.

To tell the story properly, however, I think I ought to try to recapture the point of view that I actually held — puzzled, uneasy and increasingly conscious of *something* wrong.

For one thing *was* certain, that curious sense of strain and constraint was *not* imagined. It was genuine. Even Bill Coleman the insensitive commented upon it.

'This place gets under my skin,' I heard him say. 'Are they always such a glum lot?'

It was David Emmott to whom he spoke, the other assistant. I had taken rather a fancy to Mr Emmott, his taciturnity was not, I felt sure, unfriendly. There was something about him that seemed very steadfast and reassuring in an atmosphere where one was uncertain what anyone was feeling or thinking.

'No,' he said in answer to Mr Coleman. 'It wasn't like this last year.'

But he didn't enlarge on the theme, or say any more.

'What I can't make out is what it's all about,' said Mr Coleman in an aggrieved voice.

Emmott shrugged his shoulders but didn't answer.

I had a rather enlightening conversation with Miss Johnson. I liked her very much. She was capable, practical and intelligent. She had, it was quite obvious, a distinct hero worship for Dr Leidner.

On this occasion she told me the story of his life since his young days. She knew every site he had dug, and the results of the dig. I would almost dare swear she could quote from every lecture he had ever delivered. She considered him, she told me, quite the finest field archaeologist living.

'And he's so simple. So completely unworldly. He doesn't know the meaning of the word conceit. Only a really great man could be so simple.'

'That's true enough,' I said. 'Big people don't need to throw their weight about.'

'And he's so light-hearted too, I can't tell

you what fun we used to have — he and Richard Carey and I — the first years we were out here. We were such a happy party. Richard Carey worked with him in Palestine, of course. Theirs is a friendship of ten years or so. Oh, well, I've known him for seven.'

'What a handsome man Mr Carey is,' I said.

'Yes — I suppose he is.'

She said it rather curtly.

'But he's just a little bit quiet, don't you think?'

'He usedn't to be like that,' said Miss Johnson quickly. 'It's only since — '

She stopped abruptly.

'Only since — ?' I prompted.

'Oh, well.' Miss Johnson gave a characteristic motion of her shoulders. 'A good many things are changed nowadays.'

I didn't answer. I hoped she would go on — and she did — prefacing her remarks with a little laugh as though to detract from their importance.

'I'm afraid I'm rather a conservative old fogy. I sometimes think that if an archaeologist's wife isn't really interested, it would be wiser for her not to accompany the expedition. It often leads to friction.'

'Mrs Mercado — ' I suggested.

'Oh, her!' Miss Johnson brushed the

suggestion aside. 'I was really thinking of Mrs Leidner. She's a very charming woman — and one can quite understand why Dr Leidner 'fell for her' — to use a slang term. But I can't help feeling she's out of place here. She — it unsettles things.'

So Miss Johnson agreed with Mrs Kelsey that it was Mrs Leidner who was responsible for the strained atmosphere. But then where did Mrs Leidner's own nervous fears come in?

'It unsettles *him*,' said Miss Johnson earnestly. 'Of course I'm — well, I'm like a faithful but jealous old dog. I don't like to see him so worn out and worried. His whole mind ought to be on the work — not taken up with his wife and her silly fears! If she's nervous of coming to out-of-the-way places, she ought to have stayed in America. I've no patience with people who come to a place and then do nothing but grouse about it!'

And then, a little fearful of having said more than she meant to say, she went on: 'Of course I admire her very much. She's a lovely woman and she's got great charm of manner when she chooses.'

And there the subject dropped.

I thought to myself that it was always the same way — wherever women are cooped up together, there's bound to be jealousy. Miss

Johnson clearly didn't like her chief's wife (that was perhaps natural) and unless I was much mistaken Mrs Mercado fairly hated her.

Another person who didn't like Mrs Leidner was Sheila Reilly. She came out once or twice to the dig, once in a car and twice with some young man on a horse — on two horses I mean, of course. It was at the back of my mind that she had a weakness for the silent young American, Emmott. When he was on duty at the dig she used to stay talking to him, and I thought, too, that *he* admired *her*.

One day, rather injudiciously, I thought, Mrs Leidner commented upon it at lunch.

'The Reilly girl is still hunting David down,' she said with a little laugh. 'Poor David, she chases you up on the dig even! How foolish girls are!'

Mr Emmott didn't answer, but under his tan his face got rather red. He raised his eyes and looked right into hers with a very curious expression — a straight, steady glance with something of a challenge in it.

She smiled very faintly and looked away.

I heard Father Lavigny murmur something, but when I said 'Pardon?' he merely shook his head and did not repeat his remark.

That afternoon Mr Coleman said to me:

'Matter of fact I didn't like Mrs L. any too much at first. She used to jump down my throat every time I opened my mouth. But I've begun to understand her better now. She's one of the kindest women I've ever met. You find yourself telling her all the foolish scrapes you ever got into before you know where you are. She's got her knife into Sheila Reilly, I know, but then Sheila's been damned rude to her once or twice. That's the worst of Sheila — she's got no manners. And a temper like the devil!'

That I could well believe. Dr Reilly spoilt her.

'Of course she's bound to get a bit full of herself, being the only young woman in the place. But that doesn't excuse her talking to Mrs Leidner as though Mrs Leidner were her great-aunt. Mrs L.'s not exactly a chicken, but she's a damned good-looking woman. Rather like those fairy women who come out of marshes with lights and lure you away.' He added bitterly, 'You wouldn't find Sheila luring anyone. All she does is to tick a fellow off.'

I only remember two other incidents of any kind of significance.

One was when I went to the laboratory to fetch some acetone to get the stickiness off my fingers from mending the pottery. Mr

Mercado was sitting in a corner, his head was laid down on his arms and I fancied he was asleep. I took the bottle I wanted and went off with it.

That evening, to my great surprise, Mrs Mercado tackled me.

'Did you take a bottle of acetone from the lab?'

'Yes,' I said. 'I did.'

'You know perfectly well that there's a small bottle always kept in the antika-room.'

She spoke quite angrily.

'Is there? I didn't know.'

'I think you did! You just wanted to come spying round. I know what hospital nurses are.'

I stared at her.

'I don't know what you're talking about, Mrs Mercado,' I said with dignity. 'I'm sure I don't want to spy on anyone.'

'Oh, no! Of course not. Do you think I don't know what you're here for?'

Really, for a minute or two I thought she must have been drinking. I went away without saying any more. But I thought it was very odd.

The other thing was nothing very much. I was trying to entice a pi dog pup with a piece of bread. It was very timid, however, like all Arab dogs — and was convinced I meant no good. It slunk away and I followed it — out through the archway and round the corner of the house. I came round so sharply that before I knew I had cannoned into Father Lavigny and another man who were standing together — and in a minute I realized that the second man was the same one Mrs Leidner and I had noticed that day trying to peer through the window.

I apologized and Father Lavigny smiled, and with a word of farewell greeting to the other man he returned to the house with me.

'You know,' he said. 'I am very ashamed. I am a student of Oriental languages and none of the men on the work can understand me! It is humiliating, do you not think? I was trying my Arabic on that man, who is a townsman, to see if I got on better — but it still wasn't very successful. Leidner says my Arabic is too pure.'

That was all. But it just passed through my head that it was odd the same man should still be hanging round the house.

That night we had a scare.

It must have been about two in the morning. I'm a light sleeper, as most nurses have to be. I was awake and sitting up in bed by the time that my door opened.

'Nurse, nurse!'

It was Mrs Leidner's voice, low and urgent.

I struck a match and lighted the candle.

She was standing by the door in a long blue dressing-gown. She was looking petrified with terror.

'There's someone — someone — in the room next to mine ... I heard him — scratching on the wall.'

I jumped out of bed and came to her.

'It's all right,' I said. 'I'm here. Don't be afraid, my dear.'

She whispered: 'Get Eric.'

I nodded and ran out and knocked on his door. In a minute he was with us. Mrs Leidner was sitting on my bed, her breath coming in great gasps.

'I heard him,' she said. 'I heard him — scratching on the wall.'

'Someone in the antika-room?' cried Dr Leidner.

He ran out quickly — and it just flashed across my mind how differently these two had reacted. Mrs Leidner's fear was entirely personal, but Dr Leidner's mind leaped at once to his precious treasures.

'The antika-room!' breathed Mrs Leidner. 'Of course! How stupid of me!'

And rising and pulling her gown round her, she bade me come with her. All traces of her panic-stricken fear had vanished.

We arrived in the antika-room to find Dr

Leidner and Father Lavigny. The latter had also heard a noise, had risen to investigate, and had fancied he saw a light in the antika-room. He had delayed to put on slippers and snatch up a torch and had found no one by the time he got there. The door, moreover, was duly locked, as it was supposed to be at night.

Whilst he was assuring himself that nothing had been taken, Dr Leidner had joined him.

Nothing more was to be learned. The outside archway door was locked. The guard swore nobody could have got in from outside, but as they had probably been fast asleep this was not conclusive. There were no marks or traces of an intruder and nothing had been taken.

It was possible that what had alarmed Mrs Leidner was the noise made by Father Lavigny taking down boxes from the shelves to assure himself that all was in order.

On the other hand, Father Lavigny himself was positive that he had (a) heard footsteps passing his window and (b) seen the flicker of a light, possibly a torch, in the antika-room.

Nobody else had heard or seen anything.

The incident is of value in my narrative because it led to Mrs Leidner's unburdening herself to me on the following day.

9

Mrs Leidner's Story

We had just finished lunch. Mrs Leidner went to her room to rest as usual. I settled her on her bed with plenty of pillows and her book, and was leaving the room when she called me back.

'Don't go, nurse, there's something I want to say to you.'

I came back into the room.

'Shut the door.'

I obeyed.

She got up from the bed and began to walk up and down the room. I could see that she was making up her mind to something and I didn't like to interrupt her. She was clearly in great indecision of mind.

At last she seemed to have nerved herself to the required point. She turned to me and said abruptly: 'Sit down.'

I sat down by the table very quietly. She began nervously: 'You must have wondered what all this is about?'

I just nodded without saying anything.

'I've made up my mind to tell you —

everything! I must tell someone or I shall go mad.'

'Well,' I said, 'I think really it would be just as well. It's not easy to know the best thing to do when one's kept in the dark.'

She stopped in her uneasy walk and faced me.

'Do you know what I'm frightened of?'

'Some man,' I said.

'Yes — but I didn't say whom — I said what.'

I waited.

She said: '*I'm afraid of being killed!*'

Well, it was out now. I wasn't going to show any particular concern. She was near enough to hysterics as it was.

'Dear me,' I said. 'So that's it, is it?'

Then she began to laugh. She laughed and she laughed — and the tears ran down her face.

'The way you said that!' she gasped. 'The way you said it . . . '

'Now, now,' I said. 'This won't do.' I spoke sharply. I pushed her into a chair, went over to the washstand and got a cold sponge and bathed her forehead and wrists.

'No more nonsense,' I said. 'Tell me calmly and sensibly all about it.'

That stopped her. She sat up and spoke in her natural voice.

'You're a treasure, nurse,' she said. 'You make me feel as though I'm six. I'm going to tell you.'

'That's right,' I said. 'Take your time and don't hurry.'

She began to speak, slowly and deliberately.

'When I was a girl of twenty I married. A young man in one of our State departments. It was in 1918.'

'I know,' I said. 'Mrs Mercado told me. He was killed in the war.'

But Mrs Leidner shook her head.

'That's what she thinks. That's what everybody thinks. The truth is something different. I was a queer patriotic, enthusiastic girl, nurse, full of idealism. When I'd been married a few months I discovered — by a quite unforeseeable accident — that my husband was a spy in German pay. I learned that the information supplied by him had led directly to the sinking of an American transport and the loss of hundreds of lives. I don't know what most people would have done . . . But I'll tell you what I did. I went straight to my father, who was in the War Department, and told him the truth. Frederick *was* killed in the war — but he was killed in America — shot as a spy.'

'Oh dear, dear!' I ejaculated. 'How terrible!'

'Yes,' she said. 'It was terrible. He was so kind, too — so gentle . . . And all the time . . . But I never hesitated. Perhaps I was wrong.'

'It's difficult to say,' I said. 'I'm sure I don't know what one would do.'

'What I'm telling you was never generally known outside the State department. Ostensibly my husband had gone to the Front and had been killed. I had a lot of sympathy and kindness shown me as a war widow.'

Her voice was bitter and I nodded comprehendingly.

'Lots of people wanted to marry me, but I always refused. I'd had too bad a shock. I didn't feel I could ever *trust* anyone again.'

'Yes, I can imagine feeling like that.'

'And then I became very fond of a certain young man. I wavered. An amazing thing happened! I got an anonymous letter — from Frederick — saying that if I ever married another man, he'd kill me!'

'From Frederick? From your dead husband?'

'Yes. Of course, I thought at first I was mad or dreaming . . . At last I went to my father. He told me the truth. My husband hadn't been shot after all. He'd escaped — but his escape did him no good. He was involved in a train wreck a few weeks later and his dead body was found amongst others. My father

85

had kept the fact of his escape from me, and since the man had died anyway he had seen no reason to tell me anything until now.

'But the letter I received opened up entirely new possibilities. Was it perhaps a fact that my husband was still alive?

'My father went into the matter as carefully as possible. And he declared that as far as one could humanly be sure the body that was buried as Frederick's *was* Frederick's. There had been a certain amount of disfiguration, so that he could not speak with absolute cast-iron certainty, but he reiterated his solemn belief that Frederick was dead and that this letter was a cruel and malicious hoax.

'The same thing happened more than once. If I seemed to be on intimate terms with any man, I would receive a threatening letter.'

'In your husband's handwriting?'

She said slowly: 'That is difficult to say. I had no letters of his. I had only my memory to go by.'

'There was no allusion or special form of words used that could make you sure?'

'No. There *were* certain terms — nicknames, for instance — private between us — if one of those had been used or quoted, then I should have been quite sure.'

'Yes,' I said thoughtfully. 'That is odd. It looks as though it *wasn't* your husband. But is there anyone else it could be?'

'There is a possibility. Frederick had a younger brother — a boy of ten or twelve at the time of our marriage. He worshipped Frederick and Frederick was devoted to him. What happened to this boy, William his name was, I don't know. It seems to me possible that, adoring his brother as fanatically as he did, he may have grown up regarding me as directly responsible for his death. He had always been jealous of me and may have invented this scheme by way of punishment.'

'It's possible,' I said. 'It's amazing the way children do remember if they've had a shock.'

'I know. This boy may have dedicated his life to revenge.'

'Please go on.'

'There isn't much more to tell. I met Eric three years ago. I meant never to marry. Eric made me change my mind. Right up to our wedding day I waited for another threatening letter. None came. I decided that whoever the writer might be, he was either dead, or tired of his cruel sport. *Two days after our marriage I got this.*'

Drawing a small attaché-case which was on the table towards her, she unlocked it, took out a letter and handed it to me.

The ink was slightly faded. It was written in a rather womanish hand with a forward slant.

You have disobeyed. Now you cannot escape. You must be Frederick Bosner's wife only! You have got to die.

'I was frightened — but not so much as I might have been to begin with. Being with Eric made me feel safe. Then, a month later, I got a second letter.'

I have not forgotten. I am making my plans. You have got to die. Why did you disobey?

'Does your husband know about this?'

Mrs Leidner answered slowly.

'He knows that I am threatened. I showed him both letters when the second one came. He was inclined to think the whole thing a hoax. He thought also that it might be someone who wanted to blackmail me by pretending my first husband was alive.'

She paused and then went on.

'A few days after I received the second letter we had a narrow escape from death by gas poisoning. Somebody entered our apartment after we were asleep and turned on the gas. Luckily I woke and smelled the gas in time. Then I lost my nerve. I told Eric how I had been persecuted for years, and I told him that I was sure this madman, whoever he might be, did really mean to kill me. I think that for the first time I really did think it *was* Frederick. There was always something a little ruthless behind his gentleness.

'Eric was still, I think, less alarmed than I was. He wanted to go to the police. Naturally I wouldn't hear of that. In the end we agreed that I should accompany him here, and that it might be wise if I didn't return to America in the summer but stayed in London and Paris.

'We carried out our plan and all went well. I felt sure that now everything would be all right. After all, we had put half the globe between ourselves and my enemy.

'And then — a little over three weeks ago — I received a letter — with an Iraq stamp on it.'

She handed me a third letter.

You thought you could escape. You were wrong. You shall not be false to me and live. I have always told you so. Death is coming very soon.

'And a week ago — *this*! Just lying on the table here. It had not even gone through the post.'

I took the sheet of paper from her. There was just one phrase scrawled across it.

I have arrived.

She stared at me.

'You see? You understand? He's going to

89

kill me. It may be Frederick — it may be little William — *but he's going to kill me.*'

Her voice rose shudderingly. I caught her wrist.

'Now — now,' I said warningly. 'Don't give way. We'll look after you. Have you got any sal volatile?'

She nodded towards the washstand and I gave her a good dose.

'That's better,' I said, as the colour returned to her cheeks.

'Yes, I'm better now. But oh, nurse, do you see why I'm in this state? When I saw that man looking in through my window, I thought: *he's come* . . . Even when *you* arrived I was suspicious. I thought you might be a man in disguise — '

'The idea!'

'Oh, I know it sounds absurd. But you might have been in league with him perhaps — not a hospital nurse at all.'

'But that's nonsense!'

'Yes, perhaps. But I've got beyond sense.'

Struck by a sudden idea, I said: 'You'd *recognize* your husband, I suppose?'

She answered slowly.

'I don't even know that. It's over fifteen years ago. I mightn't recognize his face.'

Then she shivered.

'I saw it one night — but it was a *dead*

face. There was a tap, tap, tap on the window. And then I saw a face, a dead face, ghastly and grinning against the pane. I screamed and screamed . . . And they said there wasn't anything there!'

I remembered Mrs Mercado's story.

'You don't think,' I said hesitatingly, 'that you *dreamt* that?'

'I'm sure I didn't!'

I wasn't so sure. It was the kind of nightmare that was quite likely under the circumstances and that easily might be taken for a waking occurrence. However, I never contradict a patient. I soothed Mrs Leidner as best I could and pointed out that if any stranger arrived in the neighbourhood it was pretty sure to be known.

I left her, I think, a little comforted, and I went in search of Dr Leidner and told him of our conversation.

'I'm glad she told you,' he said simply. 'It has worried me dreadfully. I feel sure that all those faces and tappings on the window-pane have been sheer imagination on her part. I haven't known what to do for the best. What do you think of the whole thing?'

I didn't quite understand the tone in his voice, but I answered promptly enough.

'It's possible,' I said, 'that these letters may be just a cruel and malicious hoax.'

'Yes, that is quite likely. But what are we to *do*? They are driving her mad. I don't know what to think.'

I didn't either. It had occurred to me that possibly a woman might be concerned. Those letters had a feminine note about them. Mrs Mercado was at the back of my mind.

Supposing that by some chance she had learnt the facts of Mrs Leidner's first marriage? She might be indulging her spite by terrorizing the other woman.

I didn't quite like to suggest such a thing to Dr Leidner. It's so difficult to know how people are going to take things.

'Oh, well,' I said cheerfully, 'we must hope for the best. I think Mrs Leidner seems happier already from just talking about it. That's always a help, you know. It's bottling things up that makes them get on your nerves.'

'I'm very glad she has told you,' he repeated. 'It's a good sign. It shows she likes and trusts you. I've been at my wits' end to know what to do for the best.'

It was on the tip of my tongue to ask him whether he'd thought of giving a discreet hint to the local police, but afterwards I was glad I hadn't done so.

What happened was this. On the following day Mr Coleman was going in to Hassanieh to get the workmen's pay. He was also taking in all our letters to catch the air mail.

The letters, as written, were dropped into a wooden box on the dining-room window-sill. Last thing that night Mr Coleman took them out and was sorting them out into bundles and putting rubber bands round them.

Suddenly he gave a shout.

'What is it?' I asked.

He held out a letter with a grin.

'It's our Lovely Louise — she really *is* going balmy. She's addressed a letter to someone at 42nd Street, Paris, France. I don't think that can be right, do you? Do you mind taking it to her and asking what she *does* mean? She's just gone off to bed.'

I took it from him and ran off to Mrs Leidner with it and she amended the address.

It was the first time I had seen Mrs Leidner's handwriting, and I wondered idly where I had seen it before, for it was certainly quite familiar to me.

It wasn't till the middle of the night that it suddenly came to me.

Except that it was bigger and rather more straggling, *it was extraordinarily like the writing on the anonymous letters.*

New ideas flashed through my head.

Had Mrs Leidner conceivably written those letters *herself*?

And did Dr Leidner half-suspect the fact?

10

Saturday Afternoon

Mrs Leidner told me her story on a Friday.

On the Saturday morning there was a feeling of slight anticlimax in the air.

Mrs Leidner, in particular, was inclined to be very offhand with me and rather pointedly avoided any possibility of a *tête-à-tête*. Well, *that* didn't surprise me! I've had the same thing happen to me again and again. Ladies tell their nurses things in a sudden burst of confidence, and then, afterwards, they feel uncomfortable about it and wish they hadn't! It's only human nature.

I was very careful not to hint or remind her in any way of what she had told me. I purposely kept my conversation as matter-of-fact as possible.

Mr Coleman had started in to Hassanieh in the morning, driving himself in the lorry with the letters in a knapsack. He also had one or two commissions to do for the members of the expedition. It was pay-day for the men, and he would have to go to the bank and bring out the money in coins of small denominations. All this was a long business and he did not expect to be back until the afternoon. I rather suspected he might be lunching with Sheila Reilly.

Work on the dig was usually not very busy on the afternoon of pay-day as at three-thirty the paying-out began.

The little boy, Abdullah, whose business it was to wash pots, was established as usual in the centre of the courtyard, and again, as usual, kept up his queer nasal chant. Dr Leidner and Mr Emmott were going to put in some work on the pottery until Mr Coleman returned, and Mr Carey went up to the dig.

Mrs Leidner went to her room to rest. I settled her as usual and then went to my own room, taking a book with me as I did not feel sleepy. It was then about a quarter to one, and a couple of hours passed quite pleasantly. I was reading *Death in a Nursing Home* — really a most exciting story — though I don't think the author knew much about the way nursing homes are run! At any rate I've never known a nursing home like that! I really felt inclined to write to the author and put him right about a few points.

When I put the book down at last (it was the red-haired parlourmaid and I'd never suspected her once!) and looked at my watch

I was quite surprised to find it was twenty minutes to three!

I got up, straightened my uniform, and came out into the courtyard.

Abdullah was still scrubbing and still singing his depressing chant, and David Emmott was standing by him sorting the scrubbed pots, and putting the ones that were broken into boxes to await mending. I strolled over towards them just as Dr Leidner came down the staircase from the roof.

'Not a bad afternoon,' he said cheerfully. 'I've made a bit of a clearance up there. Louise will be pleased. She's complained lately that there's not room to walk about. I'll go and tell her the good news.'

He went over to his wife's door, tapped on it and went in.

It must, I suppose, have been about a minute and a half later that he came out again. I happened to be looking at the door when he did so. It was like a nightmare. He had gone in a brisk, cheerful man. He came out like a drunken one — reeling a little on his feet, and with a queer dazed expression on his face.

'Nurse — ' he called in a queer, hoarse voice. 'Nurse — '

I saw at once something was wrong and I ran across to him. He looked awful — his face was all grey and twitching, and I saw he might collapse any minute.

'My wife . . . ' he said. 'My wife . . . Oh, my God . . . '

I pushed past him into the room. Then I caught my breath.

Mrs Leidner was lying in a dreadful huddled heap by the bed.

I bent over her. She was quite dead — must have been dead an hour at least. The cause of death was perfectly plain — a terrific blow on the front of the head just over the right temple. She must have got up from the bed and been struck down where she stood.

I didn't handle her more than I could help.

I glanced round the room to see if there was anything that might give a clue, but nothing seemed out of place or disturbed. The windows were closed and fastened, and there was no place where the murderer could have hidden. Obviously he had been and gone long ago.

I went out, closing the door behind me.

Dr Leidner had collapsed completely now. David Emmott was with him and turned a white, inquiring face to me.

In a few low words I told him what had happened.

As I had always suspected, he was a first-class person to rely on in trouble. He was perfectly calm and self-possessed. Those blue eyes of his opened very wide, but otherwise he gave no sign at all.

He considered for a moment and then said: 'I suppose we must notify the police as soon as possible. Bill ought to be back any minute. What shall we do with Leidner?'

'Help me to get him into his room.'

He nodded.

'Better lock this door first, I suppose,' he said.

He turned the key in the lock of Mrs Leidner's door, then drew it out and handed it to me.

'I guess you'd better keep this, nurse. Now then.'

Together we lifted Dr Leidner and carried him into his own room and laid him on his bed. Mr Emmott went off in search of brandy. He returned, accompanied by Miss Johnson.

Her face was drawn and anxious, but she was calm and capable, and I felt satisfied to leave Dr Leidner in her charge.

I hurried out into the courtyard. The station wagon was just coming in through the archway. I think it gave us all a shock to see Bill's pink, cheerful face as he jumped out with his familiar 'Hallo, 'allo, 'allo! Here's the oof!' He went on gaily, 'No highway robberies — '

He came to a halt suddenly. 'I say, is anything up? What's the matter with you all? You look as though the cat had killed your canary.'

Mr Emmott said shortly: 'Mrs Leidner's dead — killed.'

'*What?*' Bill's jolly face changed ludicrously. He stared, his eyes goggling. 'Mother Leidner dead! You're pulling my leg.'

'Dead?' It was a sharp cry. I turned to see Mrs Mercado behind me. 'Did you say Mrs Leidner had been *killed*?'

'Yes,' I said. 'Murdered.'

'No!' she gasped. 'Oh, no! I won't believe it. Perhaps she's committed suicide.'

'Suicides don't hit themselves on the head,' I said dryly. 'It's murder all right, Mrs Mercado.'

She sat down suddenly on an upturned packing-case.

She said, 'Oh, but this is horrible — *horrible . . .* '

Naturally it was horrible. We didn't need *her* to tell us so! I wondered if perhaps she was feeling a bit remorseful for the harsh feelings she had harboured against the dead woman, and all the spiteful things she had said.

After a minute or two she asked rather breathlessly: 'What are you going to do?'

Mr Emmott took charge in his quiet way.

'Bill, you'd better get in again to Hassanieh as quick as you can. I don't know much about the proper procedure. Better get hold of Captain Maitland, he's in charge of the police here, I think. Get Dr Reilly first. He'll know what to do.'

Mr Coleman nodded. All the facetiousness was knocked out of him. He just looked young and frightened. Without a word he jumped into the station wagon and drove off.

Mr Emmott said rather uncertainly, 'I suppose we ought to have a hunt round.' He raised his voice and called: 'Ibrahim!'

'Na'am.'

The house-boy came running. Mr Emmott spoke to him in Arabic. A vigorous colloquy passed between them. The boy seemed to be emphatically denying something.

At last Mr Emmott said in a perplexed voice, 'He says there's not been a soul here this afternoon. No stranger of any kind. I suppose the fellow must have slipped in without their seeing him.'

'Of course he did,' said Mrs Mercado. 'He slunk in when the boys weren't looking.'

'Yes,' said Mr Emmott.

The slight uncertainty in his voice made me look at him inquiringly.

He turned and spoke to the little pot-boy,

Abdullah, asking him a question.

The boy replied vehemently at length.

The puzzled frown on Mr Emmott's brow increased.

'I don't understand it,' he murmured under his breath. 'I don't understand it at all.'

But he didn't tell me what he didn't understand.

11

An Odd Business

I'm adhering as far as possible to telling only my personal part in the business. I pass over the events of the next two hours, the arrival of Captain Maitland and the police and Dr Reilly. There was a good deal of general confusion, questioning, all the routine business, I suppose.

In my opinion we began to get down to brass tacks about five o'clock when Dr Reilly asked me to come with him into the office. He shut the door, sat down in Dr Leidner's chair, motioned me to sit down opposite him, and said briskly: 'Now, then, nurse, let's get down to it. There's something damned odd here.'

I settled my cuffs and looked at him inquiringly.

He drew out a notebook.

'This is for my own satisfaction. Now, what time was it exactly when Dr Leidner found his wife's body?'

'I should say it was almost exactly a quarter to three,' I said.

'And how do you know that?'

'Well, I looked at my watch when I got up. It was twenty to three then.'

'Let's have a look at this watch of yours.'

I slipped it off my wrist and held it out to him.

'Right to the minute. Excellent woman. Good, that's *that* fixed. Now, did you form any opinion as to how long she'd been dead?'

'Oh, really, doctor,' I said, 'I shouldn't like to say.'

'Don't be so professional. I want to see if your estimate agrees with mine.'

'Well, I should say she'd been dead at least an hour.'

'Quite so. I examined the body at half-past four and I'm inclined to put the time of death between 1.15 and 1.45. We'll say half-past one at a guess. That's near enough.'

He stopped and drummed thoughtfully with his fingers on the table.

'Damned odd, this business,' he said. 'Can you tell me about it — you were resting, you say? Did you hear anything?'

'At half-past one? No, doctor. I didn't hear anything at half-past one or at any other time. I lay on my bed from a quarter to one until twenty to three and I didn't hear anything except that droning noise the Arab boy makes, and occasionally Mr Emmott shouting up to

Dr Leidner on the roof.'

'The Arab boy — yes.'

He frowned.

At that moment the door opened and Dr Leidner and Captain Maitland came in. Captain Maitland was a fussy little man with a pair of shrewd grey eyes.

Dr Reilly rose and pushed Dr Leidner into his chair.

'Sit down, man. I'm glad you've come. We shall want you. There's something very queer about this business.'

Dr Leidner bowed his head.

'I know.' He looked at me. 'My wife confided the truth to Nurse Leatheran. We mustn't keep anything back at this juncture, nurse, so please tell Captain Maitland and Dr Reilly just what passed between you and my wife yesterday.'

As nearly as possible I gave our conversation verbatim.

Captain Maitland uttered an occasional ejaculation. When I had finished he turned to Dr Leidner.

'And this is all true, Leidner — eh?'

'Every word Nurse Leatheran has told you is correct.'

'What an extraordinary story!' said Dr Reilly. 'You can produce these letters?'

'I have no doubt they will be found

amongst my wife's belongings.'

'She took them out of the attaché-case on her table,' I said.

'Then they are probably still there.'

He turned to Captain Maitland and his usually gentle face grew hard and stern.

'There must be no question of hushing this story up, Captain Maitland. The one thing necessary is for this man to be caught and punished.'

'You believe it actually is Mrs Leidner's former husband?' I asked.

'Don't you think so, nurse?' asked Captain Maitland.

'Well, I think it is open to doubt,' I said hesitatingly.

'In any case,' said Dr Leidner, 'the man is a murderer — and I should say a dangerous lunatic also. He *must* be found, Captain Maitland. He must. It should not be difficult.'

Dr Reilly said slowly: 'It may be more difficult than you think . . . eh, Maitland?'

Captain Maitland tugged at his moustache without replying.

Suddenly I gave a start.

'Excuse me,' I said, 'but there's something perhaps I ought to mention.'

I told my story of the Iraqi we had seen trying to peer through the window, and of how I had seen him hanging about the place two days ago trying to pump Father Lavigny.

'Good,' said Captain Maitland, 'we'll make a note of that. It will be something for the police to go on. The man may have some connection with the case.'

'Probably paid to act as a spy,' I suggested. 'To find out when the coast was clear.'

Dr Reilly rubbed his nose with a harassed gesture.

'That's the devil of it,' he said. 'Supposing the coast wasn't clear — eh?'

I stared at him in a puzzled fashion.

Captain Maitland turned to Dr Leidner.

'I want you to listen to me very carefully, Leidner. This is a review of the evidence we've got up to date. After lunch, which was served at twelve o'clock and was over by five and twenty to one, your wife went to her room accompanied by Nurse Leatheran, who settled her comfortably. You yourself went up to the roof, where you spent the next two hours, is that right?'

'Yes.'

'Did you come down from the roof at all during that time?'

'No.'

'Did anyone come up to you?'

'Yes, Emmott did pretty frequently. He went to and fro between me and the boy, who was washing pottery down below.'

106

'Did you yourself look over into the courtyard at all?'

'Once or twice — usually to call to Emmott about something.'

'On each occasion the boy was sitting in the middle of the courtyard washing pots?'

'Yes.'

'What was the longest period of time when Emmott was with you and absent from the courtyard?'

Dr Leidner considered.

'It's difficult to say — perhaps ten minutes. Personally I should say two or three minutes, but I know by experience that my sense of time is not very good when I am absorbed and interested in what I am doing.'

Captain Maitland looked at Dr Reilly. The latter nodded. 'We'd better get down to it,' he said.

Captain Maitland took out a small notebook and opened it.

'Look here, Leidner, I'm going to read to you exactly what every member of your expedition was doing between one and two this afternoon.'

'But surely — '

'Wait. You'll see what I'm driving at in a minute. First Mr and Mrs Mercado. Mr Mercado says he was working in his laboratory. Mrs Mercado says she was in her bedroom shampooing her hair. Miss Johnson says she was in the living-room taking impressions of cylinder seals. Mr Reiter says he was in the dark-room developing plates. Father Lavigny says he was working in his bedroom. As to the two remaining members of the expedition, Carey and Coleman, the former was up on the dig and Coleman was in Hassanieh. So much for the members of the expedition. Now for the servants. The cook — your Indian chap — was sitting immediately outside the archway chatting to the guard and plucking a couple of fowls. Ibrahim and Mansur, the house-boys, joined him there at about 1.15. They both remained there laughing and talking until 2.30 — *by which time your wife was already dead.*'

Dr Leidner leaned forward.

'I don't understand — you puzzle me. What are you hinting at?'

'Is there any means of access to your wife's room except by the door into the courtyard?'

'No. There are two windows, but they are heavily barred — and besides, I think they were shut.'

He looked at me questioningly.

'They were closed and latched on the inside,' I said promptly.

'In any case,' said Captain Maitland, 'even if they had been open, no one could have

108

entered or left the room that way. My fellows and I have assured ourselves of that. It is the same with all the other windows giving on the open country. They all have iron bars and all the bars are in good condition. To have got into your wife's room, a stranger *must* have come through the arched doorway into the courtyard. But we have the united assurance of the guard, the cook and the house-boy that *nobody did so.*'

Dr Leidner sprang up.

'What do you mean? What do you mean?'

'Pull yourself together, man,' said Dr Reilly quietly. 'I know it's a shock, but it's got to be faced. *The murderer didn't come from outside* — so he must have come from *inside.* It looks as though Mrs Leidner must have been murdered *by a member of your own expedition.*'

12

'I Didn't Believe...'

'No. No!'

Dr Leidner sprang up and walked up and down in an agitated manner.

'It's impossible what you say, Reilly. Absolutely impossible. One of *us*? Why, every single member of the expedition was devoted to Louise!'

A queer little expression pulled down the corners of Dr Reilly's mouth. Under the circumstances it was difficult for him to say anything, but if ever a man's silence was eloquent his was at that minute.

'Quite impossible,' reiterated Dr Leidner. 'They were all devoted to her, Louise had such wonderful charm. Everyone felt it.'

Dr Reilly coughed.

'Excuse me, Leidner, but after all that's only your opinion. If any member of the expedition had disliked your wife they would naturally not advertise the fact to you.'

Dr Leidner looked distressed.

'True — quite true. But all the same, Reilly, I think you are wrong. I'm sure everyone was fond of Louise.'

He was silent for a moment or two and then burst out:

'This idea of yours is infamous. It's — it's frankly incredible.'

'You can't get away from — er — the facts,' said Captain Maitland.

'Facts? Facts? Lies told by an Indian cook and a couple of Arab house-boys. You know these fellows as well as I do, Reilly, so do you, Maitland. Truth as truth means nothing to them. They say what you want them to say as a mere matter of politeness.'

'In this case,' said Dr Reilly dryly, 'they are saying what we *don't* want them to say. Besides, I know the habits of your household fairly well. Just outside the gate is a kind of social club. Whenever I've been over here in the afternoon I've always found most of your staff there. It's the natural place for them to be.'

'All the same I think you are assuming too much. Why shouldn't this man — this devil — have got in earlier and concealed himself somewhere?'

'I agree that that is not actually impossible,' said Dr Reilly coolly. 'Let us assume that a stranger *did* somehow gain admission unseen. He would have to remain concealed until the right moment (and he certainly couldn't have

111

done so in Mrs Leidner's room, there is no cover there) and take the risk of being seen entering the room and leaving it — with Emmott and the boy in the courtyard most of the time.'

'The boy. I'd forgotten the boy,' said Dr Leidner. 'A sharp little chap. But surely, Maitland, the boy *must* have seen the murderer go into my wife's room?'

'We've elucidated that. The boy was washing pots the whole afternoon with one exception. Somehow around half-past one — Emmott can't put it closer than that — he went up to the roof and was with you for ten minutes — that's right, isn't it?'

'Yes. I couldn't have told you the exact time but it must have been about that.'

'Very good. Well, during that ten minutes, the boy, seizing his chance to be idle, strolled out and joined the others outside the gate for a chat. When Emmott came down he found the boy absent and called him angrily, asking him what he meant leaving his work. As far as I can see, *your wife must have been murdered during that ten minutes.*'

With a groan Dr Leidner sat down and hid his face in his hands.

Dr Reilly took up the tale, his voice quiet and matter-of-fact.

'The time fits in with my evidence,' he said.

'She'd been dead about three hours when I examined her. The only question is — who did it?'

There was a silence. Dr Leidner sat up in his chair and passed a hand over his forehead.

'I admit the force of your reasoning, Reilly,' he said quietly. 'It certainly *seems* as though it were what people call 'an inside job'. But I feel convinced that somewhere or other there is a mistake. It's plausible but there must be a flaw in it. To begin with, you are assuming that an amazing coincidence has occurred.'

'Odd that you should use that word,' said Dr Reilly.

Without paying any attention Dr Leidner went on: 'My wife receives threatening letters. She has reason to fear a certain person. Then she is — killed. And you ask me to believe that she is killed — not by that person — but by someone entirely different! I say that that is ridiculous.'

'It seems so — yes,' said Reilly meditatively.

He looked at Captain Maitland. 'Coincidence — eh? What do you say, Maitland? Are you in favour of the idea? Shall we put it up to Leidner?'

Captain Maitland gave a nod.

'Go ahead,' he said shortly.

'Have you ever heard of a man called Hercule Poirot, Leidner?'

113

Dr Leidner stared at him, puzzled.

'I think I have heard the name, yes,' he said vaguely. 'I once heard a Mr Van Aldin speak of him in very high terms. He is a private detective, is he not?'

'That's the man.'

'But surely he lives in London, so how will that help us?'

'He lives in London, true,' said Dr Reilly, 'but this is where the coincidence comes in. He is now, not in London, but in Syria, and *he will actually pass through Hassanieh on his way to Baghdad tomorrow!*'

'Who told you this?'

'Jean Berat, the French consul. He dined with us last night and was talking about him. It seems he has been disentangling some military scandal in Syria. He's coming through here to visit Baghdad, and afterwards returning through Syria to London. How's that for a coincidence?'

Dr Leidner hesitated a moment and looked apologetically at Captain Maitland.

'What do you think, Captain Maitland?'

'Should welcome co-operation,' said Captain Maitland promptly. 'My fellows are good scouts at scouring the countryside and investigating Arab blood feuds, but frankly, Leidner, this business of your wife's seems to me rather out of my class. The whole thing looks confoundedly fishy. I'm more than willing to have the fellow take a look at the case.'

'You suggest that I should appeal to this man Poirot to help us?' said Dr Leidner. 'And suppose he refuses?'

'He won't refuse,' said Dr Reilly.

'How do you know?'

'Because I'm a professional man myself. If a really intricate case of, say, cerebro-spinal meningitis comes my way and I'm invited to take a hand, I shouldn't be able to refuse. This isn't an ordinary crime, Leidner.'

'No,' said Dr Leidner. His lips twitched with sudden pain. 'Will you then, Reilly, approach this Hercule Poirot on my behalf?'

'I will.'

Dr Leidner made a gesture of thanks.

'Even now,' he said slowly, 'I can't realize it — that Louise is really dead.'

I could bear it no longer.

'Oh! Doctor Leidner,' I burst out, 'I — I can't tell you how badly I feel about this. I've failed so badly in my duty. It was my job to watch over Mrs Leidner — to keep her from harm.'

Dr Leidner shook his head gravely.

'No, no, nurse, you've nothing to reproach yourself with,' he said slowly. 'It's *I*, God forgive me, who am to blame . . . *I didn't believe* — all along I didn't believe . . . I didn't dream for one moment that there was any *real* danger . . . '

He got up. His face twitched.

'*I let her go to her death* . . . Yes, I let her go to her death — *not believing* — '

He staggered out of the room.

Dr Reilly looked at me.

'I feel pretty culpable too,' he said. 'I thought the good lady was playing on his nerves.'

'I didn't take it really seriously either,' I confessed.

'We were all three wrong,' said Dr Reilly gravely.

'So it seems,' said Captain Maitland.

13

Hercule Poirot Arrives

I don't think I shall ever forget my first sight of Hercule Poirot. Of course, I got used to him later on, but to begin with it was a shock, and I think everyone else must have felt the same!

I don't know what I'd imagined — something rather like Sherlock Holmes — long and lean with a keen, clever face. Of course, I knew he was a foreigner, but I hadn't expected him to be *quite* as foreign as he was, if you know what I mean.

When you saw him you just wanted to laugh! He was like something on the stage or at the pictures. To begin with, he wasn't above five-foot five, I should think — an odd, plump little man, quite old, with an enormous moustache, and a head like an egg. He looked like a hairdresser in a comic play!

And this was the man who was going to find out who killed Mrs Leidner!

I suppose something of my disgust must have shown in my face, for almost straight-away he said to me with a queer kind of twinkle:

'You disapprove of me, *ma soeur*? Remember, the pudding proves itself only when you eat it.'

The proof of the pudding's in the eating, I *suppose* he meant.

Well, that's a true enough saying, but I couldn't say I felt much confidence myself!

Dr Reilly brought him out in his car soon after lunch on Sunday, and his first procedure was to ask us all to assemble together.

We did so in the dining-room, all sitting round the table. Mr Poirot sat at the head of it with Dr Leidner one side and Dr Reilly the other.

When we were all assembled, Dr Leidner cleared his throat and spoke in his gentle, hesitating voice.

'I dare say you have all heard of M. Hercule Poirot. He was passing through Hassanieh today, and has very kindly agreed to break his journey to help us. The Iraqi police and Captain Maitland are, I am sure, doing their very best, but — but there are circumstances in the case' — he floundered and shot an appealing glance at Dr Reilly — 'there may, it seems, be difficulties . . .'

'It is not all the square and overboard — no?' said the little man at the top of the table. Why, he couldn't even speak English properly!

118

'Oho, he *must* be caught!' cried Mrs Mercado. 'It would be unbearable if he got away!'

I noticed the little foreigner's eyes rest on her appraisingly.

'He? Who is *he*, madame?' he asked.

'Why, the murderer, of course.'

'Ah! the murderer,' said Hercule Poirot.

He spoke as though the murderer was of no consequence at all!

We all stared at him. He looked from one face to another.

'It is likely, I think,' he said, 'that you have none of you been brought in contact with a case of murder before?'

There was a general murmur of assent.

Hercule Poirot smiled.

'It is clear, therefore, that you do not understand the A B C of the position. There are unpleasantnesses! Yes, there are a lot of unpleasantnesses. To begin with, there is *suspicion*.'

'Suspicion?'

It was Miss Johnson who spoke. Mr Poirot looked at her thoughtfully. I had an idea that he regarded her with approval. He looked as though he were thinking: 'Here is a sensible, intelligent person!'

'Yes, mademoiselle,' he said. 'Suspicion! Let us not make the bones about it. *You are all under suspicion here in this house.* The cook, the house-boy, the scullion, the pot-boy — yes, and all the members of the expedition too.'

Mrs Mercado started up, her face working.

'How *dare* you? How dare you say such a thing? This is odious — unbearable! Dr Leidner — you can't sit here and let this man — let this man — '

Dr Leidner said wearily: 'Please try and be calm, Marie.'

Mr Mercado stood up too. His hands were shaking and his eyes were bloodshot.

'I agree. It is an outrage — an insult — '

'No, no,' said Mr Poirot. 'I do not insult you. I merely ask you all to face facts. *In a house where murder has been committed, every inmate comes in for a certain share of suspicion.* I ask you what evidence is there that the murderer came from outside at all?'

Mrs Mercado cried: 'But of course he did! It stands to reason! Why — ' She stopped and said more slowly, 'Anything else would be incredible!'

'You are doubtless correct, madame,' said Poirot with a bow. 'I explain to you only how the matter must be approached. First I assure myself of the fact that everyone in this room is innocent. After that I seek the murderer elsewhere.'

'Is it not possible that that may be a little late in the day?' asked Father Lavigny suavely.

'The tortoise, *mon père*, overtook the hare.'

Father Lavigny shrugged his shoulders.

'We are in your hands,' he said resignedly. 'Convince yourself as soon as may be of our innocence in this terrible business.'

'As rapidly as possible. It was my duty to make the position clear to you, so that you may not resent the impertinence of any questions I may have to ask. Perhaps, *mon père*, the Church will set an example?'

'Ask any questions you please of me,' said Father Lavigny gravely.

'This is your first season out here?'

'Yes.'

'And you arrived — when?'

'Three weeks ago almost to a day. That is, on the 27th of February.'

'Coming from?'

'The Order of the Pères Blancs at Carthage.'

'Thank you, *mon père*. Were you at any time acquainted with Mrs Leidner before coming here?'

'No, I had never seen the lady until I met her here.'

'Will you tell me what you were doing at the time of the tragedy?'

'I was working on some cuneiform tablets in my own room.'

I noticed that Poirot had at his elbow a rough plan of the building.

'That is the room at the south-west corner corresponding to that of Mrs Leidner on the opposite side?'

'Yes.'

'At what time did you go to your room?'

'Immediately after lunch. I should say at about twenty minutes to one.'

'And you remained there until — when?'

'Just before three o'clock. I had heard the station wagon come back — and then I heard it drive off again. I wondered why, and came out to see.'

'During the time that you were there did you leave the room at all?'

'No, not once.'

'And you heard or saw nothing that might have any bearing on the tragedy?'

'No.'

'You have no window giving on the courtyard in your room?'

'No, both the windows give on the countryside.'

'Could you hear at all what was happening in the courtyard?'

'Not very much. I heard Mr Emmott passing my room and going up to the roof.

He did so once or twice.'

'Can you remember at what time?'

'No, I'm afraid I can't. I was engrossed in my work, you see.'

There was a pause and then Poirot said:

'Can you say or suggest anything at all that might throw light on this business? Did you, for instance, notice anything in the days preceding the murder?'

Father Lavigny looked slightly uncomfortable.

He shot a half-questioning look at Dr Leidner.

'That is rather a difficult question, monsieur,' he said gravely. 'If you ask me I must reply frankly that in my opinion Mrs Leidner was clearly in dread of someone or something. She was definitely nervous about strangers. I imagine she had a reason for this nervousness of hers — but I *know* nothing. She did not confide in me.'

Poirot cleared his throat and consulted some notes that he held in his hand. 'Two nights ago I understand there was a scare of burglary.'

Father Lavigny replied in the affirmative and retailed his story of the light seen in the antika-room and the subsequent futile search.

'You believe, do you not, that some

123

unauthorized person was on the premises at that time?'

'I don't know what to think,' said Father Lavigny frankly. 'Nothing was taken or disturbed in any way. It might have been one of the house-boys — '

'Or a member of the expedition?'

'Or a member of the expedition. But in that case there would be no reason for the person not admitting the fact.'

'But it *might* equally have been a stranger from outside?'

'I suppose so.'

'Supposing a stranger *had* been on the premises, could he have concealed himself successfully during the following day and until the afternoon of the day following that?'

He asked the question half of Father Lavigny and half of Dr Leidner. Both men considered the question carefully.

'I hardly think it would be possible,' said Dr Leidner at last with some reluctance. 'I don't see where he could possibly conceal himself, do you, Father Lavigny?'

'No — no — I don't.'

Both men seemed reluctant to put the suggestion aside.

Poirot turned to Miss Johnson.

'And you, mademoiselle? Do you consider such a hypothesis feasible?'

After a moment's thought Miss Johnson shook her head.

'No,' she said. 'I don't. Where could anyone hide? The bedrooms are all in use and, in any case, are sparsely furnished. The dark-room, the drawing-office and the laboratory were all in use the next day — so were all these rooms. There are no cupboards or corners. Perhaps, if the servants were in collusion — '

'That is possible, but unlikely,' said Poirot.

He turned once more to Father Lavigny.

'There is another point. The other day Nurse Leatheran here noticed you talking to a man outside. She had previously noticed that same man trying to peer in at one of the windows on the outside. It rather looks as though the man were hanging round the place deliberately.'

'That is possible, of course,' said Father Lavigny thoughtfully.

'Did you speak to this man first, or did he speak to you?'

Father Lavigny considered for a moment or two.

'I believe — yes, I am sure, that he spoke to me.'

'What did he say?'

Father Lavigny made an effort of memory.

'He said, I think, something to the effect was this the American expedition house? And then something else about the Americans employing a lot of men on the work. I did not really understand him very well, but I endeavoured to keep up a conversation so as to improve my Arabic. I thought, perhaps, that being a townee he would understand me better than the men on the dig do.'

'Did you converse about anything else?'

'As far as I remember, I said Hassanieh was a big town — and we then agreed that Baghdad was bigger — and I think he asked whether I was an Armenian or a Syrian Catholic — something of that kind.'

Poirot nodded.

'Can you describe him?'

Again Father Lavigny frowned in thought.

'He was rather a short man,' he said at last, 'and squarely built. He had a very noticeable squint and was of fair complexion.'

Mr Poirot turned to me.

'Does that agree with the way you would describe him?' he asked.

'Not exactly,' I said hesitatingly. 'I should have said he was tall rather than short, and very dark-complexioned. He seemed to me of a rather slender build. I didn't notice any squint.'

Mr Poirot gave a despairing shrug of the shoulders.

'It is always so! If you were of the police

how well you would know it! The description of the same man by two different people — never does it agree. Every detail is contradicted.'

'I'm fairly sure about the squint,' said Father Lavigny. 'Nurse Leatheran may be right about the other points. By the way, when I said *fair*, I only meant fair for an *Iraqi*. I expect nurse would call that dark.'

'Very dark,' I said obstinately. 'A dirty dark-yellow colour.'

I saw Dr Reilly bite his lips and smile.

Poirot threw up his hands.

'*Passons!*' he said. 'This stranger hanging about, he may be important — he may not. At any rate he must be found. Let us continue our inquiry.'

He hesitated for a minute, studying the faces turned towards him round the table, then, with a quick nod, he singled out Mr Reiter.

'Come, my friend,' he said. 'Let us have your account of yesterday afternoon.'

Mr Reiter's pink, plump face flushed scarlet.

'Me?' he said.

'Yes, you. To begin with, your name and your age?'

'Carl Reiter, twenty-eight.'

'American — yes?'

'Yes, I come from Chicago.'

'This is your first season?'

'Yes. I'm in charge of the photography.'

'Ah, yes. And yesterday afternoon, how did you employ yourself?'

'Well — I was in the dark-room most of the time.'

'*Most* of the time — eh?'

'Yes. I developed some plates first. Afterwards I was fixing up some objects to photograph.'

'Outside?'

'Oh no, in the photographic-room.'

'The dark-room opens out of the photographic-room?'

'Yes.'

'And so you never came outside the photographic-room?'

'No.'

'Did you notice anything that went on in the courtyard?'

The young man shook his head.

'I wasn't noticing anything,' he explained. 'I was busy. I heard the car come back, and as soon as I could leave what I was doing I came out to see if there was any mail. It was then that I — heard.'

'And you began to work in the photographic-room — when?'

'At ten minutes to one.'

'Were you acquainted with Mrs Leidner before you joined this expedition?'

The young man shook his head.

'No, sir. I never saw her till I actually got here.'

'Can you think of *anything* — any incident — however small — that might help us?'

Carl Reiter shook his head.

He said helplessly: 'I guess I don't know anything at all, sir.'

'Mr Emmott?'

David Emmott spoke clearly and concisely in his pleasant soft American voice.

'I was working with the pottery from a quarter to one till a quarter to three — overseeing the boy Abdullah, sorting it, and occasionally going up to the roof to help Dr Leidner.'

'How often did you go up to the roof?'

'Four times, I think.'

'For how long?'

'Usually a couple of minutes — not more. But on one occasion after I'd been working a little over half an hour I stayed as long as ten minutes — discussing what to keep and what to fling away.'

'And I understand that when you came down you found the boy had left his place?'

'Yes. I called him angrily and he reappeared from outside the archway. He had gone out to gossip with the others.'

'That settles the only time he left his work?'

'Well, I sent him up once or twice to the roof with pottery.'

Poirot said gravely: 'It is hardly necessary to ask you, Mr Emmott, whether you saw anyone enter or leave Mrs Leidner's room during that time?'

Mr Emmott replied promptly.

'I saw no one at all. Nobody even came out into the courtyard during the two hours I was working.'

'And to the best of your belief it was half-past one when both you and the boy were absent and the courtyard was empty?'

'It couldn't have been far off that time. Of course, I can't say *exactly*.'

Poirot turned to Dr Reilly.

'That agrees with your estimate of the time of death, doctor?'

'It does,' said Dr Reilly.

Mr Poirot stroked his great curled moustaches.

'I think we can take it,' he said gravely, 'that Mrs Leidner met her death during that ten minutes.'

14

One of Us?

There was a little pause — and in it a wave of horror seemed to float round the room.

I think it was at that moment that I first believed Dr Reilly's theory to be right.

I *felt* that the murderer was in the room. Sitting with us — listening. *One of us . . .*

Perhaps Mrs Mercado felt it too. For she suddenly gave a short sharp cry.

'I can't help it,' she sobbed. 'I — it's so *terrible!*'

'Courage, Marie,' said her husband.

He looked at us apologetically.

'She is so sensitive. She feels things so much.'

'I — I was so fond of Louise,' sobbed Mrs Mercado.

I don't know whether something of what I felt showed in my face, but I suddenly found that Mr Poirot was looking at me, and that a slight smile hovered on his lips.

I gave him a cold glance, and at once he resumed his inquiry.

'Tell me, madame,' he said, 'of the way you

spent yesterday afternoon?'

'I was washing my hair,' sobbed Mrs Mercado. 'It seems awful not to have known anything about it. I was quite happy and busy.'

'You were in your room?'

'Yes.'

'And you did not leave it?'

'No. Not till I heard the car. Then I came out and I heard what had happened. Oh, it was *awful*!'

'Did it surprise you?'

Mrs Mercado stopped crying. Her eyes opened resentfully.

'What do you mean, M. Poirot? Are you suggesting — ?'

'What should I mean, madame? You have just told us how fond you were of Mrs Leidner. She might, perhaps, have confided in you.'

'Oh, I see . . . No — no, dear Louise never told me anything — anything *definite*, that is. Of course, I could see she was terribly worried and nervous. And there were those strange occurrences — hands tapping on the windows and all that.'

'Fancies, I remember you said,' I put in, unable to keep silent.

I was glad to see that she looked momentarily disconcerted.

Once again I was conscious of Mr Poirot's amused eye glancing in my direction.

He summed up in a businesslike way.

'It comes to this, madame, you were washing your hair — you heard nothing and you saw nothing. Is there anything at all you can think of that would be a help to us in any way?'

Mrs Mercado took no time to think.

'No, indeed there isn't. It's the deepest mystery! But I should say there is no doubt — no doubt *at all* that the murderer came from outside. Why, it stands to reason.'

Poirot turned to her husband.

'And you, monsieur, what have you to say?'

Mr Mercado started nervously. He pulled at his beard in an aimless fashion.

'Must have been. Must have been,' he said. 'Yet how could anyone wish to harm her? She was so gentle — so kind — ' He shook his head. 'Whoever killed her must have been a fiend — yes, a fiend!'

'And you yourself, monsieur, how did you pass yesterday afternoon?'

'I?' he stared vaguely.

'You were in the laboratory, Joseph,' his wife prompted him.

'Ah, yes, so I was — so I was. My usual tasks.'

'At what time did you go there?'

Again he looked helplessly and inquiringly at Mrs Mercado.

'At ten minutes to one, Joseph.'

'Ah, yes, at ten minutes to one.'

'Did you come out in the courtyard at all?'

'No — I don't think so.' He considered. 'No, I am sure I didn't.'

'When did you hear of the tragedy?'

'My wife came and told me. It was terrible — shocking. I could hardly believe it. Even now, I can hardly believe it is true.'

Suddenly he began to tremble.

'It is horrible — horrible . . . '

Mrs Mercado came quickly to his side.

'Yes, yes, Joseph, we feel that. But we mustn't give way. It makes it so much more difficult for poor Dr Leidner.'

I saw a spasm of pain pass across Dr Leidner's face, and I guessed that this emotional atmosphere was not easy for him. He gave a half-glance at Poirot as though in appeal. Poirot responded quickly.

'Miss Johnson?' he said.

'I'm afraid I can tell you very little,' said Miss Johnson. Her cultured well-bred voice was soothing after Mrs Mercado's shrill treble. She went on: 'I was working in the living-room — taking impressions of some cylinder seals on plasticine.'

'And you saw or noticed nothing?'

'No.'

Poirot gave her a quick glance. His ear had caught what mine had — a faint note of indecision.

'Are you quite sure, mademoiselle? Is there something that comes back to you vaguely?'

'No — not really — '

'Something you saw, shall we say, out of the corner of your eye hardly knowing you saw it.'

'No, certainly not,' she replied positively.

'Something you *heard* then. Ah, yes, something you are not quite sure whether you heard or not?'

Miss Johnson gave a short, vexed laugh.

'You press me very closely, M. Poirot. I'm afraid you are encouraging me to tell you what I am, perhaps, only imagining.'

'Then there was something you — shall we say — imagined?'

Miss Johnson said slowly, weighing her words in a detached way: 'I have imagined — since — that at some time during the afternoon I heard a very faint cry . . . What I mean is that I daresay I *did* hear a cry. All the windows in the living-room were open and one hears all sorts of sounds from people working in the barley fields. But you see — since — I've got the idea into my head that it was — that it was Mrs Leidner I heard.

And that's made me rather unhappy. Because if I'd jumped up and run along to her room — well, who knows? I might have been in time . . . '

Dr Reilly interposed authoritatively.

'Now, don't start getting that into your head,' he said. 'I've no doubt but that Mrs Leidner (forgive me, Leidner) was struck down almost as soon as the man entered the room, and it was that blow that killed her. No second blow was struck. Otherwise she would have had time to call for help and make a real outcry.'

'Still, I might have caught the murderer,' said Miss Johnson.

'What time was this, mademoiselle?' asked Poirot. 'In the neighbourhood of half-past one?'

'It must have been about that time — yes.' She reflected a minute.

'That would fit in,' said Poirot thoughtfully. 'You heard nothing else — the opening or shutting of a door, for instance?'

Miss Johnson shook her head.

'No, I do not remember anything of that kind.'

'You were sitting at a table, I presume. Which way were you facing? The courtyard? The antika-room? The verandah? Or the open countryside?'

'I was facing the courtyard.'

'Could you see the boy Abdullah washing pots from where you were?'

'Oh, yes, if I looked up, but of course I was very intent on what I was doing. All my attention was on that.'

'If anyone had passed the courtyard window, though, you would have noticed it?'

'Oh, yes, I am almost sure of that.'

'And nobody did so?'

'No.'

'But if anyone had walked, say, across the middle of the courtyard, would you have noticed that?'

'I think — probably not — unless, as I said before, I had happened to look up and out of the window.'

'You did not notice the boy Abdullah leave his work and go out to join the other servants?'

'No.'

'Ten minutes,' mused Poirot. 'That fatal ten minutes.'

There was a momentary silence.

Miss Johnson lifted her head suddenly and said: 'You know, M. Poirot, I think I have unintentionally misled you. On thinking it over, I do not believe that I could possibly have heard any cry uttered in Mrs Leidner's room from where I was. The antika-room lay between me and her — and I understand her windows were found closed.'

'In any case, do not distress yourself, mademoiselle,' said Poirot kindly. 'It is not really of much importance.'

'No, of course not. I understand that. But you see, it *is* of importance to me, because I feel I might have done something.'

'Don't distress yourself, dear Anne,' said Dr Leidner with affection. 'You must be sensible. What you heard was probably one Arab bawling to another some distance away in the fields.'

Miss Johnson flushed a little at the kindliness of his tone. I even saw tears spring to her eyes. She turned her head away and spoke even more gruffly than usual.

'Probably was. Usual thing after a tragedy — start imagining things that aren't so at all.'

Poirot was once more consulting his notebook.

'I do not suppose there is much more to be said. Mr Carey?'

Richard Carey spoke slowly — in a wooden mechanical manner.

'I'm afraid I can add nothing helpful. I was on duty at the dig. The news was brought to me there.'

'And you know or can think of nothing helpful that occurred in the days immediately preceding the murder?'

'Nothing at all.'

'Mr Coleman?'

'I was right out of the whole thing,' said Mr Coleman with — was it just a shade of regret — in his tone. 'I went into Hassanieh yesterday morning to get the money for the men's wages. When I came back Emmott told me what had happened and I went back in the bus to get the police and Dr Reilly.'

'And beforehand?'

'Well, sir, things were a bit jumpy — but you know that already. There was the antika-room scare and one or two before that — hands and faces at the window — you remember, sir,' he appealed to Dr Leidner, who bent his head in assent. 'I think, you know, that you'll find some Johnny *did* get in from outside. Must have been an artful sort of beggar.'

Poirot considered him for a minute or two in silence.

'You are an Englishman, Mr Coleman?' he asked at last.

'That's right, sir. All British. See the trade-mark. Guaranteed genuine.'

'This is your first season?'

'Quite right.'

'And you are passionately keen on archaeology?'

This description of himself seemed to cause Mr Coleman some embarrassment. He got rather pink and shot the side look of a guilty schoolboy at Dr Leidner.

'Of course — it's all very interesting,' he stammered. 'I mean — I'm not exactly a brainy chap . . .'

He broke off rather lamely. Poirot did not insist.

He tapped thoughtfully on the table with the end of his pencil and carefully straightened an inkpot that stood in front of him.

'It seems then,' he said, 'that that is as near as we can get for the moment. If any one of you thinks of something that has for the time being slipped his or her memory, do not hesitate to come to me with it. It will be well now, I think, for me to have a few words alone with Dr Leidner and Dr Reilly.'

It was the signal for a breaking up of the party. We all rose and filed out of the door. When I was half-way out, however, a voice recalled me.

'Perhaps,' said M. Poirot, 'Nurse Leatheran will be so kind as to remain. I think her assistance will be valuable to us.'

I came back and resumed my seat at the table.

15

Poirot Makes a Suggestion

Dr Reilly had risen from his seat. When everyone had gone out he carefully closed the door. Then, with an inquiring glance at Poirot, he proceeded to shut the window giving on the courtyard. The others were already shut. Then he, too, resumed his seat at the table.

'*Bien!*' said Poirot. 'We are now private and undisturbed. We can speak freely. We have heard what the members of the expedition have to tell us and — But yes, *ma soeur*, what is it that you think?'

I got rather red. There was no denying that the queer little man had sharp eyes. He'd seen the thought passing through my mind — I suppose my face *had* shown a bit too clearly what I was thinking!

'Oh, it's nothing — ' I said hesitating.

'Come on, nurse,' said Dr Reilly. 'Don't keep the specialist waiting.'

'It's nothing really,' I said hurriedly. 'It only just passed through my mind, so to speak, that perhaps even if anyone did know or suspect something it wouldn't be easy to bring it out in front of everybody else — or even, perhaps, in front of Dr Leidner.'

Rather to my astonishment, M. Poirot nodded his head in vigorous agreement.

'Precisely. Precisely. It is very just what you say there. But I will explain. That little reunion we have just had — it served a purpose. In England before the races you have a parade of the horses, do you not? They go in front of the grandstand so that everyone may have an opportunity of seeing and judging them. That is the purpose of my little assembly. In the sporting phrase, I run my eye over the possible starters.'

Dr Leidner cried out violently, 'I do not believe for one minute that *any* member of my expedition is implicated in this crime!'

Then, turning to me, he said authoritatively: 'Nurse, I should be much obliged if you would tell M. Poirot here and now exactly what passed between my wife and you two days ago.'

Thus urged, I plunged straightaway into my own story, trying as far as possible to recall the exact words and phrases Mrs Leidner had used.

When I had finished, M. Poirot said: 'Very good. Very good. You have the mind neat and orderly. You will be of great service to me here.'

He turned to Dr Leidner.

'You have these letters?'

'I have them here. I thought that you would want to see them first thing.'

Poirot took them from him, read them, and scrutinized them carefully as he did so. I was rather disappointed that he didn't dust powder over them or examine them with a microscope or anything like that — but I realized that he wasn't a very young man and that his methods were probably not very up to date. He just read them in the way that anyone might read a letter.

Having read them he put them down and cleared his throat.

'Now,' he said, 'let us proceed to get our facts clear and in order. The first of these letters was received by your wife shortly after her marriage to you in America. There had been others but these she destroyed. The first letter was followed by a second. A very short time after the second arrived you both had a near escape from coal-gas poisoning. You then came abroad and for nearly two years no further letters were received. They started again at the beginning of your season this year — that is to say within the last three weeks. That is correct?'

'Absolutely.'

'Your wife displayed every sign of panic and, after consulting Dr Reilly, you engaged Nurse Leatheran here to keep your wife company and allay her fears?'

'Yes.'

'Certain incidents occurred — hands tapping at the window — a spectral face — noises in the antika-room. You did not witness any of these phenomena yourself?'

'No.'

'In fact nobody did except Mrs Leidner?'

'Father Lavigny saw a light in the antika-room.'

'Yes, I have not forgotten that.'

He was silent for a minute or two, then he said: 'Had your wife made a will?'

'I do not think so.'

'Why was that?'

'It did not seem worth it from her point of view.'

'Is she not a wealthy woman?'

'Yes, during her lifetime. Her father left her a considerable sum of money in trust. She could not touch the principal. At her death it was to pass to any children she might have — and failing children to the Pittstown Museum.'

Poirot drummed thoughtfully on the table.

'Then we can, I think,' he said, 'eliminate

one motive from the case. It is, you comprehend, what I look for first. *Who benefits by the deceased's death?* In this case it is a museum. Had it been otherwise, had Mrs Leidner died intestate but possessed of a considerable fortune, I should imagine that it would prove an interesting question as to who inherited the money — you — or a former husband. But there would have been this difficulty, the former husband would have had to resurrect himself in order to claim it, and I should imagine that he would then be in danger of arrest, though I hardly fancy that the death penalty would be exacted so long after the war. However, these speculations need not arise. As I say, I settle first the question of money. For the next step I proceed always to suspect the husband or wife of the deceased! In this case, in the first place, you are proved never to have gone near your wife's room yesterday afternoon, in the second place you lose instead of gain by your wife's death, and in the third place — '

He paused.

'Yes?' said Dr Leidner.

'In the third place,' said Poirot slowly, 'I can, I think, appreciate devotion when I see it. I believe, Dr Leidner, that your love for your wife was the ruling passion of your life. It is so, is it not?'

Dr Leidner answered quite simply: 'Yes.'

Poirot nodded.

'Therefore,' he said, 'we can proceed.'

'Hear, hear, let's get down to it,' said Dr Reilly with some impatience.

Poirot gave him a reproving glance.

'My friend, do not be impatient. In a case like this everything must be approached with order and method. In fact, that is my rule in every case. Having disposed of certain possibilities, we now approach a very important point. It is vital that, as you say — all the cards should be on the table — there must be nothing kept back.'

'Quite so,' said Dr Reilly.

'That is why I demand the whole truth,' went on Poirot.

Dr Leidner looked at him in surprise.

'I assure you, M. Poirot, that I have kept nothing back. I have told you everything that I know. There have been no reserves.'

'*Tout de même*, you have not told me *everything.*'

'Yes, indeed. I cannot think of any detail that has escaped me.'

He looked quite distressed.

Poirot shook his head gently.

'No,' he said. '*You have not told me, for instance, why you installed Nurse Leatheran in the house.*'

Dr Leidner looked completely bewildered.

'But I have explained that. It is obvious. My wife's nervousness — her fears . . . '

Poirot leaned forward. Slowly and emphatically he wagged a finger up and down.

'No, no, no. There is something there that is not clear. Your wife is in danger, yes — she is threatened with death, yes. You send — *not for the police* — not for a private detective even — but for a *nurse*! It does not make the sense, that!'

'I — I — ' Dr Leidner stopped. The colour rose in his cheeks. 'I thought — ' He came to a dead stop.

'Now we are coming to it,' Poirot encouraged him. 'You thought — what?'

Dr Leidner remained silent. He looked harassed and unwilling.

'See you,' Poirot's tone became winning and appealing, 'it all rings true what you have told me, *except for that*. Why a *nurse*? There is an answer — yes. In fact, there can be only one answer. *You did not believe yourself in your wife's danger.*'

And then with a cry Dr Leidner broke down.

'God help me,' he groaned. 'I didn't. I didn't.'

Poirot watched him with the kind of attention a cat gives a mouse-hole — ready to pounce when the mouse shows itself.

'What *did* you think then?' he asked.

'I don't know. I don't know . . . '

'But you do know. You know perfectly. Perhaps I can help you — with a guess. *Did you, Dr Leidner, suspect that these letters were all written by your wife herself?*'

There wasn't any need for him to answer. The truth of Poirot's guess was only too apparent. The horrified hand he held up, as though begging for mercy, told its own tale.

I drew a deep breath. So I *had* been right in my half-formed guess! I recalled the curious tone in which Dr Leidner had asked me what I thought of it all. I nodded my head slowly and thoughtfully, and suddenly awoke to the fact that M. Poirot's eyes were on me.

'Did you think the same, nurse?'

'The idea did cross my mind,' I said truthfully.

'For what reason?'

I explained the similarity of the handwriting on the letter that Mr Coleman had shown me.

Poirot turned to Dr Leidner.

'Had you, too, noticed that similarity?'

Dr Leidner bowed his head.

'Yes, I did. The writing was small and cramped — not big and generous like Louise's, but several of the letters were formed the same way. I will show you.'

From an inner breast pocket he took out some letters and finally selected a sheet from one, which he handed to Poirot. It was part of a letter written to him by his wife. Poirot compared it carefully with the anonymous letters.

'Yes,' he murmured. 'Yes. There are several similarities — a curious way of forming the letter s, a distinctive e. I am not a handwriting expert — I cannot pronounce definitely (and for that matter, I have never found two handwriting experts who agree on any point whatsoever) — but one can at least say this — the similarity between the two handwritings is very marked. It seems highly probable that they were all written by the same person. But it is not *certain*. We must take all contingencies into mind.'

He leaned back in his chair and said thoughtfully: 'There are three possibilities. First, the similarity of the handwriting is pure coincidence. Second, that these threatening letters were written by Mrs Leidner herself for some obscure reason. Third, that they were written by someone *who deliberately copied her handwriting*. Why? There seems no sense in it. One of these three possibilities must be the correct one.'

He reflected for a minute or two and then,

turning to Dr Leidner, he asked, with a resumal of his brisk manner: 'When the possibility that Mrs Leidner herself was the author of these letters first struck you, what theory did you form?'

Dr Leidner shook his head.

'I put the idea out of my head as quickly as possible. I felt it was monstrous.'

'Did you search for no explanation?'

'Well,' he hesitated. 'I wondered if worrying and brooding over the past had perhaps affected my wife's brain slightly. I thought she might possibly have written those letters to herself without being conscious of having done so. That is possible, isn't it?' he added, turning to Dr Reilly.

Dr Reilly pursed up his lips.

'The human brain is capable of almost anything,' he replied vaguely.

But he shot a lightning glance at Poirot, and as if in obedience to it, the latter abandoned the subject.

'The letters are an interesting point,' he said. 'But we must concentrate on the case as a whole. There are, as I see it, three possible solutions.'

'Three?'

'Yes. Solution one: the simplest. Your wife's first husband is still alive. He first threatens her and then proceeds to carry out his threats. If we accept this solution, our problem is to discover how he got in or out without being seen.

'Solution two: Mrs Leidner, for reasons of her own (reasons probably more easily understood by a medical man than a layman), writes herself threatening letters. The gas business is staged by her (remember, it was she who roused you by telling you she smelt gas). But, *if Mrs Leidner wrote herself the letters, she cannot be in danger from the supposed writer.* We must, therefore, look elsewhere for the murderer. We must look, in fact, amongst the members of your staff. Yes,' in answer to a murmur of protest from Dr Leidner, 'that is the only logical conclusion. To satisfy a private grudge one of them killed her. That person, I may say, was probably aware of the letters — or was at any rate aware that Mrs Leidner feared or was pretending to fear someone. That fact, in the murderer's opinion, rendered the murder quite safe for him. He felt sure it would be put down to a mysterious outsider — the writer of the threatening letters.'

'A variant of this solution is that the murderer actually wrote the letters himself, being aware of Mrs Leidner's past history. But in that case it is not quite clear *why* the criminal should have copied Mrs Leidner's

151

own handwriting since, as far as we can see, it would be more to his or her advantage that they should appear to be written by an outsider.

'The third solution is the most interesting to my mind. I suggest that the letters are genuine. They are written by Mrs Leidner's first husband (or his younger brother), *who is actually one of the expedition staff.*'

16

The Suspects

Dr Leidner sprang to his feet.

'Impossible! Absolutely impossible! The idea is absurd!'

Mr Poirot looked at him quite calmly but said nothing.

'You mean to suggest that my wife's former husband is one of the expedition *and that she didn't recognize him?*'

'Exactly. Reflect a little on the facts. Some fifteen years ago your wife lived with this man for a few months. Would she know him if she came across him after that lapse of time? I think not. His face will have changed, his build will have changed — his voice may not have changed so much, but that is a detail he can attend to himself. And remember, *she is not looking for him amongst her own household*. She visualizes him as somewhere *outside* — a stranger. No, I do not think she would recognize him. And there is a second possibility. The young brother — the child of those days who was so passionately devoted to his elder brother. He is now a man. Will

153

she recognize a child of ten or twelve years old in a man nearing thirty? Yes, there is young William Bosner to be reckoned with. Remember, his brother in his eyes may not loom as a traitor but as a patriot, a martyr for his own country — Germany. In his eyes *Mrs Leidner* is the traitor — the monster who sent his beloved brother to death! A susceptible child is capable of great hero worship, and a young mind can easily be obsessed by an idea which persists into adult life.'

'Quite true,' said Dr Reilly. 'The popular view that a child forgets easily is not an accurate one. Many people go right through life in the grip of an idea which has been impressed on them in very tender years.'

'*Bien*. You have these two possibilities. Frederick Bosner, a man by now of fifty odd, and William Bosner, whose age would be something short of thirty. Let us examine the members of your staff from these two points of view.'

'This is fantastic,' murmured Dr Leidner. '*My* staff! The members of my own expedition.'

'And consequently considered above suspicion,' said Poirot dryly. 'A very useful point of view. *Commençons!* Who could emphatically *not* be Frederick or William?'

'The women.'

'Naturally. Miss Johnson and Mrs Mercado are crossed off. Who else?'

'Carey. He and I have worked together for years before I even met Louise — '

'And also he is the wrong age. He is, I should judge, thirty-eight or nine, too young for Frederick, too old for William. Now for the rest. There is Father Lavigny and Mr Mercado. Either of them might be Frederick Bosner.'

'But, my dear sir,' cried Dr Leidner in a voice of mingled irritation and amusement, 'Father Lavigny is known all over the world as an epigraphist and Mercado has worked for years in a well-known museum in New York. It is *impossible* that either of them should be the man you think!'

Poirot waved an airy hand.

'Impossible — impossible — I take no account of the word! The impossible, always I examine it very closely! But we will pass on for the moment. Who else have you? Carl Reiter, a young man with a German name, David Emmott — '

'He has been with me two seasons, remember.'

'He is a young man with the gift of patience. *If* he committed a crime, it would not be in a hurry. All would be very well prepared.'

Dr Leidner made a gesture of despair.

'And lastly, William Coleman,' continued Poirot.

'He is an Englishman.'

'*Pourquoi pas?* Did not Mrs Leidner say that the boy left America and could not be traced? He might easily have been brought up in England.'

'You have an answer to everything,' said Dr Leidner.

I was thinking hard. Right from the beginning I had thought Mr Coleman's manner rather more like a P. G. Wodehouse book than like a real live young man. Had he really been playing a part all the time?

Poirot was writing in a little book.

'Let us proceed with order and method,' he said. 'On the first count we have two names. Father Lavigny and Mr Mercado. On the second we have Coleman, Emmott and Reiter.'

'Now let us pass to the opposite aspect of the matter — means and opportunity. *Who amongst the expedition had the means and the opportunity of committing the crime?* Carey was on the dig, Coleman was in Hassanieh, you yourself were on the roof. That leaves us Father Lavigny, Mr Mercado, Mrs Mercado, David Emmott, Carl Reiter, Miss Johnson and Nurse Leatheran.'

'Oh!' I exclaimed, and I bounded in my chair.

Mr Poirot looked at me with twinkling eyes.

'Yes, I'm afraid, *ma soeur*, that you have got to be included. It would have been quite easy for you to have gone along and killed Mrs Leidner while the courtyard was empty. You have plenty of muscle and strength, and she would have been quite unsuspicious until the moment the blow was struck.'

I was so upset that I couldn't get a word out. Dr Reilly, I noticed, was looking highly amused.

'Interesting case of a nurse who murdered her patients one by one,' he murmured.

Such a look as I gave him!

Dr Leidner's mind had been running on a different tack.

'Not Emmott, M. Poirot,' he objected. 'You can't include him. He was on the roof with me, remember, during that ten minutes.'

'Nevertheless we cannot exclude him. He could have come down, gone straight to Mrs Leidner's room, killed her, and *then* called the boy back. Or he might have killed her on one of the occasions when he had *sent the boy up to you*.'

Dr Leidner shook his head, murmuring: 'What a nightmare! It's all so — fantastic.'

157

To my surprise Poirot agreed.

'Yes, that's true. *This is a fantastic crime.* One does not often come across them. Usually murder is very sordid — very simple. But this is unusual murder . . . I suspect, Dr Leidner, that your wife was an unusual woman.'

He had hit the nail on the head with such accuracy that I jumped.

'Is that true, nurse?' he asked.

Dr Leidner said quietly: 'Tell him what Louise was like, nurse. You are unprejudiced.'

I spoke quite frankly.

'She was very lovely,' I said. 'You couldn't help admiring her and wanting to do things for her. I've never met anyone like her before.'

'Thank you,' said Dr Leidner and smiled at me.

'That is valuable testimony coming from an outsider,' said Poirot politely. 'Well, let us proceed. Under the heading of *means and opportunity* we have seven names. Nurse Leatheran, Miss Johnson, Mrs Mercado, Mr Mercado, Mr Reiter, Mr Emmott and Father Lavigny.'

Once more he cleared his throat. I've always noticed that foreigners can make the oddest noises.

'Let us for the moment assume that our third theory is correct. That is that the murderer is Frederick or William Bosner, and that Frederick or William Bosner is a member of the expedition staff. By comparing both lists we can narrow down our suspects on this count to four. Father Lavigny, Mr Mercado, Carl Reiter and David Emmott.'

'Father Lavigny is out of the question,' said Dr Leidner with decision. 'He is one of the Pères Blancs in Carthage.'

'And his beard's quite real,' I put in.

'*Ma soeur*,' said Poirot, 'a murderer of the first class *never* wears a false beard!'

'How do you know the murderer is of the first class?' I asked rebelliously.

'Because if he were not, the whole truth would be plain to me at this instant — and it is not.'

That's pure conceit, I thought to myself.

'Anyway,' I said, reverting to the beard, 'it must have taken quite a time to grow.'

'That is a practical observation,' said Poirot.

Dr Leidner said irritably: 'But it's ridiculous — quite ridiculous. Both he and Mercado are well-known men. They've been known for years.'

Poirot turned to him.

'You have not the true version. You do not appreciate an important point. *If Frederick Bosner is not dead — what has he been doing all these years?* He must have taken a different name. He must have built himself up a career.'

'As a Père Blanc?' asked Dr Reilly sceptically.

'It is a little fantastic that, yes,' confessed Poirot. 'But we cannot put it right out of court. Besides, these other possibilities.'

'The young 'uns?' said Reilly. 'If you want my opinion, on the face of it there's only one of your suspects that's even plausible.'

'And that is?'

'Young Carl Reiter. There's nothing actually against him, but come down to it and you've got to admit a few things — he's the right age, he's got a German name, he's new this year and he had the opportunity all right. He'd only got to pop out of his photographic place, cross the courtyard to do his dirty work and hare back again while the coast was clear. If anyone were to have dropped into the photographic-room while he was out of it, he can always say later that he was in the dark-room. I don't say he's your man but if you are going to suspect someone I say he's by far and away the most likely.'

M. Poirot didn't seem very receptive. He nodded gravely but doubtfully.

'Yes,' he said. 'He is the most plausible, but it may not be so simple as all that.'

160

Then he said: 'Let us say no more at present. I would like now, if I may, to examine the room where the crime took place.'

'Certainly.' Dr Leidner fumbled in his pockets, then looked at Dr Reilly.

'Captain Maitland took it,' he said.

'Maitland gave it to me,' said Reilly. 'He had to go off on that Kurdish business.'

He produced the key.

Dr Leidner said hesitatingly: 'Do you mind — if I don't — Perhaps, nurse — '

'Of course. Of course,' said Poirot. 'I quite understand. Never do I wish to cause you unnecessary pain. If you will be good enough to accompany me, *ma soeur*.'

'Certainly,' I said.

17

The Stain by the Washstand

Mrs Leidner's body had been taken to Hassanieh for the postmortem, but otherwise her room had been left exactly as it was. There was so little in it that it had not taken the police long to go over it.

To the right of the door as you entered was the bed. Opposite the door were the two barred windows giving on the countryside. Between them was a plain oak table with two drawers that served Mrs Leidner as a dressing-table. On the east wall there was a line of hooks with dresses hung up protected by cotton bags and a deal chest of drawers. Immediately to the left of the door was the washstand. In the middle of the room was a good-sized plain oak table with a blotter and inkstand and a small attaché-case. It was in the latter that Mrs Leidner had kept the anonymous letters. The curtains were short strips of native material — white striped with orange. The floor was of stone with some goatskin rugs on it, three narrow ones of brown striped with white in front of the two windows and the washstand, and a larger better quality one of white with brown stripes lying between the bed and the writing-table.

There were no cupboards or alcoves or long curtains — nowhere, in fact, where anyone could have hidden. The bed was a plain iron one with a printed cotton quilt. The only trace of luxury in the room were three pillows all made of the best soft and billowy down. Nobody but Mrs Leidner had pillows like these.

In a few brief words Dr Reilly explained where Mrs Leidner's body had been found — in a heap on the rug beside the bed.

To illustrate his account, he beckoned me to come forward.

'If you don't mind, nurse?' he said.

I'm not squeamish. I got down on the floor and arranged myself as far as possible in the attitude in which Mrs Leidner's body had been found.

'Leidner lifted her head when he found her,' said the doctor. 'But I questioned him closely and it's obvious that he didn't actually change her position.'

'It seems quite straightforward,' said Poirot. 'She was lying on the bed, asleep or resting — someone opens the door, she looks up, rises to her feet — '

'And he struck her down,' finished the

163

doctor. 'The blow would produce unconsciousness and death would follow very shortly. You see — '

He explained the injury in technical language.

'Not much blood, then?' said Poirot.

'No, the blood escaped internally into the brain.'

'*Eh bien*,' said Poirot, 'that seems straightforward enough — except for one thing. *If the man who entered was a stranger, why did not Mrs Leidner cry out at once for help? If she had screamed she would have been heard. Nurse Leatheran here would have heard her, and Emmott and the boy.*'

'That's easily answered,' said Dr Reilly dryly. '*Because it wasn't a stranger.*'

Poirot nodded.

'Yes,' he said meditatively. 'She may have been *surprised* to see the person — but she was not *afraid*. Then, as he struck, she *may* have uttered a half-cry — too late.'

'The cry Miss Johnson heard?'

'Yes, if she *did* hear it. But on the whole I doubt it. These mud walls are thick and the windows were closed.'

He stepped up to the bed.

'You left her actually lying down?' he asked me.

I explained exactly what I had done.

'Did she mean to sleep or was she going to read?'

'I gave her two books — a light one and a volume of memoirs. She usually read for a while and then sometimes dropped off for a short sleep.'

'And she was — what shall I say — quite as usual?'

I considered.

'Yes. She seemed quite normal and in good spirits,' I said. 'Just a shade off-hand, perhaps, but I put that down to her having confided in me the day before. It makes people a little uncomfortable sometimes.'

Poirot's eyes twinkled.

'Ah, yes, indeed, me, I know that well.'

He looked round the room.

'And when you came in here after the murder, was everything as you had seen it before?'

I looked round also.

'Yes, I think so. I don't remember anything being different.'

'There was no sign of the weapon with which she was struck?'

'No.'

Poirot looked at Dr Reilly.

'What was it in your opinion?'

The doctor replied promptly:

'Something pretty powerful, of a fair size

and without any sharp corners or edges. The rounded base of a statue, say — something like that. Mind you, I'm not suggesting that that *was* it. But that type of thing. The blow was delivered with great force.'

'Struck by a strong arm? A man's arm?'

'Yes — unless — '

'Unless — what?'

Dr Reilly said slowly: 'It is just possible that Mrs Leidner might have been on her knees — in which case, the blow being delivered from above with a heavy implement, the force needed would not have been so great.'

'*On her knees*,' mused Poirot. 'It is an idea — that.'

'It's only an idea, mind,' the doctor hastened to point out. 'There's absolutely nothing to indicate it.'

'But it's possible.'

'Yes. And after all, in view of the circumstances, it's not fantastic. Her fear might have led her to kneel in supplication rather than to scream when her instinct would tell her it was too late — that nobody could get there in time.'

'Yes,' said Poirot thoughtfully. 'It is an idea . . . '

It was a very poor one, I thought. I couldn't for one moment imagine Mrs Leidner on her knees to anyone.

Poirot made his way slowly round the room. He opened the windows, tested the bars, passed his head through and satisfied himself that by no means could his shoulders be made to follow his head.

'The windows were shut when you found her,' he said. 'Were they also shut when you left her at a quarter to one?'

'Yes, they were always shut in the afternoon. There is no gauze over these windows as there is in the living-room and dining-room. They are kept shut to keep out the flies.'

'And in any case no one could get in that way,' mused Poirot. 'And the walls are of the most solid — mud-brick — and there are no trap-doors and no sky-lights. No, there is only one way into this room — *through the door*. And there is only one way to the door *through the courtyard*. And there is only one entrance to the courtyard — *through the archway*. And outside the archway there were five people and they all tell the same story, and I do not think, me, that they are lying . . . No, they are not lying. They are not bribed to silence. The murderer was *here* . . . '

I didn't say anything. Hadn't I felt the same thing just now when we were all cooped up round the table?

Slowly Poirot prowled round the room. He

took up a photograph from the chest of drawers. It was of an elderly man with a white goatee beard. He looked inquiringly at me.

'Mrs Leidner's father,' I said. 'She told me so.'

He put it down again and glanced over the articles on the dressing-table — all of plain tortoiseshell — simple but good. He looked up at a row of books on a shelf, repeating the titles aloud.

'*Who were the Greeks? Introduction to Relativity. Life of Lady Hester Stanhope. Crewe Traine. Back to Methuselah. Linda Condon.* Yes, they tell us something, perhaps. She was not a fool, your Mrs Leidner. She had a mind.'

'Oh! she was a *very* clever woman,' I said eagerly. 'Very well read and up in everything. She wasn't a bit ordinary.'

He smiled as he looked over at me.

'No,' he said. 'I've already realized that.'

He passed on. He stood for some moments at the washstand, where there was a big array of bottles and toilet creams.

Then, suddenly, he dropped on his knees and examined the rug.

Dr Reilly and I came quickly to join him. He was examining a small dark brown stain, almost invisible on the brown of the rug. In fact it was only just noticeable where it impinged on one of the white stripes.

'What do you say, doctor?' he said. 'Is that blood?'

Dr Reilly knelt down.

'Might be,' he said. 'I'll make sure if you like?'

'If you would be so amiable.'

Mr Poirot examined the jug and basin. The jug was standing on the side of the washstand. The basin was empty, but beside the washstand there was an empty kerosene tin containing slop water.

He turned to me.

'Do you remember, nurse? Was this jug *out* of the basin or *in* it when you left Mrs Leidner at a quarter to one?'

'I can't be sure,' I said after a minute or two. 'I rather think it was standing in the basin.'

'Ah?'

'But you see,' I said hastily, 'I only think so because it usually was. The boys leave it like that after lunch. I just feel that if it hadn't been in I should have noticed it.'

He nodded quite appreciatively.

'Yes. I understand that. It is your hospital training. If everything had not been just so in the room, you would quite unconsciously have set it to rights hardly noticing what you were doing. And after the murder? Was it like it is now?'

I shook my head.

'I didn't notice then,' I said. 'All I looked for was whether there was any place anyone could be hidden or if there was anything the murderer had left behind him.'

'It's blood all right,' said Dr Reilly, rising from his knees. 'Is it important?'

Poirot was frowning perplexedly. He flung out his hands with petulance.

'I cannot tell. How can I tell? It may mean nothing at all. I can say, if I like, that the murderer touched her — that there was blood on his hands — very little blood, but still blood — and so he came over here and washed them. Yes, it may have been like that. But I cannot jump to conclusions and say that it *was* so. That stain may be of no importance at all.'

'There would have been very little blood,' said Dr Reilly dubiously. 'None would have spurted out or anything like that. It would have just oozed a little from the wound. Of course, if he'd probed it at all . . . '

I gave a shiver. A nasty sort of picture came up in my mind. The vision of somebody — perhaps that nice pig-faced photographic boy, striking down that lovely woman and then bending over her probing the wound with his finger in an awful gloating fashion and his face, perhaps, quite different . . . all fierce and mad . . .

Dr Reilly noticed my shiver.

'What's the matter, nurse?' he said.

'Nothing — just goose-flesh,' I said. 'A goose walking over my grave.'

Mr Poirot turned round and looked at me.

'I know what you need,' he said. 'Presently when we have finished here and I go back with the doctor to Hassanieh we will take you with us. You will give Nurse Leatheran tea, will you not, doctor?'

'Delighted.'

'Oh, no doctor,' I protested. 'I couldn't think of such a thing.'

M. Poirot gave me a little friendly tap on the shoulder. Quite an English tap, not a foreign one.

'You, *ma soeur*, will do as you are told,' he said. 'Besides, it will be of advantage to me. There is a good deal more that I want to discuss, and I cannot do it here where one must preserve the decencies. The good Dr Leidner he worshipped his wife and he is sure — oh, so sure — that everybody else felt the same about her! But that, in my opinion, would not be human nature! No, we want to discuss Mrs Leidner with — how do you say? — the gloves removed. That is settled then. When we have finished here, we take you with us to Hassanieh.'

'I suppose,' I said doubtfully, 'that I ought to be leaving anyway. It's rather awkward.'

'Do nothing for a day or two,' said Dr Reilly. 'You can't very well go until after the funeral.'

'That's all very well,' I said. 'And supposing *I* get murdered too, doctor?'

I said it half jokingly and Dr Reilly took it in the same fashion and would, I think, have made some jocular response.

But M. Poirot, to my astonishment, stood stock-still in the middle of the floor and clasped his hands to his head.

'Ah! if that were possible,' he murmured. 'It is a danger — yes — a great danger — and what can one do? How can one guard against it?'

'Why, M. Poirot,' I said, 'I was only joking! Who'd want to murder me, I should like to know?'

'You — or another,' he said, and I didn't like the way he said it at all. Positively creepy.

'But why?' I persisted.

He looked at me very straight then.

'I joke, mademoiselle,' he said, 'and I laugh. *But there are some things that are no joke.* There are things that my profession has taught me. And one of these things, the most terrible thing, is this: *Murder is a habit . . .* '

18

Tea at Dr Reilly's

Before leaving, Poirot made a round of the expedition house and the outbuildings. He also asked a few questions of the servants at second hand — that is to say, Dr Reilly translated the questions and answers from English to Arabic and *vice versa*.

These questions dealt mainly with the appearance of the stranger Mrs Leidner and I had seen looking through the window and to whom Father Lavigny had been talking on the following day.

'Do you really think that fellow had anything to do with it?' asked Dr Reilly when we were bumping along in his car on our way to Hassanieh.

'I like all the information there is,' was Poirot's reply.

And really, that described his methods very well. I found later that there wasn't anything — no small scrap of insignificant gossip — in which he wasn't interested. Men aren't usually so gossipy.

I must confess I was glad of my cup of tea

when we got to Dr Reilly's house. M. Poirot, I noticed, put five lumps of sugar in his.

Stirring it carefully with his teaspoon he said: 'And now we can talk, can we not? We can make up our minds who is likely to have committed the crime.'

'Lavigny, Mercado, Emmott or Reiter?' asked Dr Reilly.

'No, no — that was theory number three. I wish to concentrate now on theory number two — leaving aside all question of a mysterious husband or brother-in-law turning up from the past. Let us discuss now quite simply which member of the expedition had the means and opportunity to kill Mrs Leidner, and who is likely to have done so.'

'I thought you didn't think much of that theory.'

'Not at all. But I have some natural delicacy,' said Poirot reproachfully. 'Can I discuss in the presence of Dr Leidner the motives likely to lead to the murder of his wife by a member of the expedition? That would not have been delicate at all. I had to sustain the fiction that his wife was adorable and that everyone adored her!

'But naturally it was not like that at all. Now we can be brutal and impersonal and say what we think. We have no longer to consider people's feelings. And that is where

Nurse Leatheran is going to help us. She is, I am sure, a very good observer.'

'Oh, I don't know about that,' I said.

Dr Reilly handed me a plate of hot scones — 'To fortify yourself,' he said. They were very good scones.

'Come now,' said M. Poirot in a friendly, chatty way. 'You shall tell me, *ma soeur*, exactly what each member of the expedition felt towards Mrs Leidner.'

'I was only there a week, M. Poirot,' I said.

'Quite long enough for one of your intelligence. A nurse sums up quickly. She makes her judgments and abides by them. Come, let us make a beginning. Father Lavigny, for instance?'

'Well, there now, I really couldn't say. He and Mrs Leidner seemed to like talking together. But they usually spoke French and I'm not very good at French myself though I learnt it as a girl at school. I've an idea they talked mainly about books.'

'They were, as you might say, companionable together — yes?'

'Well, yes, you might put it that way. But, all the same, I think Father Lavigny was puzzled by her and — well — almost annoyed by being puzzled, if you know what I mean.'

And I told him of the conversation I had had with him out on the dig that first day when he had called Mrs Leidner a 'dangerous woman.'

'Now that is very interesting,' M. Poirot said. 'And she — what do you think she thought of him?'

'That's rather difficult to say, too. It wasn't easy to know what Mrs Leidner thought of people. Sometimes, I fancy, *he* puzzled *her*. I remember her saying to Dr Leidner that he was unlike any priest she had ever known.'

'A length of hemp to be ordered for Father Lavigny,' said Dr Reilly facetiously.

'My dear friend,' said Poirot. 'Have you not, perhaps, some patients to attend? I would not for the world detain you from your professional duties.'

'I've got a whole hospital of them,' said Dr Reilly.

And he got up and said a wink was as good as a nod to a blind horse, and went out laughing.

'That is better,' said Poirot. 'We will have now an interesting conversation *tête-à-tête*. But you must not forget to eat your tea.'

He passed me a plate of sandwiches and suggested my having a second cup of tea. He really had very pleasant, attentive manners.

'And now,' he said, 'let us continue with your impressions. Who was there who in your opinion did *not* like Mrs Leidner?'

'Well,' I said, 'it's only my opinion and I don't want it repeated as coming from me.'

'Naturally not.'

'But in my opinion little Mrs Mercado fairly hated her!'

'Ah! And Mr Mercado?'

'He was a bit soft on her,' I said. 'I shouldn't think women, apart from his wife, had ever taken much notice of him. And Mrs Leidner had a nice kind way of being interested in people and the things they told her. It rather went to the poor man's head, I fancy.'

'And Mrs Mercado — she was not pleased?'

'She was just plain jealous — that's the truth of it. You've got to be very careful when there's a husband and wife about, and that's a fact. I could tell you some surprising things. You've no idea the extraordinary things women get into their heads when it's a question of their husbands.'

'I do not doubt the truth of what you say. So Mrs Mercado was jealous? And she hated Mrs Leidner?'

'I've seen her look at her as though she'd have liked to kill her — oh, gracious!' I pulled myself up. 'Indeed, M. Poirot, I didn't mean to say — I mean, that is, not for one moment — '

'No, no. I quite understand. The phrase slipped out. A very convenient one. And Mrs Leidner, was she worried by this animosity of Mrs Mercado's?'

'Well,' I said, reflecting, 'I don't really think she was worried at all. In fact, I don't even know whether she noticed it. I thought once of just giving her a hint — but I didn't like to. Least said soonest mended. That's what I say.'

'You are doubtless wise. Can you give me any instances of how Mrs Mercado showed her feelings?'

I told him about our conversation on the roof.

'So she mentioned Mrs Leidner's first marriage,' said Poirot thoughtfully. 'Can you remember — in mentioning it — did she look at you as though she wondered whether you had heard a different version?'

'You think she may have known the truth about it?'

'It is a possibility. She may have written those letters — and engineered a tapping hand and all the rest of it.'

'I wondered something of the same kind myself. It seemed the kind of petty revengeful thing she might do.'

'Yes. A cruel streak, I should say. But hardly the temperament for cold-blooded, brutal murder unless, of course — '

He paused and then said: 'It is odd, that curious thing she said to you. '*I know why you are here.*' What did she mean by it?'

'I can't imagine,' I said frankly.

'She thought you were there for some ulterior reason apart from the declared one. What reason? And why should she be so concerned in the matter. Odd, too, the way you tell me she stared at you all through tea the day you arrived.'

'Well, she's not a lady, M. Poirot,' I said primly.

'That, *ma soeur*, is an excuse but not an explanation.'

I wasn't quite sure for the minute what he meant. But he went on quickly.

'And the other members of the staff?'

I considered.

'I don't think Miss Johnson liked Mrs Leidner either very much. But she was quite open and above-board about it. She as good as admitted she was prejudiced. You see, she's very devoted to Dr Leidner and had worked with him for years. And of course, marriage does change things — there's no denying it.'

'Yes,' said Poirot. 'And from Miss Johnson's point of view it would be an unsuitable marriage. It would really have been much more suitable if Dr Leidner had married *her*.'

'It would really,' I agreed. 'But there, that's a man all over. Not one in a hundred considers suitability. And one can't really blame Dr Leidner. Miss Johnson, poor soul, isn't so much to look at. Now Mrs Leidner was really beautiful — not young, of course — but oh! I wish you'd known her. There was something about her . . . I remember Mr Coleman saying she was like a thingummyjig that came to lure people into marshes. That wasn't a very good way of putting it, but — oh, well — you'll laugh at me, but there *was* something about her that was — well — unearthly.'

'She could cast a spell — yes, I understand,' said Poirot.

'Then I don't think she and Mr Carey got on very well either,' I went on. 'I've an idea *he* was jealous just like Miss Johnson. He was always very stiff with her and so was she with him. You know — she passed him things and was very polite and called him Mr Carey rather formally. He was an old friend of her husband's of course, and some women can't stand their husband's old friends. They don't like to think that anyone knew them before they did — at least that's rather a muddled way of putting it — '

'I quite understand. And the three young men? Coleman, you say, was inclined to be poetic about her.'

I couldn't help laughing.

'It was funny, M. Poirot,' I said. 'He's such a matter-of-fact young man.'

'And the other two?'

'I don't really know about Mr Emmott. He's always so quiet and never says much. She was very nice to him always. You know — friendly — called him David and used to tease him about Miss Reilly and things like that.'

'Ah, really? And did he enjoy that?'

'I don't quite know,' I said doubtfully. 'He'd just look at her. Rather funnily. You couldn't tell what he was thinking.'

'And Mr Reiter?'

'She wasn't always very kind to him,' I said slowly. 'I think he got on her nerves. She used to say quite sarcastic things to him.'

'And did he mind?'

'He used to get very pink, poor boy. Of course, she didn't *mean* to be unkind.'

And then suddenly, from feeling a little sorry for the boy, it came over me that he was very likely a cold-blooded murderer and had been playing a part all the time.

'Oh, M. Poirot,' I exclaimed. 'What do you think *really* happened?'

He shook his head slowly and thoughtfully.

'Tell me,' he said. 'You are not afraid to go back there tonight?'

'Oh *no*,' I said. 'Of course, I remember what you said, but who would want to murder *me*?'

'I do not think that anyone could,' he said slowly. 'That is partly why I have been so anxious to hear all you could tell me. No, I think — I am sure — you are quite safe.'

'If anyone had told me in Baghdad — ' I began and stopped.

'Did you hear any gossip about the Leidners and the expedition before you came here?' he asked.

I told him about Mrs Leidner's nickname and just a little of what Mrs Kelsey had said about her.

In the middle of it the door opened and Miss Reilly came in. She had been playing tennis and had her racquet in her hand.

I gathered Poirot had already met her when he arrived in Hassanieh.

She said how-do-you-do to me in her usual off-hand manner and picked up a sandwich.

'Well, M. Poirot,' she said. 'How are you getting on with our local mystery?'

'Not very fast, mademoiselle.'

'I see you've rescued nurse from the wreck.'

'Nurse Leatheran has been giving me valuable information about the various members of the expedition. Incidentally I have learnt a good deal — about the victim. And the victim, mademoiselle, is very often the clue to the mystery.'

Miss Reilly said: 'That's rather clever of you, M. Poirot. It's certainly true that if ever a woman deserved to be murdered Mrs Leidner was that woman!'

'Miss Reilly!' I cried, scandalized.

She laughed, a short, nasty laugh.

'Ah!' she said. 'I thought you hadn't been hearing quite the truth. Nurse Leatheran, I'm afraid, was quite taken in, like many other people. Do you know, M. Poirot, I rather hope that this case isn't going to be one of your successes. I'd quite like the murderer of Louise Leidner to get away with it. In fact, I wouldn't much have objected to putting her out of the way myself.'

I was simply disgusted with the girl. M. Poirot, I must say, didn't turn a hair. He just bowed and said quite pleasantly:

'I hope, then, that you have an alibi for yesterday afternoon?'

There was a moment's silence and Miss Reilly's racquet went clattering down on to the floor. She didn't bother to pick it up. Slack and untidy like all her sort! She said in a rather breathless voice: 'Oh, yes, I was playing tennis at the club. But, seriously, M. Poirot, I wonder if you know anything at all about Mrs Leidner and the kind of woman she was?'

Again he made a funny little bow and said: 'You shall inform me, mademoiselle.'

She hesitated a minute and then spoke with a callousness and lack of decency that really sickened me.

'There's a convention that one doesn't speak ill of the dead. That's stupid, I think. The truth's always the truth. On the whole it's better to keep your mouth shut about living people. You might conceivably injure them. The dead are past that. But the harm they've done lives after them sometimes. Not quite a quotation from Shakespeare but very nearly! Has nurse told you of the queer atmosphere there was at Tell Yarimjah? Has she told you how jumpy they all were? And how they all used to glare at each other like enemies? That was Louise Leidner's doing. When I was a kid out here three years ago they were the happiest, jolliest lot imaginable. Even last year they were pretty well all right. But this year there was a blight over them — and it was *her* doing. She was the kind of woman who won't let anybody else be happy! There *are* women like that and she was one of them! She wanted to break up things always. Just for fun — or for the sense of power — or perhaps just because she was made that way. And she was the kind of woman who had to get hold of every male creature within reach!'

'Miss Reilly,' I cried, 'I don't think that's true. In fact I *know* it isn't.'

She went on without taking the least notice of me.

'It wasn't enough for her to have her husband adore her. She had to make a fool of that long-legged shambling idiot of a Mercado. Then she got hold of Bill. Bill's a sensible cove, but she was getting him all mazed and bewildered. Carl Reiter she just amused herself by tormenting. It was easy. He's a sensitive boy. And she had a jolly good go at David.

'David was better sport to her because he put up a fight. He felt her charm — but he wasn't having any. I think because he'd got sense enough to know that she didn't really care a damn. And that's why I hate her so. She's not sensual. She doesn't *want* affairs. It's just cold-blooded experiment on her part and the fun of stirring people up and setting them against each other. She dabbled in that too. She's the sort of woman who's never had a row with anyone in her life — but rows always happen where she is! She *makes* them happen. She's a kind of female Iago. She *must* have drama. But she doesn't want to be involved *herself*. She's always outside pulling strings — looking on — enjoying it. Oh, do you see *at all* what I mean?'

'I see, perhaps, more than you know, mademoiselle,' said Poirot.

I couldn't make his voice out. He didn't sound indignant. He sounded — oh, well, I can't explain it.

Sheila Reilly seemed to understand, for she flushed all over her face.

'You can think what you choose,' she said. 'But I'm right about her. She was a clever woman and she was bored and she experimented — with people — like other people experiment with chemicals. She enjoyed working on poor old Johnson's feelings and seeing her bite on the bullet and control herself like the old sport she is. She liked goading little Mercado into a white-hot frenzy. She liked flicking *me* on the raw — and she could do it too, every time! She liked finding out things about people and holding it over them. Oh, I don't mean crude blackmail — I mean just letting them know that she *knew* — and leaving them uncertain what she meant to do about it. My God, though, that woman was an artist! There was nothing crude about *her* methods!'

'And her husband?' asked Poirot.

'She never wanted to hurt him,' said Miss Reilly slowly. 'I've never known her anything but sweet to him. I suppose she was fond of him. He's a dear — wrapped up in his own world — his digging and his theories. And he worshipped her and thought her perfection. That might have annoyed some women. It didn't annoy her. In a sense he lived in a fool's paradise — and yet it wasn't a fool's paradise because to him she was what he thought her. Though it's hard to reconcile that with — '

She stopped.

'Go on, mademoiselle,' said Poirot.

She turned suddenly on me.

'What have you said about Richard Carey?'

'About Mr Carey?' I asked, astonished.

'About her and Carey?'

'Well,' I said, 'I've mentioned that they didn't hit it off very well — '

To my surprise she broke into a fit of laughter.

'Didn't hit it off very well! You fool! He's head over ears in love with her. And it's tearing him to pieces — because he worships Leidner too. He's been his friend for years. That would be enough for her, of course. She's made it her business to come between them. But all the same I've fancied — '

'*Eh bien?*'

She was frowning, absorbed in thought.

'I've fancied that she'd gone too far for once — that she was not only biter but bit! Carey's attractive. He's as attractive as hell . . . She was a cold devil — but I believe she could have lost her coldness with him . . . '

'I think it's just scandalous what you're saying,' I cried. 'Why, they hardly spoke to each other!'

'Oh, didn't they?' She turned on me. 'A hell of a lot you know about it. It was 'Mr Carey' and 'Mrs Leidner' in the house, but they used to meet outside. She'd walk down the path to the river. And he'd leave the dig for an hour at a time. They used to meet among the fruit trees.

'I saw him once just leaving her, striding back to the dig, and she was standing looking after him. I was a female cad, I suppose. I had some glasses with me and I took them out and had a good look at her face. If you ask me, I believe she cared like hell for Richard Carey . . . '

She broke off and looked at Poirot.

'Excuse my butting in on your case,' she said with a sudden rather twisted grin, 'but I thought you'd like to have the local colour correct.'

And she marched out of the room.

188

'M. Poirot,' I cried. 'I don't believe one word of it all!'

He looked at me and he smiled, and he said (very queerly I thought): 'You can't deny, nurse, that Miss Reilly has shed a certain — illumination on the case.'

19

A New Suspicion

We couldn't say any more just then because Dr Reilly came in, saying jokingly that he'd killed off the most tiresome of his patients.

He and M. Poirot settled down to a more or less medical discussion of the psychology and mental state of an anonymous letter-writer. The doctor cited cases that he had known professionally, and M. Poirot told various stories from his own experience.

'It is not so simple as it seems,' he ended. 'There is the desire for power and very often a strong inferiority complex.'

Dr Reilly nodded.

'That's why you often find that the author of anonymous letters is the last person in the place to be suspected. Some quiet inoffensive little soul who apparently can't say boo to a goose — all sweetness and Christian meekness on the outside — and seething with all the fury of hell underneath!'

Poirot said thoughtfully: 'Should you say Mrs Leidner had any tendency to an inferiority complex?'

Dr Reilly scraped out his pipe with a chuckle.

'Last woman on earth I'd describe that way. No repressions about her. Life, life and more life — that's what she wanted — and got, too!'

'Do you consider it a possibility, psychologically speaking, that she wrote those letters?'

'Yes, I do. But if she did, the reason arose out of her instinct to dramatize herself. Mrs Leidner was a bit of a film star in private life! She *had* to be the centre of things — in the limelight. By the law of opposites she married Leidner, who's about the most retiring and modest man I know. He adored her — but adoration by the fireside wasn't enough for her. She had to be the persecuted heroine as well.'

'In fact,' said Poirot, smiling, 'you don't subscribe to his theory that she wrote them and retained no memory of her act?'

'No, I don't. I didn't turn down the idea in front of him. You can't very well say to a man who's just lost a dearly loved wife that that same wife was a shameless exhibitionist, and that she drove him nearly crazy with anxiety to satisfy her sense of the dramatic. As a matter of fact it wouldn't be safe to tell any man the truth about his wife! Funnily

191

enough, I'd trust most women with the truth about their husbands. Women can accept the fact that a man is a rotter, a swindler, a drug-taker, a confirmed liar, and a general swine without batting an eyelash and without its impairing their affection for the brute in the least! Women are wonderful realists.'

'Frankly, Dr Reilly, what *was* your exact opinion of Mrs Leidner?'

Dr Reilly lay back in his chair and puffed slowly at his pipe.

'Frankly — it's hard to say! I didn't know her well enough. She'd got charm — any amount of it. Brains, sympathy . . . What else? She hadn't any of the ordinary unpleasant vices. She wasn't sensual or lazy or even particularly vain. She was, I've always thought (but I've no proofs of it), a most accomplished liar. What I don't know (and what I'd like to know) is whether she lied to herself or only to other people. I'm rather partial to liars myself. A woman who doesn't lie is a woman without imagination and without sympathy. I don't think she was really a man-hunter — she just liked the sport of bringing them down 'with my bow and arrow.' If you get my daughter on the subject — '

'We have had that pleasure,' said Poirot with a slight smile.

'H'm,' said Dr Reilly. 'She hasn't wasted much time! Shoved her knife into her pretty thoroughly, I should imagine! The younger generation has no sentiment towards the dead. It's a pity all young people are prigs! They condemn the 'old morality' and then proceed to set up a much more hard-and-fast code of their own. If Mrs Leidner had had half a dozen affairs Sheila would probably have approved of her as 'living her life fully' — or 'obeying her blood instincts'. What she doesn't see is that Mrs Leidner was acting true to type — *her* type. The cat *is* obeying its blood instinct when it plays with the mouse! It's made that way. Men aren't little boys to be shielded and protected. They've got to meet cat women — and faithful spaniel, yours-till-death adoring women, and hen-pecking nagging bird women — and all the rest of it! Life's a battlefield — not a picnic! I'd like to see Sheila honest enough to come off her high horse and admit that she hated Mrs Leidner for good old thorough-going personal reasons. Sheila's about the only young girl in this place and she naturally assumes that she ought to have it all her own way with the young things in trousers. Naturally it annoys her when a woman, who in her view is middle-aged and who has already two husbands to her credit, comes along and licks her on her own ground. Sheila's a nice child, healthy and reasonably good-looking and attractive to the other sex as she should be. But Mrs Leidner was something out of the ordinary in that line. She'd got just that sort of calamitous magic that plays the deuce with things — a kind of Belle Dame sans Merci.'

I jumped in my chair. What a coincidence his saying that!

'Your daughter — I am not indiscreet — she has perhaps a *tendresse* for one of the young men out there?'

'Oh, I don't suppose so. She's had Emmott and Coleman dancing attendance on her as a matter of course. I don't know that she cares for one more than the other. There are a couple of young Air Force chaps too. I fancy all's fish that comes to her net at present. No, I think it's age daring to defeat youth that annoys her so much! She doesn't know as much of the world as I do. It's when you get to my age that you really appreciate a schoolgirl complexion and a clear eye and a firmly knit young body. But a woman over thirty can listen with rapt attention and throw in a word here and there to show the talker what a fine fellow he is — and few young men can resist that! Sheila's a pretty girl — but Louise Leidner was beautiful. Glorious eyes and that amazing golden fairness. Yes, she was a beautiful woman.'

Yes, I thought to myself, he's right. Beauty's a wonderful thing. She *had* been beautiful. It wasn't the kind of looks you were jealous of — you just sat back and admired. I felt that first day I met her that I'd do *anything* for Mrs Leidner!

All the same, that night as I was being driven back to Tell Yarimjah (Dr Reilly made me stay for an early dinner) one or two things came back to my mind and made me rather uncomfortable. At the time I hadn't believed a word of all Sheila Reilly's outpouring. I'd taken it for sheer spite and malice.

But now I suddenly remembered the way Mrs Leidner had insisted on going for a stroll by herself that afternoon and wouldn't hear of me coming with her. I couldn't help wondering if perhaps, after all, she *had* been going to meet Mr Carey . . . And of course, it *was* a little odd, really, the way he and she spoke to each other so formally. Most of the others she called by their Christian names.

He never seemed to look at her, I remembered. That might be because he disliked her — or it might be just the opposite . . .

I gave myself a little shake. Here I was

fancying and imagining all sorts of things —
all because of a girl's spiteful outburst! It just
showed how unkind and dangerous it was to
go about saying that kind of thing.

Mrs Leidner *hadn't* been like that at all . . .

Of course, she *hadn't* liked Sheila Reilly.
She'd really been — almost catty about her
that day at lunch to Mr Emmott.

Funny, the way he'd looked at her. The sort
of way that you couldn't possibly tell what he
was thinking. You never could tell what Mr
Emmott was thinking. He was so quiet. But
very nice. A nice dependable person.

Now Mr Coleman was a foolish young man
if there ever was one!

I'd got to that point in my meditations
when we arrived. It was just on nine o'clock
and the big door was closed and barred.

Ibrahim came running with his great key to
let me in.

We all went to bed early at Tell Yarimjah.
There weren't any lights showing in the
living-room. There was a light in the
drawing-office and one in Dr Leidner's office,
but nearly all the other windows were dark.
Everyone must have gone to bed even earlier
than usual.

As I passed the drawing-office to go to my
room I looked in. Mr Carey was in his shirt
sleeves working over his big plan.

Terribly ill, he looked, I thought. So strained and worn. It gave me quite a pang. I don't know what there was about Mr Carey — it wasn't what he *said* because he hardly said anything — and that of the most ordinary nature, and it wasn't what he *did*, for that didn't amount to much either — and yet you just couldn't help noticing him, and everything about him seemed to matter more than it would have about anyone else. He just *counted*, if you know what I mean.

He turned his head and saw me. He removed his pipe from his mouth and said: 'Well, nurse, back from Hassanieh?'

'Yes, Mr Carey. You're up working late. Everybody else seems to have gone to bed.'

'I thought I might as well get on with things,' he said. 'I was a bit behind-hand. And I shall be out on the dig all tomorrow. We're starting digging again.'

'Already?' I asked, shocked.

He looked at me rather queerly.

'It's the best thing, I think. I put it up to Leidner. He'll be in Hassanieh most of tomorrow seeing to things. But the rest of us will carry on here. You know it's not too easy all sitting round and looking at each other as things are.'

He was right there, of course. Especially in the nervy, jumped state everyone was in.

'Well, of course you're right in a way,' I said. 'It takes one's mind off if one's got something to do.'

The funeral, I knew, was to be the day after tomorrow.

He had bent over his plan again. I don't know why, but my heart just ached for him. I felt certain that he wasn't going to get any sleep.

'If you'd like a sleeping draught, Mr Carey?' I said hesitatingly.

He shook his head with a smile.

'I'll carry on, nurse. Bad habit, sleeping draughts.'

'Well, good night, Mr Carey,' I said. 'If there's anything I can do — '

'Don't think so, thank you, nurse. Good night.'

'I'm terribly sorry,' I said, rather too impulsively I suppose.

'Sorry?' He looked surprised.

'For — for everybody. It's all so dreadful. But especially for you.'

'For me? Why for me?'

'Well, you're such an old friend of them both.'

'I'm an old friend of Leidner's. I wasn't a friend of hers particularly.'

He spoke as though he had actually disliked her. Really, I wished Miss Reilly could have heard him!

'Well, good night,' I said and hurried along to my room.

I fussed around a bit in my room before undressing. Washed out some handkerchiefs and a pair of wash-leather gloves and wrote up my diary. I just looked out of my door again before I really started to get ready for bed. The lights were still on in the drawing-office and in the south building.

I suppose Dr Leidner was still up and working in his office. I wondered whether I ought to go and say goodnight to him. I hesitated about it — I didn't want to seem officious. He might be busy and not want to be disturbed. In the end, however, a sort of uneasiness drove me on. After all, it couldn't do any harm. I'd just say goodnight, ask if there was anything I could do and come away.

But Dr Leidner wasn't there. The office itself was lit up but there was no one in it except Miss Johnson. She had her head down on the table and was crying as though her heart would break.

It gave me quite a turn. She was such a quiet, self-controlled woman. It was pitiful to see her.

'Whatever is it, my dear?' I cried. I put my arm round her and patted her. 'Now, now, this won't do at all . . . You mustn't sit here crying all by yourself.'

She didn't answer and I felt the dreadful shuddering sobs that were racking her.

'Don't, my dear, don't,' I said. 'Take a hold on yourself. I'll go and make you a cup of nice hot tea.'

She raised her head and said: 'No, no, its all right, nurse. I'm being a fool.'

'What's upset you, my dear?' I asked.

She didn't answer at once, then she said: 'It's all too awful . . . '

'Now don't start thinking of it,' I told her. 'What's happened has happened and can't be mended. It's no use fretting.'

She sat up straight and began to pat her hair.

'I'm making rather a fool of myself,' she said in her gruff voice. 'I've been clearing up and tidying the office. Thought it was best to *do* something. And then — it all came over me suddenly — '

'Yes, yes,' I said hastily. 'I know. A nice strong cup of tea and a hot-water bottle in your bed is what you want,' I said.

And she had them too. I didn't listen to any protests.

'Thank you, nurse,' she said when I'd settled her in bed, and she was sipping her tea and the hot-water bottle was in. 'You're a nice kind sensible woman. It's not often I make such a fool of myself.'

'Oh, anybody's liable to do that at a time like this,' I said. 'What with one thing and another. The strain and the shock and the police here, there and everywhere. Why, I'm quite jumpy myself.'

She said slowly in rather a queer voice: 'What you said in there is true. What's happened has happened and can't be mended . . . '

She was silent for a minute or two and then said — rather oddly, I thought: 'She was never a nice woman!'

Well, I didn't argue the point. I'd always felt it was quite natural for Miss Johnson and Mrs Leidner not to hit it off.

I wondered if, perhaps, Miss Johnson had secretly had a feeling that she was pleased Mrs Leidner was dead, and had then been ashamed of herself for the thought.

I said: 'Now you go to sleep and don't worry about anything.'

I just picked up a few things and set the room to rights. Stockings over the back of the chair and coat and skirt on a hanger. There was a little ball of crumpled paper on the floor where it must have fallen out of a pocket.

I was just smoothing it out to see whether I

could safely throw it away when she quite startled me.

'Give that to me!'

I did so — rather taken aback. She'd called out so peremptorily. She snatched it from me — fairly snatched it — and then held it in the candle flame till it was burnt to ashes.

As I say, I was startled — and I just stared at her.

I hadn't had time to see what the paper was — she'd snatched it so quick. But funnily enough, as it burned it curled over towards me and I just saw that there were words written in ink on the paper.

It wasn't till I was getting into bed that I realized why they'd looked sort of familiar to me.

It was the same handwriting as that of the anonymous letters.

Was *that* why Miss Johnson had given way to a fit of remorse? Had it been her all along who had written those anonymous letters?

20

Miss Johnson, Mrs Mercado, Mr Reiter

I don't mind confessing that the idea came as a complete shock to me. I'd never thought of associating *Miss Johnson* with the letters. Mrs Mercado, perhaps. But Miss Johnson was a real lady, and so self-controlled and sensible.

But I reflected, remembering the conversation I had listened to that evening between M. Poirot and Dr Reilly, that that might be just *why*.

If it were Miss Johnson who had written the letters it explained a lot, mind you. I didn't think for a minute Miss Johnson had had anything to do with the murder. But I *did* see that her dislike of Mrs Leidner might have made her succumb to the temptation of, well — putting the wind up her — to put it vulgarly.

She might have hoped to frighten away Mrs Leidner from the dig.

But then Mrs Leidner had been murdered and Miss Johnson had felt terrible pangs of remorse — first for her cruel trick and also, perhaps, because she realized that those letters were acting as a very good shield to the actual murderer. No wonder she had broken down so utterly. She was, I was sure, a decent soul at heart. And it explained, too, why she had caught so eagerly at my consolation of 'what's happened's happened and can't be mended.'

And then her cryptic remark — her vindication of herself — 'she was never a nice woman!'

The question was, what was *I* to do about it?

I tossed and turned for a good while and in the end decided I'd let M. Poirot know about it at the first opportunity.

He came out next day, but I didn't get a chance of speaking to him what you might call privately.

We had just a minute alone together and before I could collect myself to know how to begin, he had come close to me and was whispering instructions in my ear.

'Me, I shall talk to Miss Johnson — and others, perhaps, in the living-room. You have the key of Mrs Leidner's room still?'

'Yes,' I said.

'Très bien. Go there, shut the door behind you and give a cry — not a scream — a cry. You understand what I mean — it is alarm — surprise that I want you to express — not mad terror. As for the excuse if you are heard — I leave that to you — the stepped toe or what you will.'

At that moment Miss Johnson came out into the courtyard and there was no time for more.

I understood well enough what M. Poirot was after. As soon as he and Miss Johnson had gone into the living-room I went across to Mrs Leidner's room and, unlocking the door, went in and pulled the door to behind me.

I can't say I didn't feel a bit of a fool standing up in an empty room and giving a yelp all for nothing at all. Besides, it wasn't so easy to know just how loud to do it. I gave a pretty loud 'Oh' and then tried it a bit higher and a bit lower.

Then I came out again and prepared my excuse of a stepped (stubbed I *suppose* he meant!) toe.

But it soon appeared that no excuse would be needed. Poirot and Miss Johnson were talking together earnestly and there had clearly been no interruption.

'Well,' I thought, 'that settles that. Either Miss Johnson imagined that cry she heard or else it was something quite different.'

I didn't like to go in and interrupt them. There was a deck-chair on the porch so I sat down there. Their voices floated out to me.

'The position is delicate, you understand,' Poirot was saying. 'Dr Leidner — obviously he adored his wife — '

'He worshipped her,' said Miss Johnson.

'He tells me, naturally, how fond all his staff was of her! As for them, what can they say? Naturally they say the same thing. It is politeness. It is decency. It *may* also be the truth! But also it may *not!* And I am convinced, mademoiselle, that the key to this enigma lies in a complete understanding of Mrs Leidner's character. If I could get the opinion — the honest opinion — of every member of the staff, I might, from the whole, build up a picture. Frankly, that is why I am here today. I knew Dr Leidner would be in Hassanieh. That makes it easy for me to have an interview with each of you here in turn, and beg your help.'

'That's all very well,' began Miss Johnson and stopped.

'Do not make me the British *clichés*,' Poirot begged. 'Do not say it is not the cricket or the football, that to speak anything but well of the dead is not done — that — *enfin* — there is loyalty! Loyalty it is a pestilential thing in crime. Again and again it obscures the truth.'

'I've no particular loyalty to Mrs Leidner,'

said Miss Johnson dryly. There was indeed a sharp and acid tone in her voice. 'Dr Leidner's a different matter. And, after all, she was his wife.'

'Precisely — precisely. I understand that you would not wish to speak against your chief's wife. But this is not a question of a testimonial. It is a question of sudden and mysterious death. If I am to believe that it is a martyred angel who has been killed it does not add to the easiness of my task.'

'I certainly shouldn't call her an angel,' said Miss Johnson and the acid tone was even more in evidence.

'Tell me your opinion, frankly, of Mrs Leidner — as a woman.'

'H'm! To begin with, M. Poirot, I'll give you this warning. I'm prejudiced. I am — we all were — devoted to Dr Leidner. And, I suppose, when Mrs Leidner came along, we were jealous. We resented the demands she made on his time and attention. The devotion he showed her irritated us. I'm being truthful, M. Poirot, and it isn't very pleasant for me. I resented her presence here — yes, I did, though, of course, I tried never to show it. It made a difference to us, you see.'

'Us? You say us?'

'I mean Mr Carey and myself. We're the two old-timers, you see. And we didn't much care for the new order of things. I suppose that's natural, though perhaps it was rather petty of us. But it *did* make a difference.'

'What kind of a difference?'

'Oh! to everything. We used to have such a happy time. A good deal of fun, you know, and rather silly jokes, like people do who work together. Dr Leidner was quite light-hearted — just like a boy.'

'And when Mrs Leidner came she changed all that?'

'Well, I suppose it wasn't her *fault*. It wasn't so bad last year. And please believe, M. Poirot, that it wasn't anything she *did*. She's always been charming to me — quite charming. That's why I've felt ashamed sometimes. It wasn't her fault that little things she said and did seemed to rub me up the wrong way. Really, nobody could be nicer than she was.'

'But nevertheless things were changed this season? There was a different atmosphere.'

'Oh, entirely. Really. I don't know what it was. Everything seemed to go wrong — not with the work — I mean with us — our tempers and our nerves. All on edge. Almost the sort of feeling you get when there is a thunderstorm coming.'

'And you put that down to Mrs Leidner's influence?'

'Well, it was never like that before she came,' said Miss Johnson dryly. 'Oh! I'm a cross-grained, complaining old dog. Conservative — liking things always the same. You really mustn't take any notice of me, M. Poirot.'

'How would you describe to me Mrs Leidner's character and temperament?'

Miss Johnson hesitated for a moment. Then she said slowly: 'Well, of course, she was temperamental. A lot of ups and downs. Nice to people one day and perhaps wouldn't speak to them the next. She was very kind, I think. And very thoughtful for others. All the same you could see she had been thoroughly spoilt all her life. She took Dr Leidner's waiting on her hand and foot as perfectly natural. And I don't think she ever really appreciated what a very remarkable — what a really great — man she had married. That used to annoy me sometimes. And of course she was terribly highly strung and nervous. The things she used to imagine and the states she used to get into! I was thankful when Dr Leidner brought Nurse Leatheran here. It was too much for him having to cope both with his work and with his wife's fears.'

'What is your own opinion of these anonymous letters she received?'

I had to do it. I leaned forward in my chair

till I could just catch sight of Miss Johnson's profile turned to Poirot in answer to his question.

She was looking perfectly cool and collected.

'I think someone in America had a spite against her and was trying to frighten or annoy her.'

'*Pas plus sérieux que ça?*'

'That's my opinion. She was a very handsome woman, you know, and might easily have had enemies. I think, those letters were written by some spiteful woman. Mrs Leidner being of a nervous temperament took them seriously.'

'She certainly did that,' said Poirot. 'But remember — the last of them arrived by hand.'

'Well, I suppose that *could* have been managed if anyone had given their minds to it. Women will take a lot of trouble to gratify their spite, M. Poirot.'

They will indeed, I thought to myself!

'Perhaps you are right, mademoiselle. As you say, Mrs Leidner was handsome. By the way, you know Miss Reilly, the doctor's daughter?'

'Sheila Reilly? Yes, of course.'

Poirot adopted a very confidential, gossipy tone.

'I have heard a rumour (naturally I do not like to ask the doctor) that there was a *tendresse* between her and one of the members of Dr Leidner's staff. Is that so, do you know?'

Miss Johnson appeared rather amused.

'Oh, young Coleman and David Emmott were both inclined to dance attendance. I believe there was some rivalry as to who was to be her partner in some event at the club. Both the boys went in on Saturday evenings to the club as a general rule. But I don't know that there was anything in it on her side. She's the only young creature in the place, you know, and so she's by way of being the belle of it. She's got the Air Force dancing attendance on her as well.'

'So you think there is nothing in it?'

'Well — I don't know.' Miss Johnson became thoughtful. 'It is true that she comes out this way fairly often. Up to the dig and all that. In fact, Mrs Leidner was chaffing David Emmott about it the other day — saying the girl was running after him. Which was rather a catty thing to say, I thought, and I don't think he liked it . . . Yes, she was here a good deal. I saw her riding towards the dig on that awful afternoon.' She nodded her head towards the open window. 'But neither David Emmott nor Coleman were on duty that afternoon. Richard Carey was in charge. Yes, perhaps she *is* attracted to one of the boys — but she's such a modern unsentimental young woman that one doesn't know quite how seriously to take her. I'm sure I don't know which of them it is. Bill's a nice boy, and not nearly such a fool as he pretends to be. David Emmott is a dear — and there's a lot to him. He is the deep, quiet kind.'

Then she looked quizzically at Poirot and said: 'But has this any bearing on the crime, M. Poirot?'

M. Poirot threw up his hands in a very French fashion.

'You make me blush, mademoiselle,' he said. 'You expose me as a mere gossip. But what will you, I am interested always in the love affairs of young people.'

'Yes,' said Miss Johnson with a little sigh. 'It's nice when the course of true love runs smooth.'

Poirot gave an answering sigh. I wondered if Miss Johnson was thinking of some love affair of her own when she was a girl. And I wondered if M. Poirot had a wife, and if he went on in the way you always hear foreigners do, with mistresses and things like that. He looked so comic I couldn't imagine it.

'Sheila Reilly has a lot of character,' said Miss Johnson. 'She's young and she's crude, but she's the right sort.'

'I take your word for it, mademoiselle,' said Poirot.

He got up and said, 'Are there any other members of the staff in the house?'

'Marie Mercado is somewhere about. All the men are up on the dig today. I think they wanted to get out of the house. I don't blame them. If you'd like to go up to the dig — '

She came out on the verandah and said, smiling to me: 'Nurse Leatheran won't mind taking you, I dare say.'

'Oh, certainly, Miss Johnson,' I said.

'And you'll come back to lunch, won't you, M. Poirot?'

'Enchanted, mademoiselle.'

Miss Johnson went back into the living-room where she was engaged in cataloguing.

'Mrs Mercado's on the roof,' I said. 'Do you want to see her first?'

'It would be as well, I think. Let us go up.'

As we went up the stairs I said: 'I did what you told me. Did you hear anything?'

'Not a sound.'

'That will be a weight off Miss Johnson's mind at any rate,' I said. 'She's been worrying that she might have done something about it.'

Mrs Mercado was sitting on the parapet, her head bent down, and she was so deep in thought that she never heard us till Poirot halted opposite her and bade her good morning.

Then she looked up with a start.

She looked ill this morning, I thought, her small face pinched and wizened and great dark circles under her eyes.

'*Encore moi*,' said Poirot. 'I come today with a special object.'

And he went on much in the same way as he had done to Miss Johnson, explaining how necessary it was that he should get a true picture of Mrs Leidner.

Mrs Mercado, however, wasn't as honest as Miss Johnson had been. She burst into fulsome praise which, I was pretty sure, was quite far removed from her real feelings.

'Dear, *dear* Louise! It's so hard to explain her to someone who didn't know her. She was such an *exotic* creature. Quite different from anyone else. You felt that, I'm sure, nurse? A martyr to nerves, of course, and full of fancies, but one put up with things in her one wouldn't from anyone else. And she was so *sweet* to us all, wasn't she, nurse? And so *humble* about herself — I mean she didn't know anything about archaeology, and she was so eager to learn. Always asking my husband about the chemical processes for treating the metal objects and helping Miss

Johnson to mend pottery. Oh, we were all *devoted* to her.'

'Then it is not true, madame, what I have heard, that there was a certain tenseness — an uncomfortable atmosphere — here?'

Mrs Mercado opened her opaque black eyes very wide.

'Oh! who *can* have been telling you that? Nurse? Dr Leidner? I'm sure *he* would never notice anything, poor man.'

And she shot a thoroughly unfriendly glance at me.

Poirot smiled easily.

'I have my spies, madame,' he declared gaily. And just for a minute I saw her eyelids quiver and blink.

'Don't you think,' asked Mrs Mercado with an air of great sweetness, 'that after an event of this kind, everyone always pretends a lot of things that never were? You know — tension, atmosphere, a 'feeling that something was going to happen'? I think people just *make up* these things afterwards.'

'There is a lot in what you say, madame,' said Poirot.

'And it really *wasn't* true! We were a thoroughly happy family here.'

'That woman is one of the most utter liars I've ever known,' I said indignantly, when M. Poirot and I were clear of the house and walking along the path to the dig. 'I'm sure she simply hated Mrs Leidner really!'

'She is hardly the type to whom one would go for the truth,' Poirot agreed.

'Waste of time talking to her,' I snapped.

'Hardly that — hardly that. If a person tells you lies with her lips she is sometimes telling you truth with her eyes. What is she afraid of, little Madame Mercado? I saw fear in her eyes. Yes — decidedly she is afraid of something. It is very interesting.'

'I've got something to tell you, M. Poirot,' I said.

Then I told him all about my return the night before and my strong belief that Miss Johnson was the writer of the anonymous letters.

'So *she's* a liar too!' I said. 'The cool way she answered you this morning about these same letters!'

'Yes,' said Poirot. 'It was interesting, that. *For she let out the fact she knew all about those letters.* So far they have not been spoken of in the presence of the staff. Of course, it is quite possible that Dr Leidner told her about them yesterday. They are old friends, he and she. But if he did not — well — then it is curious and interesting, is it not?'

My respect for him went up. It was clever

the way he had tricked her into mentioning the letters.

'Are you going to tackle her about them?' I asked.

M. Poirot seemed quite shocked by the idea.

'No, no, indeed. Always it is unwise to parade one's knowledge. Until the last minute I keep everything here,' he tapped his forehead. 'At the right moment — I make the spring — like the panther — and, *mon Dieu!* the consternation!'

I couldn't help laughing to myself at little M. Poirot in the role of a panther.

We had just reached the dig. The first person we saw was Mr Reiter, who was busy photographing some walling.

It's my opinion that the men who were digging just hacked out walls wherever they wanted them. That's what it looked like anyway. Mr Carey explained to me that you could feel the difference at once with a pick, and he tried to show me — but I never saw. When the man said '*Libn*' — mud-brick — it was just ordinary dirt and mud as far as I could see.

Mr Reiter finished his photographs and handed over the camera and the plate to his boy and told him to take them back to the house.

Poirot asked him one or two questions about exposures and film packs and so on which he answered very readily. He seemed pleased to be asked about his work.

He was just tendering his excuses for leaving us when Poirot plunged once more into his set speech. As a matter of fact it wasn't quite a set speech because he varied it a little each time to suit the person he was talking to. But I'm not going to write it all down every time. With sensible people like Miss Johnson he went straight to the point, and with some of the others he had to beat about the bush a bit more. But it came to the same in the end.

'Yes, yes, I see what you mean,' said Mr Reiter. 'But indeed, I do not see that I can be much help to you. I am new here this season and I did not speak much with Mrs Leidner. I regret, but indeed I can tell you nothing.'

There was something a little stiff and foreign in the way he spoke, though, of course, he hadn't got any accent — except an American one, I mean.

'You can at least tell me whether you liked or disliked her?' said Poirot with a smile.

Mr Reiter got quite red and stammered: 'She was a charming person — most charming. And intellectual. She had a very fine brain — yes.'

'*Bien!* You liked her. And she liked you?'

Mr Reiter got redder still.

'Oh, I — I don't know that she noticed me much. And I was unfortunate once or twice. I was always unlucky when I tried to do anything for her. I'm afraid I annoyed her by my clumsiness. It was quite unintentional . . . I would have done *anything* — '

Poirot took pity on his flounderings.

'Perfectly — perfectly. Let us pass to another matter. Was it a happy atmosphere in the house?'

'Please?'

'Were you all happy together? Did you laugh and talk?'

'No — no, not exactly that. There was a little — stiffness.'

He paused, struggling with himself, and then said: 'You see, I am not very good in company. I am clumsy. I am shy. Dr Leidner always he has been most kind to me. But — it is stupid — I cannot overcome my shyness. I say always the wrong thing. I upset water jugs. I am unlucky.'

He really looked like a large awkward child.

'We all do these things when we are young,' said Poirot, smiling. 'The poise, the *savoir faire*, it comes later.'

Then with a word of farewell we walked on.

He said: 'That, *ma soeur*, is either an extremely simple young man or a very remarkable actor.'

I didn't answer. I was caught up once more by the fantastic notion that one of these people was a dangerous and cold-blooded murderer. Somehow, on this beautiful still sunny morning it seemed impossible.

21

Mr Mercado, Richard Carey

'They work in two separate places, I see,' said Poirot, halting.

Mr Reiter had been doing his photography on an outlying portion of the main excavation. A little distance away from us a second swarm of men were coming and going with baskets.

'That's what they call the deep cut,' I explained. 'They don't find much there, nothing but rubbishy broken pottery, but Dr Leidner always says it's very interesting, so I suppose it must be.'

'Let us go there.'

We walked together slowly, for the sun was hot.

Mr Mercado was in command. We saw him below us talking to the foreman, an old man like a tortoise who wore a tweed coat over his long striped cotton gown.

It was a little difficult to get down to them as there was only a narrow path or stair and basket-boys were going up and down it constantly, and they always seemed to be as blind as bats and never to think of getting out of the way.

As I followed Poirot down he said suddenly over his shoulder: 'Is Mr Mercado right-handed or left-handed?'

Now that was an extraordinary question if you like!

I thought a minute, then: 'Right-handed,' I said decisively.

Poirot didn't condescend to explain. He just went on and I followed him.

Mr Mercado seemed rather pleased to see us.

His long melancholy face lit up.

M. Poirot pretended to an interest in archaeology that I'm sure he couldn't have really felt, but Mr Mercado responded at once.

He explained that they had already cut down through twelve levels of house occupation.

'We are now definitely in the fourth millennium,' he said with enthusiasm.

I always thought a millennium was in the future — the time when everything comes right.

Mr Mercado pointed out belts of ashes (how his hand did shake! I wondered if he might possibly have malaria) and he explained how the pottery changed in character, and about burials — and how they had had one level almost entirely composed of infant burials — poor little things — and about flexed position and orientation, which seemed to mean the way the bones were lying.

And then suddenly, just as he was stooping down to pick up a kind of flint knife that was lying with some pots in a corner, he leapt into the air with a wild yell.

He spun round to find me and Poirot staring at him in astonishment.

He clapped his hand to his left arm.

'Something stung me — like a red-hot needle.'

Immediately Poirot was galvanized into energy.

'Quick, *mon cher*, let us see. Nurse Leatheran!'

I came forward.

He seized Mr Mercado's arm and deftly rolled back the sleeve of his khaki shirt to the shoulder.

'There,' said Mr Mercado pointing.

About there inches below the shoulder there was a minute prick from which the blood was oozing.

'Curious,' said Poirot. He peered into the rolled-up sleeve. 'I can see nothing. It was an ant, perhaps?'

'Better put on a little iodine,' I said.

I always carry an iodine pencil with me, and I whipped it out and applied it. But I was a little absent-minded as I did so, for my attention had been caught by something quite different. Mr Mercado's arm, all the way up the forearm to the elbow, was marked all over by tiny punctures. I knew well enough what *they* were — *the marks of a hypodermic needle.*

Mr Mercado rolled down his sleeve again and recommenced his explanations. Mr Poirot listened, but didn't try to bring the conversation round to the Leidners. In fact, he didn't ask Mr Mercado anything at all.

Presently we said goodbye to Mr Mercado and climbed up the path again.

'It was neat that, did you not think so?' my companion asked.

'Neat?' I asked.

M. Poirot took something from behind the lapel of his coat and surveyed it affectionately. To my surprise I saw that it was a long sharp darning needle with a blob of sealing wax making it into a pin.

'M. Poirot,' I cried, 'did you do that?'

'I was the stinging insect — yes. And very neatly I did it, too, do you not think so? You did not see me.'

That was true enough. I never saw him do it. And I'm sure Mr Mercado hadn't suspected. He must have been quick as lightning.

'But, M. Poirot, why?' I asked.

He answered me by another question.

'Did you notice anything, sister?' he asked.

I nodded my head slowly.

'Hypodermic marks,' I said.

'So now we know something about Mr Mercado,' said Poirot. 'I suspected — but I did not *know*. It is always necessary to *know*.'

'And you don't care how you set about it!' I thought, but didn't say.

Poirot suddenly clapped his hand to his pocket.

'Alas, I have dropped my handkerchief down there. I concealed the pin in it.'

'I'll get it for you,' I said and hurried back.

I'd got the feeling, you see, by this time, that M. Poirot and I were the doctor and nurse in charge of a case. At least, it was more like an operation and he was the surgeon. Perhaps I oughtn't to say so, but in a queer way I was beginning to enjoy myself.

I remember just after I'd finished my training, I went to a case in a private house and the need for an immediate operation arose, and the patient's husband was cranky about nursing homes. He just wouldn't hear of his wife being taken to one. Said it had to be done in the house.

Well, of course it was just splendid for me! Nobody else to have a look in! I was in charge of everything. Of course, I was terribly nervous — I thought of everything conceivable that doctor could want, but even then I was afraid I might have forgotten something. You never know with doctors. They ask for absolutely anything sometimes! But everything went splendidly! I had each thing ready as he asked for it, and he actually told me I'd done first-rate after it was over — and that's a thing most doctors wouldn't bother to do! The G.P. was very nice too. And I ran the whole thing myself!

The patient recovered, too, so everybody was happy.

Well, I felt rather the same now. In a way M. Poirot reminded me of that surgeon. *He* was a little man, too. Ugly little man with a face like a monkey, but a wonderful surgeon. He knew instinctively just where to go. I've seen a lot of surgeons and I know what a lot of difference there is.

Gradually I'd been growing a kind of confidence in M. Poirot. I felt that he, too, knew exactly what he was doing. And I was getting to feel that it was my job to help him — as you might say — to have the forceps and the swabs and all handy just when he wanted them. That's why it seemed just as natural for me to run off and look for his handkerchief as it would have been to pick up a towel that a doctor had thrown on the floor.

When I'd found it and got back I couldn't see him at first. But at last I caught sight of him. He was sitting a little way from the mound talking to Mr Carey. Mr Carey's boy was standing near with that great big rod thing with metres marked on it, but just at that moment he said something to the boy and the boy took it away. It seemed he had finished with it for the time being.

I'd like to get this next bit quite clear. You see, I wasn't quite sure what M. Poirot did or didn't want me to do. He might, I mean, have sent me back for that handkerchief *on purpose*. To get me out of the way.

It was just like an operation over again. You've got to be careful to hand the doctor just what he wants and not what he *doesn't* want. I mean, suppose you gave him the artery forceps at the wrong moment, and were late with them at the right moment! Thank goodness I know my work in the theatre well enough. I'm not likely to make mistakes there. But in this business I was really the rawest of raw little probationers. And so I had to be particularly careful not to make any silly mistakes.

Of course, I didn't for one moment

imagine that M. Poirot didn't want me to hear what he and Mr Carey were saying. But he might have thought he'd get Mr Carey to talk better if I wasn't there.

Now I don't want anybody to get it into their heads that I'm the kind of woman who goes about eavesdropping on private conversations. I wouldn't do such a thing. Not for a moment. Not however much I wanted to.

And what I mean is if it *had* been a private conversation I wouldn't for a moment have done what, as a matter of fact, I actually did do.

As I looked at it I was in a privileged position. After all, you hear many a thing when a patient's coming round after an anaesthetic. The patient wouldn't want you to hear it — and usually has no idea you *have* heard it — but the fact remains you *do* hear it. I just took it that Mr Carey was the patient. He'd be none the worse for what he didn't know about. And if you think that I was just curious, well, I'll admit that I *was* curious. I didn't want to miss anything I could help.

All this is just leading up to the fact that I turned aside and went by a roundabout way up behind the big dump until I was a foot from where they were, but concealed from them by the corner of the dump. And if anyone says it was dishonourable I just beg to disagree. *Nothing* ought to be hidden from the nurse in charge of the case, though, of course, it's for the doctor to say what shall be *done*.

I don't know, of course, what M. Poirot's line of approach had been, but by the time I'd got there he was aiming straight for the bull's eye, so to speak.

'Nobody appreciates Dr Leidner's devotion to his wife more than I do,' he was saying. 'But it is often the case that one learns more about a person from their enemies than from their friends.'

'You suggest that their faults are more important than their virtues?' said Mr Carey. His tone was dry and ironic.

'Undoubtedly — when it comes to murder. It seems odd that as far as I know nobody has yet been murdered for having too perfect a character! And yet perfection is undoubtedly an irritating thing.'

'I'm afraid I'm hardly the right person to help you,' said Mr Carey. 'To be perfectly honest, Mrs Leidner and I didn't hit it off particularly well. I don't mean that we were in any sense of the word enemies, but we were not exactly friends. Mrs Leidner was, perhaps, a shade jealous of my old friendship with her husband. I, for my part, although I admired her very much and thought she was an extremely attractive woman, was just a shade resentful of her influence over Leidner. As a result we were quite polite to each other, but not intimate.'

'Admirably explained,' said Poirot.

I could just see their heads, and I saw Mr Carey's turn sharply as though something in M. Poirot's detached tone struck him disagreeably.

M. Poirot went on: 'Was not Dr Leidner distressed that you and his wife did not get on together better?'

Carey hesitated a minute before saying: 'Really — I'm not sure. He never said anything. I always hoped he didn't notice it. He was very wrapped up in his work, you know.'

'So the truth, according to you, is that you did not really like Mrs Leidner?'

Carey shrugged his shoulders.

'I should probably have liked her very much if she hadn't been Leidner's wife.'

He laughed as though amused by his own statement.

Poirot was arranging a little heap of broken potsherds. He said in a dreamy, far-away voice: 'I talked to Miss Johnson this morning. She admitted that she was prejudiced against Mrs Leidner and did not like her very much, although she hastened to add that Mrs Leidner had always been charming to her.'

'All quite true, I should say,' said Carey.

'So I believed. Then I had a conversation with Mrs Mercado. She told me at great length how devoted she had been to Mrs Leidner and how much she had admired her.'

Carey made no answer to this, and after waiting a minute or two Poirot went on: 'That — I did not believe! Then I come to you and that which you tell me — well, again — I do *not believe* . . . '

Carey stiffened. I could hear the anger — repressed anger — in his voice.

'I really cannot help your beliefs — or your disbeliefs, M. Poirot. You've heard the truth and you can take it or leave it as far as I am concerned.'

Poirot did not grow angry. Instead he sounded particularly meek and depressed.

'Is it my fault what I do — or do not believe? I have a sensitive ear, you know. And then — there are always plenty of stories going about — rumours floating in the air. One listens — and perhaps — one learns something! Yes, there *are* stories . . . '

Carey sprang to his feet. I could see clearly a little pulse that beat in his temple. He looked simply splendid! So lean and so brown — and that wonderful jaw, hard and square. I don't wonder women fell for that man.

'What stories?' he asked savagely.

Poirot looked sideways at him.

'Perhaps you can guess. The usual sort of story — about you and Mrs Leidner.'

'What foul minds people have!'

'*N'est-ce pas?* They are like dogs. However deep you bury an unpleasantness a dog will always root it up again.'

'And you believe these stories?'

'I am willing to be convinced — of the truth,' said Poirot gravely.

'I doubt if you'd know the truth if you heard it,' Carey laughed rudely.

'Try me and see,' said Poirot, watching him.

'I will then! You shall have the truth! I hated Louise Leidner — there's the truth for you! I hated her like hell!'

22

David Emmott, Father Lavigny
and a Discovery

Turning abruptly away, Carey strode off with
long, angry strides.

Poirot sat looking after him and presently
he murmured: 'Yes — I see . . . '

Without turning his head he said in a
slightly louder voice: 'Do not come round the
corner for a minute, nurse. In case he turns
his head. Now it is all right. You have my
handkerchief? Many thanks. You are most
amiable.'

He didn't say anything at all about my
having been listening — and how he knew I
was listening I can't think. He'd never once
looked in that direction. I was rather relieved
he didn't say anything. I mean, I felt all right
with *myself* about it, but it might have been a
little awkward explaining to him. So it was a
good thing he didn't seem to want explanations.

'Do you think he did hate her, M. Poirot?' I
asked.

Nodding his head slowly with a curious

expression on his face, Poirot answered.

'Yes — I think he did.'

Then he got up briskly and began to walk to where the men were working on the top of the mound. I followed him. We couldn't see anyone but Arabs at first, but we finally found Mr Emmott lying face downwards blowing dust off a skeleton that had just been uncovered.

He gave his pleasant, grave smile when he saw us.

'Have you come to see round?' he asked. 'I'll be free in a minute.'

He sat up, took his knife and began daintily cutting the earth away from round the bones, stopping every now and then to use either a bellows or his own breath. A very insanitary proceeding the latter, I thought.

'You'll get all sorts of nasty germs in your mouth, Mr Emmott,' I protested.

'Nasty germs are my daily diet, nurse,' he said gravely. 'Germs can't do anything to an archaeologist — they just get naturally discouraged trying.'

He scraped a little more away round the thigh bone. Then he spoke to the foreman at his side, directing him exactly what he wanted done.

'There,' he said, rising to his feet. 'That's ready for Reiter to photograph after lunch.

Rather nice stuff she had in with her.'

He showed us a little verdigris copper bowl and some pins. And a lot of gold and blue things that had been her necklace of beads.

The bones and all the objects were brushed and cleaned with a knife and kept in position ready to be photographed.

'Who is she?' asked Poirot.

'First millennium. A lady of some consequence perhaps. Skull looks rather odd — I must get Mercado to look at it. It suggests death by foul play.'

'A Mrs Leidner of two thousand odd years ago?' said Poirot.

'Perhaps,' said Mr Emmott.

Bill Coleman was doing something with a pick to a wall face.

David Emmott called something to him which I didn't catch and then started showing M. Poirot round.

When the short explanatory tour was over, Emmott looked at his watch.

'We knock off in ten minutes,' he said. 'Shall we walk back to the house?'

'That will suit me excellently,' said Poirot.

We walked slowly along the well-worn path.

'I expect you are all glad to get back to work again,' said Poirot.

Emmott replied gravely: 'Yes, it's much the

best thing. It's not been any too easy loafing about the house and making conversation.'

'Knowing all the time *that one of you was a murderer.'*

Emmott did not answer. He made no gesture of dissent. I knew now that he had had a suspicion of the truth from the very first when he had questioned the house-boys.

After a few minutes he asked quietly: 'Are you getting anywhere, M. Poirot?'

Poirot said gravely: 'Will you help me to get somewhere?'

'Why, naturally.'

Watching him closely, Poirot said: 'The hub of the case is Mrs Leidner. I want to know about Mrs Leidner.'

David Emmott said slowly: 'What do you mean by know about her?'

'I do not mean where she came from and what her maiden name was. I do not mean the shape of her face and the colour of her eyes. I mean her — herself.'

'You think that counts in the case?'

'I am quite sure of it.'

Emmott was silent for a moment or two, then he said: 'Maybe you're right.'

'And that is where you can help me. You can tell me what sort of a woman she was.'

'Can I? I've often wondered about it myself.'

'Didn't you make up your mind on the subject?'

'I think I did in the end.'

'*Eh bien?*'

But Mr Emmott was silent for some minutes, then he said: 'What did nurse think of her? Women are said to sum up other women quickly enough, and a nurse has a wide experience of types.'

Poirot didn't give me any chance of speaking even if I had wanted to. He said quickly: 'What I want to know is what a *man* thought of her?'

Emmott smiled a little.

'I expect they'd all be much the same.' He paused and said, 'She wasn't young, but I think she was about the most beautiful woman I've ever come across.'

'That's hardly an answer, Mr Emmott.'

'It's not so far off one, M. Poirot.'

He was silent a minute or two and then he went on: 'There used to be a fairy story I read when I was a kid. A Northern fairy tale about the Snow Queen and Little Kay. I guess Mrs Leidner was rather like that — always taking Little Kay for a ride.'

'Ah yes, a tale of Hans Andersen, is it not? And there was a girl in it. Little Gerda, was that her name?'

'Maybe. I don't remember much of it.'

'Can't you go a little further, Mr Emmott?'

David Emmott shook his head.

'I don't even know if I've summed her up correctly. She wasn't easy to read. She'd do a devilish thing one day, and a really fine one the next. But I think you're about right when you say that she's the hub of the case. That's what she always wanted to be — *at the centre of things*. And she liked to get *at* other people — I mean, she wasn't just satisfied with being passed the toast and the peanut butter, she wanted you to turn your mind and soul inside out for her to look at it.'

'And if one did not give her that satisfaction?' asked Poirot.

'Then she could turn ugly!'

I saw his lips close resolutely and his jaw set.

'I suppose, Mr Emmott, you would not care to express a plain unofficial opinion as to who murdered her?'

'I don't know,' said Emmott. 'I really haven't the slightest idea. I rather think that, if I'd been Carl — Carl Reiter, I mean — I would have had a shot at murdering her. She was a pretty fair devil to him. But, of course, he asks for it by being so darned sensitive. Just invites you to give him a kick in the pants.'

'And did Mrs Leidner give him — a kick in

the pants?' inquired Poirot.

Emmott gave a sudden grin.

'No. Pretty little jabs with an embroidery needle — that was her method. He *was* irritating, of course. Just like some blubbering, poor-spirited kid. But a needle's a painful weapon.'

I stole a glance at Poirot and thought I detected a slight quiver of his lips.

'But you don't really believe that Carl Reiter killed her?' he asked.

'No. I don't believe you'd kill a woman because she persistently made you look a fool at every meal.'

Poirot shook his head thoughtfully.

Of course, Mr Emmott made Mrs Leidner sound quite inhuman. There was something to be said on the other side too.

There had been something terribly irritating about Mr Reiter's attitude. He jumped when she spoke to him, and did idiotic things like passing her the marmalade again and again when he knew she never ate it. I'd have felt inclined to snap at him a bit myself.

Men don't understand how their mannerisms can get on women's nerves so that you feel you just have to snap.

I thought I'd just mention that to Mr Poirot some time.

We had arrived back now and Mr Emmott

offered Poirot a wash and took him into his room.

I hurried across the courtyard to mine.

I came out again about the same time they did and we were all making for the dining-room when Father Lavigny appeared in the doorway of his room and invited Poirot in.

Mr Emmott came on round and he and I went into the dining-room together. Miss Johnson and Mrs Mercado were there already, and after a few minutes Mr Mercado, Mr Reiter and Bill Coleman joined us.

We were just sitting down and Mercado had told the Arab boy to tell Father Lavigny lunch was ready when we were all startled by a faint, muffled cry.

I suppose our nerves weren't very good yet, for we all jumped, and Miss Johnson got quite pale and said: '*What was that*? What's happened?'

Mrs Mercado stared at her and said: 'My dear, what *is* the matter with you? It's some noise outside in the fields.'

But at that minute Poirot and Father Lavigny came in.

'We thought someone was hurt,' Miss Johnson said.

'A thousand pardons, mademoiselle,' cried Poirot. 'The fault is mine. Father Lavigny, he explains to me some tablets, and I take one to the window to see better — and, *ma foi*, not looking where I was going, I steb the toe, and the pain is sharp for the moment and I cry out.'

'We thought it was another murder,' said Mrs Mercado, laughing.

'Marie!' said her husband.

His tone was reproachful and she flushed and bit her lip.

Miss Johnson hastily turned the conversation to the dig and what objects of interest had turned up that morning. Conversation all through lunch was sternly archaeological.

I think we all felt it was the safest thing.

After we had had coffee we adjourned to the living-room. Then the men, with the exception of Father Lavigny, went off to the dig again.

Father Lavigny took Poirot through into the antika-room and I went with them. I was getting to know the things pretty well by now and I felt a thrill of pride — almost as though it were my own property — when Father Lavigny took down the gold cup and I heard Poirot's exclamation of admiration and pleasure.

'How beautiful! What a work of art!'

Father Lavigny agreed eagerly and began to point out its beauties with real enthusiasm and knowledge.

'No wax on it today,' I said.

'Wax?' Poirot stared at me.

'Wax?' So did Father Lavigny.

I explained my remark.

'Ah, *je comprends*,' said Father Lavigny. 'Yes, yes, candle grease.'

That led direct to the subject of the midnight visitor. Forgetting my presence they both dropped into French, and I left them together and went back into the living-room.

Mrs Mercado was darning her husband's socks and Miss Johnson was reading a book. Rather an unusual thing for her. She usually seemed to have something to work at.

After a while Father Lavigny and Poirot came out, and the former excused himself on the score of work. Poirot sat down with us.

'A most interesting man,' he said, and asked how much work there had been for Father Lavigny to do so far.

Miss Johnson explained that tablets had been scarce and that there had been very few inscribed bricks or cylinder seals. Father Lavigny, however, had done his share of work on the dig and was picking up colloquial Arabic very fast.

That led the talk to cylinder seals, and presently Miss Johnson fetched from a cupboard a sheet of impressions made by rolling them out on plasticine.

I realized as we bent over them, admiring the spirited designs, that these must be what she had been working at on that fatal afternoon.

As we talked I noticed that Poirot was rolling and kneading a little ball of plasticine between his fingers.

'You use a lot of plasticine, mademoiselle?' he asked.

'A fair amount. We seem to have got through a lot already this year — though I can't imagine how. But half our supply seems to have gone.'

'Where is it kept, mademoiselle?'

'Here — in this cupboard.'

As she replaced the sheet of impressions she showed him the shelf with rolls of plasticine, Durofix, photographic paste and other stationery supplies.

Poirot stooped down.

'And this — what is this, mademoiselle?'

He had slipped his hand right to the back and had brought out a curious crumpled object.

As he straightened it out we could see that it was a kind of mask, with eyes and mouth crudely painted on it in Indian ink and the whole thing roughly smeared with plasticine.

'How perfectly extraordinary!' cried Miss Johnson. 'I've never seen it before. How did it get there? And what is it?'

'As to how it got there, well, one hiding-place is as good as another, and I presume that this cupboard would not have been turned out till the end of the season. As to what it *is* — that, too, I think, is not difficult to say. *We have here the face that Mrs Leidner described.* The ghostly face seen in the semi-dusk outside her window — without body attached.'

Mrs Mercado gave a little shriek.

Miss Johnson was white to the lips. She murmured: 'Then it was *not* fancy. It was a trick — a wicked trick! But who played it?'

'Yes,' cried Mrs Mercado. 'Who could have done such a wicked, wicked thing?'

Poirot did not attempt a reply. His face was very grim as he went into the next room, returned with an empty cardboard box in his hand and put the crumpled mask into it.

'The police must see this,' he explained.

'It's horrible,' said Miss Johnson in a low voice. 'Horrible!'

'Do you think everything's hidden here somewhere?' cried Mrs Mercado shrilly. 'Do you think perhaps the weapon — the club she was killed with — all covered with blood still, perhaps . . . Oh! I'm frightened — I'm frightened . . . '

Miss Johnson gripped her by the shoulder.

'Be quiet,' she said fiercely. 'Here's Dr Leidner. We mustn't upset him.'

Indeed, at that very moment the car had driven into the courtyard. Dr Leidner got out of it and came straight across and in at the living-room door. His face was set in lines of fatigue and he looked twice the age he had three days ago.

He said in a quiet voice: 'The funeral will be at eleven o'clock tomorrow. Major Deane will read the service.'

Mrs Mercado faltered something, then slipped out of the room.

Dr Leidner said to Miss Johnson: 'You'll come, Anne?'

And she answered: 'Of course, my dear, we'll all come. Naturally.'

She didn't say anything else, but her face must have expressed what her tongue was powerless to do, for his face lightened up with affection and a momentary ease.

'Dear Anne,' he said. 'You are such a wonderful comfort and help to me. My dear old friend.'

He laid his hand on her arm and I saw the red colour creep up in her face as she muttered, gruff as ever: 'That's all right.'

But I just caught a glimpse of her expression and knew that, for one short moment, Anne Johnson was a perfectly happy woman.

And another idea flashed across my mind. Perhaps soon, in the natural course of things, turning to his old friend for sympathy, a new and happy state of things might come about.

Not that I'm really a matchmaker, and of course it was indecent to think of such a thing before the funeral even. But after all, it *would* be a happy solution. He was very fond of her, and there was no doubt she was absolutely devoted to him and would be perfectly happy devoting the rest of her life to him. That is, if she could bear to hear Louise's perfections sung all the time. But women can put up with a lot when they've got what they want.

Dr Leidner then greeted Poirot, asking him if he had made any progress.

Miss Johnson was standing behind Dr Leidner and she looked hard at the box in Poirot's hand and shook her head, and I realized that she was pleading with Poirot not to tell him about the mask. She felt, I was sure, that he had enough to bear for one day.

Poirot fell in with her wish.

'These things march slowly, monsieur,' he said.

Then, after a few desultory words, he took his leave.

I accompanied him out to his car.

There were half a dozen things I wanted to ask him, but somehow, when he turned and looked at me, I didn't ask anything after all. I'd as soon have asked a surgeon if he thought he'd made a good job of an operation. I just stood meekly waiting for instructions.

Rather to my surprise he said: 'Take care of yourself, my child.'

And then he added: 'I wonder if it is well for you to remain here?'

'I must speak to Dr Leidner about leaving,' I said. 'But I thought I'd wait until after the funeral.'

He nodded in approval.

'In the meantime,' he said, 'do not try to find out too much. You understand, I do not want you to be clever!' And he added with a smile, 'It is for you to hold the swabs and for me to do the operation.'

Wasn't it funny, his actually saying that?

Then he said quite irrelevantly: 'An interesting man, that Father Lavigny.'

'A monk being an archaeologist seems odd to me,' I said.

'Ah, yes, you are a Protestant. Me, I am a good Catholic. I know something of priests and monks.'

He frowned, seemed to hesitate, then said:

'Remember, he is quite clever enough to turn you inside out if he likes.'

If he was warning me against gossiping I felt that I didn't need any warning!

It annoyed me, and though I didn't like to ask him any of the things I really wanted to know, I didn't see why I shouldn't at any rate say one thing.

'You'll excuse me, M. Poirot,' I said. 'But it's 'stubbed your toe', not *stepped* or *stebbed*.'

'Ah! Thank you, *ma soeur*.'

'Don't mention it. But it's just as well to get a phrase right.'

'I will remember,' he said — quite meekly for him.

And he got in the car and was driven away, and I went slowly back across the courtyard wondering about a lot of things.

About the hypodermic marks on Mr Mercado's arm, and what drug it was he took. And about that horrid yellow smeared mask. And how odd it was that Poirot and Miss Johnson hadn't heard my cry in the living-room that morning, whereas we had all heard Poirot perfectly well in the dining-room at lunch-time — and yet Father Lavigny's room and Mrs Leidner's were just the same distance from the living-room and the dining-room respectively.

And then I felt rather pleased that I'd taught *Doctor* Poirot one English phrase correctly!

Even if he *was* a great detective he'd realize he *didn't* know *everything*!

23

I Go Psychic

The funeral was, I thought, a very affecting affair. As well as ourselves, all the English people in Hassanieh attended it. Even Sheila Reilly was there, looking quiet and subdued in a dark coat and skirt. I hoped that she was feeling a little remorseful for all the unkind things she had said.

When we got back to the house I followed Dr Leidner into the office and broached the subject of my departure. He was very nice about it, thanked me for what I had done (Done! I had been worse than useless) and insisted on my accepting an extra week's salary.

I protested because really I felt I'd done nothing to earn it.

'Indeed, Dr Leidner, I'd rather not have any salary at all. If you'll just refund me my travelling expenses, that's all I want.'

But he wouldn't hear of that.

'You see,' I said, 'I don't feel I deserve it, Dr Leidner. I mean, I've — well, I've failed. She — my coming didn't save her.'

'Now don't get that idea into your head, nurse,' he said earnestly. 'After all, I didn't engage you as a female detective. I never dreamt my wife's life was in danger. I was convinced it was all nerves and that she'd worked herself up into a rather curious mental state. You did all anyone could do. She liked and trusted you. And I think in her last days she felt happier and safer because of your being here. There's nothing for you to reproach yourself with.'

His voice quivered a little and I knew what he was thinking. *He* was the one to blame for not having taken Mrs Leidner's fears seriously.

'Dr Leidner,' I said curiously. 'Have you ever come to any conclusion about those anonymous letters?'

He said with a sigh: 'I don't know what to believe. Has M. Poirot come to any definite conclusion?'

'He hadn't yesterday,' I said, steering rather neatly, I thought, between truth and fiction. After all, he hadn't until I told him about Miss Johnson.

It was on my mind that I'd like to give Dr Leidner a hint and see if he reacted. In the pleasure of seeing him and Miss Johnson together the day before, and his affection and reliance on her, I'd forgotten all about the letters. Even now I felt it was perhaps rather mean of me to bring it up. Even if she had written them, she had had a bad time after Mrs Leidner's death. Yet I did want to see whether that particular possibility had ever entered Dr Leidner's head.

'Anonymous letters are usually the work of a woman,' I said. I wanted to see how he'd take it.

'I suppose they are,' he said with a sigh. 'But you seem to forget, nurse, that these may be genuine. They may actually be written by Frederick Bosner.'

'No, I haven't forgotten,' I said. 'But I can't believe somehow that that's the real explanation.'

'I do,' he said. 'It's all nonsense, his being one of the expedition staff. That is just an ingenious theory of M. Poirot's. I believe that the truth is much simpler. The man is a madman, of course. He's been hanging round the place — perhaps in disguise of some kind. And somehow or other he got in on that fatal afternoon. The servants may be lying — they may have been bribed.'

'I suppose it's possible,' I said doubtfully.

Dr Leidner went on with a trace of irritability.

'It is all very well for M. Poirot to suspect the members of my expedition. I am perfectly certain *none* of them have anything to do with it! I have worked with them. I *know* them!'

He stopped suddenly, then he said: 'Is that your experience, nurse? That anonymous letters are usually written by women?'

'It isn't always the case,' I said. 'But there's a certain type of feminine spitefulness that finds relief that way.'

'I suppose you are thinking of Mrs Mercado?' he said.

Then he shook his head.

'Even if she were malicious enough to wish to hurt Louise she would hardly have the necessary knowledge,' he said.

I remembered the earlier letters in the attaché-case.

If Mrs Leidner had left that unlocked and Mrs Mercado had been alone in the house one day pottering about, she might easily have found them and read them. Men never seem to think of the simplest possibilities!

'And apart from her there is only Miss Johnson,' I said, watching him.

'That would be quite ridiculous!'

The little smile with which he said it was quite conclusive. The idea of Miss Johnson being the author of the letters had never entered his head! I hesitated just for a minute — but I didn't say anything. One doesn't like giving away a fellow woman, and besides, I had been a witness of Miss Johnson's genuine and moving remorse. What was done was done. Why expose Dr Leidner to a fresh disillusion on top of all his other troubles?

It was arranged that I should leave on the following day, and I had arranged through Dr Reilly to stay for a day or two with the matron of the hospital whilst I made arrangements for returning to England either via Baghdad or direct via Nissibin by car and train.

Dr Leidner was kind enough to say that he would like me to choose a memento from amongst his wife's things.

'Oh, no, really, Dr Leidner,' I said. 'I couldn't. It's much too kind of you.'

He insisted.

'But I should like you to have something. And Louise, I am sure, would have wished it.'

Then he went on to suggest that I should have her tortoiseshell toilet set!

'Oh, no, Dr Leidner! Why, that's a most *expensive* set. I couldn't, really.'

'She had no sisters, you know — no one who wants these things. There is no one else to have them.'

I could quite imagine that he wouldn't want them to fall into Mrs Mercado's greedy little hands. And I didn't think he'd want to offer them to Miss Johnson.

He went on kindly: 'You just think it over. By the way, here is the key of Louise's jewel case. Perhaps you will find something there you would rather have. And I should be very grateful if you would pack up — all her clothes. I daresay Reilly can find a use for them amongst some of the poor Christian families in Hassanieh.'

I was very glad to be able to do that for him, and I expressed my willingness.

I set about it at once.

Mrs Leidner had only had a very simple wardrobe with her and it was soon sorted and packed up into a couple of suitcases. All her papers had been in the small attaché-case. The jewel case contained a few simple trinkets — a pearl ring, a diamond brooch, a small string of pearls, and one or two plain gold bar brooches of the safety-pin type, and a string of large amber beads.

Naturally I wasn't going to take the pearls or the diamonds, but I hesitated a bit between the amber beads and the toilet set. In the end, however, I didn't see why I shouldn't take the latter. It was a kindly thought on Dr Leidner's part, and I was sure there wasn't any patronage about it. I'd take it in the spirit it had been offered, without any false pride. After all, I *had* been fond of her.

Well, that was all done and finished with. The suitcases packed, the jewel case locked up again and put separate to give to Dr Leidner with the photograph of Mrs Leidner's father and one or two other personal little odds and ends.

The room looked bare and forlorn emptied of all its accoutrements, when I'd finished. There was nothing more for me to do — and yet somehow or other I shrank from leaving the room. It seemed as though there was something still to do there — something I ought to *see* — or something I ought to have *known*. I'm not superstitious, but the idea *did* pop into my head that perhaps Mrs Leidner's spirit was hanging about the room and trying to get in touch with me.

I remember once at the hospital some of us girls got a planchette and really it wrote some very remarkable things.

Perhaps, although I'd never thought of such a thing, I might be mediumistic.

As I say, one gets all worked up to imagine all sorts of foolishness sometimes.

I prowled round the room uneasily, touching this and that. But, of course, there wasn't anything in the room but bare furniture. There was nothing slipped behind drawers or tucked away. I couldn't hope for anything of that kind.

In the end (it sounds rather batty, but as I say, one gets worked up) I did rather a queer thing.

I went and lay down in the bed and closed my eyes.

I deliberately tried to forget who and what I was. I tried to think myself back to that fatal afternoon. I was Mrs Leidner lying here resting, peaceful and unsuspicious.

It's extraordinary how you *can* work yourself up.

I'm a perfectly normal matter-of-fact individual — not the least bit spooky, but I tell you that after I'd lain there about five minutes I began to *feel* spooky.

I didn't try to resist. I deliberately encouraged the feeling.

I said to myself: 'I'm Mrs Leidner. I'm Mrs Leidner. I'm lying here — half asleep. Presently — very soon now — the door's going to open.'

I kept on saying that — as though I were hypnotizing myself.

'It's just about half-past one . . . it's just about the time . . . The door is going to open . . . *the door is going to open* . . . I shall see who comes in . . . '

I kept my eyes glued on that door. Presently it was going to open. I should *see* it open. And I should see *the person who opened it*.

I must have been a little over-wrought that afternoon to imagine I could solve the mystery that way.

But I did believe it. A sort of chill passed down my back and settled in my legs. They felt numb — paralysed.

'You're going into a trance,' I said. 'And in that trance you'll see . . . '

And once again I repeated monotonously again and again:

'The door is going to open — the door is going to open . . . '

The cold numbed feeling grew more intense.

And then, slowly, *I saw the door just beginning to open.*

It was horrible.

I've never known anything so horrible before or since.

I was paralysed — chilled through and through. I couldn't move. For the life of me I couldn't have moved.

And I was terrified. Sick and blind and dumb with terror.

That slowly opening door.

So noiseless.

In a minute I should see . . .

Slowly — slowly — wider and wider.

Bill Coleman came quietly in.

He must have had the shock of his life!

I bounded off the bed with a scream of terror and hurled myself across the room.

He stood stock-still, his blunt pink face pinker and his mouth opened wide with surprise.

'Hallo, 'allo, 'allo,' he said. 'What's up, nurse?'

I came back to reality with a crash.

'Goodness, Mr Coleman,' I said. 'How you startled me!'

'Sorry,' he said with a momentary grin.

I saw then that he was holding a little bunch of scarlet ranunculus in his hand. They were pretty little flowers and they grew wild on the sides of the Tell. Mrs Leidner had been fond of them.

He blushed and got rather red as he said: 'One can't get any flowers or things in Hassanieh. Seemed rather rotten not to have any flowers for the grave. I thought I'd just nip in here and put a little posy in that little pot thing she always had flowers in on her table. Sort of show she wasn't forgotten — eh? A bit asinine, I know, but — well — I mean to say.'

I thought it was very nice of him. He was all pink with embarrassment like Englishmen are when they've done anything sentimental. I thought it was a very sweet thought.

'Why, I think that's a very nice idea, Mr Coleman,' I said.

And I picked up the little pot and went and got some water in it and we put the flowers in.

I really thought much more of Mr Coleman for this idea of his. It showed he had a heart and nice feelings about things.

He didn't ask me again what made me let out such a squeal and I'm thankful he didn't. I should have felt a fool explaining.

'Stick to common sense in future, woman,' I said to myself as I settled my cuffs and smoothed my apron. 'You're not cut out for this psychic stuff.'

I bustled about doing my own packing and kept myself busy for the rest of the day.

Father Lavigny was kind enough to express great distress at my leaving. He said my cheerfulness and common sense had been such a help to everybody. Common sense! I'm glad he didn't know about my idiotic behaviour in Mrs Leidner's room.

'We have not seen M. Poirot today,' he remarked.

I told him that Poirot had said he was going to be busy all day sending off telegrams.

Father Lavigny raised his eyebrows.

'Telegrams? To America?'

'I suppose so. He said, 'All over the world!' but I think that was rather a foreign exaggeration.'

And then I got rather red, remembering that Father Lavigny was a foreigner himself.

He didn't seem offended though, just laughed quite pleasantly and asked me if there were any news of the man with the squint.

I said I didn't know but I hadn't heard of any.

Father Lavigny asked me again about the time Mrs Leidner and I had noticed the man and how he had seemed to be standing on tiptoe and peering through the window.

'It seems clear the man had some overwhelming interest in Mrs Leidner,' he said thoughtfully. 'I have wondered since whether the man could possibly have been a European got up to look like an Iraqi?'

That was a new idea to me and I considered it carefully. I had taken it for granted that the man was a native, but of course when I came to think of it, I was really going by the cut of his clothes and the yellowness of his skin.

Father Lavigny declared his intention of going round outside the house to the place where Mrs Leidner and I had seen the man standing.

'You never know, he might have dropped something. In the detective stories the criminal always does.'

'I expect in real life criminals are more careful,' I said.

I fetched some socks I had just finished darning and put them on the table in the living-room for the men to sort out when they came in, and then, as there was nothing much more to do, I went up on the roof.

Miss Johnson was standing there but she didn't hear me. I got right up to her before she noticed me.

But long before that I'd seen that there was something very wrong.

She was standing in the middle of the roof staring straight in front of her, and there was the most awful look on her face. As though she'd seen something she couldn't possibly believe.

It gave me quite a shock.

Mind you, I'd seen her upset the other evening, but this was quite different.

'My dear,' I said, hurrying to her, 'whatever's the matter?'

She turned her head at that and stood looking at me — almost as if she didn't see me.

'What is it?' I persisted.

She made a queer sort of grimace — as though she were trying to swallow but her throat were too dry. She said hoarsely: 'I've just seen something.'

'What have you seen? Tell me. Whatever can it be? You look all in.'

She gave an effort to pull herself together, but she still looked pretty dreadful.

She said, still in that same dreadful choked voice: *'I've seen how someone could come in from outside — and no one would ever guess.'*

I followed the direction of her eyes but I couldn't see anything.

Mr Reiter was standing in the door of the photographic-room and Father Lavigny was just crossing the courtyard — but there was nothing else.

I turned back puzzled and found her eyes fixed on mine with the strangest expression in them.

'Really,' I said, 'I don't see what you mean. Won't you explain?'

But she shook her head.

'Not now. Later. We *ought* to have seen. Oh, we ought to have seen!'

'If you'd only tell me — '

But she shook her head.

'I've got to think it out first.'

And pushing past me, she went stumbling down the stairs.

I didn't follow her as she obviously didn't want me with her. Instead I sat down on the parapet and tried to puzzle things out. But I didn't get anywhere. There was only the one way into the courtyard — through the big arch. Just outside it I could see the water-boy and his horse and the Indian cook talking to him. Nobody could have passed them and come in without their seeing him.

I shook my head in perplexity and went downstairs again.

24

Murder is a Habit

We all went to bed early that night. Miss Johnson had appeared at dinner and had behaved more or less as usual. She had, however, a sort of dazed look, and once or twice quite failed to take in what other people said to her.

It wasn't somehow a very comfortable sort of meal. You'd say, I suppose, that that was natural enough in a house where there'd been a funeral that day. But I know what I mean.

Lately our meals had been hushed and subdued, but for all that there had been a feeling of comradeship. There had been sympathy with Dr Leidner in his grief and a fellow feeling of being all in the same boat amongst the others.

But tonight I was reminded of my first meal there — when Mrs Mercado had watched me and there had been that curious feeling as though something might snap any minute.

I'd felt the same thing — only very much intensified — when we'd sat round the dining-room table with Poirot at the head of it.

Tonight it was particularly strong. Everyone was on edge — jumpy — on tenterhooks. If anyone had dropped something I'm sure somebody would have screamed.

As I say, we all separated early afterwards. I went to bed almost at once. The last thing I heard as I was dropping off to sleep was Mrs Mercado's voice saying goodnight to Miss Johnson just outside my door.

I dropped off to sleep at once — tired by my exertions and even more by my silly experience in Mrs Leidner's room. I slept heavily and dreamlessly for several hours.

I awoke when I did awake with a start and a feeling of impending catastrophe. Some sound had woken me, and as I sat up in bed listening I heard it again.

An awful sort of agonized choking groan.

I had lit my candle and was out of bed in a twinkling. I snatched up a torch, too, in case the candle should blow out. I came out of my door and stood listening. I knew the sound wasn't far away. It came again — from the room immediately next to mine — Miss Johnson's room.

I hurried in. Miss Johnson was lying in bed, her whole body contorted in agony. As I set down the candle and bent over her, her lips moved and she tried to speak — but only an awful hoarse whisper came. I saw that the corners of her mouth and the skin of her chin were burnt a kind of greyish white.

Her eyes went from me to a glass that lay on the floor evidently where it had dropped from her hand. The light rug was stained a bright red where it had fallen. I picked it up and ran a finger over the inside, drawing back my hand with a sharp exclamation. Then I examined the inside of the poor woman's mouth.

There wasn't the least doubt what was the matter. Somehow or other, intentionally or otherwise, she'd swallowed a quantity of corrosive acid — oxalic or hydrochloric, I suspected.

I ran out and called to Dr Leidner and he woke the others, and we worked over her for all we were worth, but all the time I had an awful feeling it was no good. We tried a strong solution of carbonate of soda — and followed it with olive oil. To ease the pain I gave her a hypodermic of morphine sulphate.

David Emmott had gone off to Hassanieh to fetch Dr Reilly, but before he came it was over.

I won't dwell on the details. Poisoning by a strong solution of hydrochloric acid (which is what it proved to be) is one of the most painful deaths possible.

It was when I was bending over her to give her the morphia that she made one ghastly effort to speak. It was only a horrible strangled whisper when it came.

'*The window . . .* ' she said. '*Nurse . . . the window . . .* '

But that was all — she couldn't go on. She collapsed completely.

I shall never forget that night. The arrival of Dr Reilly. The arrival of Captain Maitland. And finally with the dawn, Hercule Poirot.

He it was who took me gently by the arm and steered me into the dining-room, where he made me sit down and have a cup of good strong tea.

'There, *mon enfant*,' he said, 'that is better. You are worn out.'

Upon that, I burst into tears.

'It's too awful,' I sobbed. 'It's been like a nightmare. Such awful suffering. And her eyes . . . Oh, M. Poirot — her eyes . . . '

He patted me on the shoulder. A woman couldn't have been kinder.

'Yes, yes — do not think of it. You did all you could.'

'It was one of the corrosive acids.'

'It was a strong solution of hydrochloric acid.'

'The stuff they use on the pots?'

'Yes. Miss Johnson probably drank it off before she was fully awake. That is — unless she took it on purpose.'

'Oh, M. Poirot, what an awful idea!'

'It is a possibility, after all. What do you think?'

I considered for a moment and then shook my head decisively.

'I don't believe it. No, I don't believe it for a moment.' I hesitated and then said, 'I think she found out something yesterday afternoon.'

'What is that you say? She found out something?'

I repeated to him the curious conversation we had had together.

Poirot gave a low soft whistle.

'*La pauvre femme!*' he said. 'She said she wanted to think it over — eh? That is what signed her death warrant. If she had only spoken out — then — at once.'

He said: 'Tell me again her exact words.'

I repeated them.

'She saw how someone could have come in from outside without any of you knowing? Come, *ma soeur*, let us go up to the roof and you shall show me just where she was standing.'

We went up to the roof together and I showed Poirot the exact spot where Miss Johnson had stood.

'Like this?' said Poirot. 'Now what do I see? I see half the courtyard — and the archway — and the doors of the drawing-office and the photographic-room and the laboratory. Was there anyone in the courtyard?'

'Father Lavigny was just going towards the archway and Mr Reiter was standing in the door of the photographic-room.'

'And still I do not see in the least how anyone could come in from outside and none of you know about it . . . But *she* saw . . . '

He gave it up at last, shaking his head.

'*Sacré nom d'un chien* — *va*! What *did* she see?'

The sun was just rising. The whole eastern sky was a riot of rose and orange and pale, pearly grey.

'What a beautiful sunrise!' said Poirot gently.

The river wound away to our left and the Tell stood up outlined in gold colour. To the south were the blossoming trees and the peaceful cultivation. The water-wheel groaned in the distance — a faint unearthly sound. In the north were the slender minarets and the clustering fairy whiteness of Hassanieh.

It was incredibly beautiful.

And then, close at my elbow, I heard Poirot give a long deep sigh.

'Fool that I have been,' he murmured. 'When the truth is so clear — so clear.'

25

Suicide or Murder?

I hadn't time to ask Poirot what he meant, for Captain Maitland was calling up to us and asking us to come down.

We hurried down the stairs.

'Look here, Poirot,' he said. 'Here's another complication. The monk fellow is missing.'

'Father Lavigny?'

'Yes. Nobody noticed it till just now. Then it dawned on somebody that he was the only one of the party not around, and we went to his room. His bed's not been slept in and there's no sign of him.'

The whole thing was like a bad dream. First Miss Johnson's death and then the disappearance of Father Lavigny.

The servants were called and questioned, but they couldn't throw any light on the mystery. He had last been seen at about eight o'clock the night before. Then he had said he was going out for a stroll before going to bed.

Nobody had seen him come back from that stroll.

The big doors had been closed and barred

at nine o'clock as usual. Nobody, however, remembered unbarring them in the morning. The two house-boys each thought the other one must have done the unfastening.

Had Father Lavigny ever returned the night before? Had he, in the course of his earlier walk, discovered anything of a suspicious nature, gone out to investigate it later, and perhaps fallen a third victim?

Captain Maitland swung round as Dr Reilly came up with Mr Mercado behind him.

'Hallo, Reilly. Got anything?'

'Yes. The stuff came from the laboratory here. I've just been checking up the quantities with Mercado. It's H.C.L. from the lab.'

'The laboratory — eh? Was it locked up?'

Mr Mercado shook his head. His hands were shaking and his face was twitching. He looked a wreck of a man.

'It's never been the custom,' he stammered. 'You see — just now — we're using it all the time. I — nobody ever dreamt — '

'Is the place locked up at night?'

'Yes — all the rooms are locked. The keys are hung up just inside the living-room.'

'So if anyone had a key to that they could get the lot.'

'Yes.'

'And it's a perfectly ordinary key, I suppose?'

'Oh, yes.'

'Nothing to show whether she took it herself from the laboratory?' asked Captain Maitland.

'She didn't,' I said loudly and positively.

I felt a warning touch on my arm. Poirot was standing close behind me.

And then something rather ghastly happened.

Not ghastly in itself — in fact it was just the incongruousness that made it seem worse than anything else.

A car drove into the courtyard and a little man jumped out. He was wearing a sun helmet and a short thick trench coat.

He came straight to Dr Leidner, who was standing by Dr Reilly, and shook him warmly by the hand.

'*Vous voilà, mon cher,*' he cried. 'Delighted to see you. I passed this way on Saturday afternoon — en route to the Italians at Fugima. I went to the dig but there wasn't a single European about and alas! I cannot speak Arabic. I had not time to come to the house. This morning I leave Fugima at five — two hours here with you — and then I catch the convoy on. *Eh bien,* and how is the season going?'

It was ghastly.

The cheery voice, the matter-of-fact

manner, all the pleasant sanity of an everyday world now left far behind. He just bustled in, knowing nothing and noticing nothing — full of cheerful bonhomie.

No wonder Dr Leidner gave an inarticulate gasp and looked in mute appeal at Dr Reilly.

The doctor rose to the occasion.

He took the little man (he was a French archaeologist called Verrier who dug in the Greek islands, I heard later) aside and explained to him what had occurred.

Verrier was horrified. He himself had been staying at an Italian dig right away from civilization for the last few days and had heard nothing.

He was profuse in condolences and apologies, finally striding over to Dr Leidner and clasping him warmly by both hands.

'What a tragedy! My God, what a tragedy! I have no words. *Mon pauvre collègue.*'

And shaking his head in one last ineffectual effort to express his feelings, the little man climbed into his car and left us.

As I say, that momentary introduction of comic relief into tragedy seemed really more gruesome than anything else that had happened.

'The next thing,' said Dr Reilly firmly, 'is breakfast. Yes, I insist. Come, Leidner, you must eat.'

Poor Dr Leidner was almost a complete wreck. He came with us to the dining-room and there a funereal meal was served. I think the hot coffee and fried eggs did us all good, though no one actually felt they wanted to eat. Dr Leidner drank some coffee and sat twiddling his bread. His face was grey, drawn with pain and bewilderment.

After breakfast, Captain Maitland got down to things.

I explained how I had woken up, heard a queer sound and had gone into Miss Johnson's room.

'You say there was a glass on the floor?'

'Yes. She must have dropped it after drinking.'

'Was it broken?'

'No, it had fallen on the rug. (I'm afraid the acid's ruined the rug, by the way.) I picked the glass up and put it back on the table.'

'I'm glad you've told us that. There are only two sets of fingerprints on it, and one set is certainly Miss Johnson's own. The other must be yours.'

He was silent for a moment, then he said: 'Please go on.'

I described carefully what I'd done and the methods I had tried, looking rather anxiously at Dr Reilly for approval. He gave it with a nod.

'You tried everything that could possibly have done any good,' he said. And though I was pretty sure I had done so, it was a relief to have my belief confirmed.

'Did you know exactly what she had taken?' Captain Maitland asked.

'No — but I could see, of course, that it was a corrosive acid.'

Captain Maitland asked gravely: 'Is it your opinion, nurse, that Miss Johnson deliberately administered this stuff to herself?'

'Oh, no,' I exclaimed. 'I never thought of such a thing!'

I don't know why I was so sure. Partly, I think, because of M. Poirot's hints. His 'murder is a habit' had impressed itself on my mind. And then one doesn't readily believe that anyone's going to commit suicide in such a terribly painful way.

I said as much and Captain Maitland nodded thoughtfully. 'I agree that it isn't what one would choose,' he said. 'But if anyone were in great distress of mind and this stuff were easily obtainable it might be taken for that reason.'

'Was she in great distress of mind?' I asked doubtfully.

'Mrs Mercado says so. She says that Miss Johnson was quite unlike herself at dinner last night — that she hardly replied to anything that was said to her. Mrs Mercado is quite sure that Miss Johnson was in terrible distress over something and that the idea of making away with herself had already occurred to her.'

'Well, I don't believe it for a moment,' I said bluntly.

Mrs Mercado indeed! Nasty slinking little cat!

'Then what *do* you think?'

'I think she was murdered,' I said bluntly.

He rapped out his next question sharply. I felt rather that I was in the orderly room.

'Any reasons?'

'It seems to me by far and away the most possible solution.'

'That's just your private opinion. There was no reason why the lady should be murdered?'

'Excuse me,' I said, 'there was. She found out something.'

'Found out something? What did she find out?'

I repeated our conversation on the roof word for word.

'She refused to tell you what her discovery was?'

'Yes. She said she must have time to think it over.'

'But she was very excited by it?'

'Yes.'

'*A way of getting in from outside.*' Captain Maitland puzzled over it, his brows knit. 'Had you no idea at all of what she was driving at?'

'Not in the least. I puzzled and puzzled over it but I couldn't even get a glimmering.'

Captain Maitland said: 'What do you think, M. Poirot?'

Poirot said: 'I think you have there a possible motive.'

'For murder?'

'For murder.'

Captain Maitland frowned.

'She wasn't able to speak before she died?'

'Yes, she just managed to get out two words.'

'What were they?'

'*The window . . .* '

'The window?' repeated Captain Maitland. 'Did you understand to what she was referring?'

I shook my head.

'How many windows were there in her bedroom?'

'Just the one.'

'Giving on the courtyard?'

'Yes.'

'Was it open or shut? Open, I seem to remember. But perhaps one of you opened it?'

'No, it was open all the time. I wondered — '

I stopped.

'Go on, nurse.'

'I examined the window, of course, but I couldn't see anything unusual about it. I wondered whether, perhaps, somebody changed the glasses that way.'

'Changed the glasses?'

'Yes. You see, Miss Johnson always takes a glass of water to bed with her. I think that glass must have been tampered with and a glass of acid put in its place.'

'What do you say, Reilly?'

'If it's murder, that was probably the way it was done,' said Dr Reilly promptly. 'No ordinary moderately observant human being would drink a glass of acid in mistake for one of water — if they were in full possession of their waking faculties. But if anyone's accustomed to drinking off a glass of water in the middle of the night, that person might easily stretch out an arm, find the glass in the accustomed place, and still half asleep, toss off enough of the stuff to be fatal before realizing what had happened.'

Captain Maitland reflected a minute.

'I'll have to go back and look at that window. How far is it from the head of the bed?'

I thought.

'With a very long stretch you could just reach the little table that stands by the head of the bed.'

'The table on which the glass of water was?'

'Yes.'

'Was the door locked?'

'No.'

'So whoever it was could have come in that way and made the substitution?'

'Oh, yes.'

'There would be more risk that way,' said Dr Reilly. 'A person who is sleeping quite soundly will often wake up at the sound of a footfall. If the table could be reached from the window it would be the safer way.'

'I'm not only thinking of the glass,' said Captain Maitland absent-mindedly.

Rousing himself, he addressed me once again.

'It's your opinion that when the poor lady felt she was dying she was anxious to let you know that somebody had substituted acid for water through the open window? Surely the person's *name* would have been more to the point?'

'She mayn't have known the name,' I pointed out.

'Or it would have been more to the point if

she'd managed to hint what it was that she had discovered the day before?'

Dr Reilly said: 'When you're dying, Maitland, you haven't always got a sense of proportion. One particular fact very likely obsesses your mind. That a murderous hand had come through the window may have been the principal fact obsessing her at the minute. It may have seemed to her important that she should let people know that. In my opinion she wasn't far wrong either. It *was* important! She probably jumped to the fact that you'd think it was suicide. If she could have used her tongue freely, she'd probably have said 'It wasn't suicide. I didn't take it myself. Somebody else must have put it near my bed *through the window.*''

Captain Maitland drummed with his fingers for a minute or two without replying. Then he said:

'There are certainly two ways of looking at it. It's either suicide or murder. Which do you think, Dr Leidner?'

Dr Leidner was silent for a minute or two, then he said quietly and decisively: 'Murder. Anne Johnson wasn't the sort of woman to kill herself.'

'No,' allowed Captain Maitland. 'Not in the normal run of things. But there might be circumstances in which it would be quite a

281

natural thing to do.'

'Such as?'

Captain Maitland stooped to a bundle which I had previously noticed him place by the side of his chair. He swung it on to the table with something of an effort.

'There's something here that none of you know about,' he said. 'We found it under her bed.'

He fumbled with the knot of the covering, then threw it back, revealing a heavy great quern or grinder.

That was nothing in itself — there were a dozen or so already found in the course of the excavations.

What riveted our attention on this particular specimen was a dull, dark stain and a fragment of something that looked like hair.

'That'll be your job, Reilly,' said Captain Maitland. 'But I shouldn't say that there's much doubt about this being the instrument with which Mrs Leidner was killed!'

26

Next It Will Be Me!

It was rather horrible. Dr Leidner looked as though he were going to faint and I felt a bit sick myself.

Dr Reilly examined it with professional gusto.

'No fingerprints, I presume?' he threw out.

'No fingerprints.'

Dr Reilly took out a pair of forceps and investigated delicately.

'H'm — a fragment of human tissue — and hair — fair blonde hair. That's the unofficial verdict. Of course, I'll have to make a proper test, blood group, etc., but there's not much doubt. Found under Miss Johnson's bed? Well, well — so *that's* the big idea. She did the murder, and then, God rest her, remorse came to her and she finished herself off. It's a theory — a pretty theory.'

Dr Leidner could only shake his head helplessly.

'Not Anne — not Anne,' he murmured.

'I don't know where she hid this to begin with,' said Captain Maitland. 'Every room was searched after the first crime.'

Something jumped into my mind and I thought, 'In the stationery cupboard,' but I didn't say anything.

'Wherever it was, she became dissatisfied with its hiding-place and took it into her own room, which had been searched with all the rest. Or perhaps she did that after making up her mind to commit suicide.'

'I don't believe it,' I said aloud.

And I couldn't somehow believe that kind nice Miss Johnson had battered out Mrs Leidner's brains. I just couldn't *see* it happening! And yet it *did* fit in with some things — her fit of weeping that night, for instance. After all, I'd said 'remorse' myself — only I'd never thought it was remorse for anything but the smaller, more insignificant crime.

'I don't know what to believe,' said Captain Maitland. 'There's the French Father's disappearance to be cleared up too. My men are out hunting around in case he's been knocked on the head and his body rolled into a convenient irrigation ditch.'

'Oh! I remember now — ' I began.

Everyone looked towards me inquiringly.

'It was yesterday afternoon,' I said. 'He'd been cross-questioning me about the man with a squint who was looking in at the window that day. He asked me just where he'd stood on the path and then he said he was going out to have a look round. He said in detective stories the criminal always dropped a convenient clue.'

'Damned if any of my criminals ever do,' said Captain Maitland. 'So that's what he was after, was it? By Jove, I wonder if he *did* find anything. A bit of a coincidence if both he and Miss Johnson discovered a clue to the identity of the murderer at practically the same time.'

He added irritably, 'Man with a squint? Man with a squint? There's more in this tale of that fellow with a squint than meets the eye. I don't know why the devil my fellows can't lay hold of him!'

'Probably because he hasn't got a squint,' said Poirot quietly.

'Do you mean he faked it? Didn't know you could fake an actual squint.'

Poirot merely said: 'A squint can be a very useful thing.'

'The devil it can! I'd give a lot to know where that fellow is now, squint or no squint!'

'At a guess,' said Poirot, 'he has already passed the Syrian frontier.'

'We've warned Tell Kotchek and Abu Kemal — all the frontier posts, in fact.'

'I should imagine that he took the route

through the hills. The route lorries sometimes take when running contraband.'

Captain Maitland grunted.

'Then we'd better telegraph Deir ez Zor?'

'I did so yesterday — warning them to look out for a car with two men in it whose passports will be in the most impeccable order.'

Captain Maitland favoured him with a stare.

'*You* did, did you? Two men — eh?'

Poirot nodded.

'There are two men in this.'

'It strikes me, M. Poirot, that you've been keeping quite a lot of things up your sleeve.'

Poirot shook his head.

'No,' he said. 'Not really. The truth came to me only this morning when I was watching the sunrise. A very beautiful sunrise.'

I don't think that any of us had noticed that Mrs Mercado was in the room. She must have crept in when we were all taken aback by the production of that horrible great bloodstained stone.

But now, without the least warning, she set up a noise like a pig having its throat cut.

'Oh, my God!' she cried. 'I see it all. I see it all now. *It was Father Lavigny.* He's mad — religious mania. He thinks women are sinful. *He's killing them all.* First Mrs

Leidner — then Miss Johnson. And next it will be *me* . . . '

With a scream of frenzy she flung herself across the room and clutched Dr Reilly's coat.

'I won't stay here, I tell you! I won't stay here a day longer. There's danger. There's danger all round. He's hiding somewhere — waiting his time. He'll spring out on me!'

Her mouth opened and she began screaming again.

I hurried over to Dr Reilly, who had caught her by the wrists. I gave her a sharp slap on each cheek and with Dr Reilly's help I sat her down in a chair.

'Nobody's going to kill you,' I said. 'We'll see to that. Sit down and behave yourself.'

She didn't scream any more. Her mouth closed and she sat looking at me with startled, stupid eyes.

Then there was another interruption. The door opened and Sheila Reilly came in.

Her face was pale and serious. She came straight to Poirot.

'I was at the post office early, M. Poirot,' she said, 'and there was a telegram there for you — so I brought it along.'

'Thank you, mademoiselle.'

He took it from her and tore it open while she watched his face.

It did not change, that face. He read the

telegram, smoothed it out, folded it up neatly and put it in his pocket.

Mrs Mercado was watching him. She said in a choked voice: 'Is that — from America?'

'No, madame,' he said. 'It is from Tunis.'

She stared at him for a moment as though she did not understand, then with a long sigh, she leant back in her seat.

'Father Lavigny,' she said. 'I *was* right. I've always thought there was something queer about him. He said things to me once — I suppose he's mad . . . ' She paused and then said, 'I'll be quiet. But I *must* leave this place. Joseph and I can go in and sleep at the Rest House.'

'Patience, madame,' said Poirot. 'I will explain everything.'

Captain Maitland was looking at him curiously.

'Do you consider you've definitely got the hang of this business?' he demanded.

Poirot bowed.

It was a most theatrical bow. I think it rather annoyed Captain Maitland.

'Well,' he barked. 'Out with it, man.'

But that wasn't the way Hercule Poirot did things. I saw perfectly well that he meant to make a song and dance of it. I wondered if he really *did* know the truth, or if he was just showing off.

He turned to Dr Reilly.

'Will you be so good, Dr Reilly, as to summon the others?'

Dr Reilly jumped up and went off obligingly. In a minute or two the other members of the expedition began to file into the room. First Reiter and Emmott. Then Bill Coleman. Then Richard Carey and finally Mr Mercado.

Poor man, he really looked like death. I suppose he was mortally afraid that he'd get hauled over the coals for carelessness in leaving dangerous chemicals about.

Everyone seated themselves round the table very much as we had done on the day M. Poirot arrived. Both Bill Coleman and David Emmott hesitated before they sat down, glancing towards Sheila Reilly. She had her back to them and was standing looking out of the window.

'Chair, Sheila?' said Bill.

David Emmott said in his low pleasant drawl, 'Won't you sit down?'

She turned then and stood for a minute looking at them. Each was indicating a chair, pushing it forward. I wondered whose chair she would accept.

In the end she accepted neither.

'I'll sit here,' she said brusquely. And she sat down on the edge of a table quite close to the window.

'That is,' she added, 'if Captain Maitland doesn't mind my staying?'

I'm not quite sure what Captain Maitland would have said. Poirot forestalled him.

'Stay by all means, mademoiselle,' he said. 'It is, indeed, necessary that you should.'

She raised her eyebrows.

'Necessary?'

'That is the word I used, mademoiselle. There are some questions I shall have to ask you.'

Again her eyebrows went up but she said nothing further. She turned her face to the window as though determined to ignore what went on in the room behind her.

'And now,' said Captain Maitland, 'perhaps we shall get at the truth!'

He spoke rather impatiently. He was essentially a man of action. At this very moment I felt sure that he was fretting to be out and doing things — directing the search for Father Lavigny's body, or alternatively sending out parties for his capture and arrest.

He looked at Poirot with something akin to dislike.

'If the beggar's got anything to say, why doesn't he say it?'

I could see the words on the tip of his tongue.

Poirot gave a slow appraising glance at us

all, then rose to his feet.

I don't know what I expected him to say — something dramatic certainly. He was that kind of person.

But I certainly didn't expect him to start off with a phrase in Arabic.

Yet that is what happened. He said the words slowly and solemnly — and really quite religiously, if you know what I mean.

'*Bismillahi ar rahman ar rahim.*'

And then he gave the translation in English.

'In the name of Allah, the Merciful, the Compassionate.'

27

Beginning of a Journey

'*Bismillahi ar rahman ar rahim*. That is the Arab phrase used before starting out on a journey. *Eh bien*, we too start on a journey. A journey into the past. A journey into the strange places of the human soul.'

I don't think that up till that moment I'd ever felt any of the so-called 'glamour of the East'. Frankly, what had struck me was the *mess* everywhere. But suddenly, with M. Poirot's words, a queer sort of vision seemed to grow up before my eyes. I thought of words like Samarkand and Ispahan — and of merchants with long beards — and kneeling camels — and staggering porters carrying great bales on their backs held by a rope round the forehead — and women with henna-stained hair and tattooed faces kneeling by the Tigris and washing clothes, and I heard their queer wailing chants and the far-off groaning of the water-wheel.

They were mostly things I'd seen and heard and thought nothing much of. But now, somehow they seemed *different* — like a piece of fusty old stuff you take into the light and suddenly see the rich colours of an old embroidery . . .

Then I looked round the room we were sitting in and I got a queer feeling that what M. Poirot said was true — we *were* all starting on a journey. We were here together now, but we were all going our different ways.

And I looked at everyone as though, in a sort of way, I were seeing them for the first time — *and* for the last time — which sounds stupid, but it was what I felt all the same.

Mr Mercado was twisting his fingers nervously — his queer light eyes with their dilated pupils were staring at Poirot. Mrs Mercado was looking at her husband. She had a strange watchful look like a tigress waiting to spring. Dr Leidner seemed to have shrunk in some curious fashion. This last blow had just crumpled him up. You might almost say he wasn't in the room at all. He was somewhere far away in a place of his own. Mr Coleman was looking straight at Poirot. His mouth was slightly open and his eyes protruded. He looked almost idiotic. Mr Emmott was looking down at his feet and I couldn't see his face properly. Mr Reiter looked bewildered. His mouth was pushed out in a pout and that made him look more like a nice clean pig than ever. Miss Reilly was looking steadily out of the window. I don't know what she was thinking or feeling. Then I looked at Mr Carey, and somehow his face hurt me and I looked away. There we were, all of us. And somehow I felt that when M. Poirot had finished we'd all be somewhere quite different . . .

It was a queer feeling . . .

Poirot's voice went quietly on. It was like a river running evenly between its banks . . . running to the sea . . .

'From the very beginning I have felt that to understand this case one must seek not for external signs or clues, but for the truer clues of the clash of personalities and the secrets of the heart.

'And I may say that though I have now arrived at what I believe to be the true solution of the case, *I have no material proof of it*. I *know* it is so, because it *must* be so, because *in no other way* can every single fact fit into its ordered and recognized place.

'And that, to my mind, is the most satisfying solution there can be.'

He paused and then went on:

'I will start my journey at the moment when I myself was brought into the case — when I had it presented to me as an accomplished happening. Now, every case, in my opinion, has a definite *shape* and *form*.

The pattern of this case, to my mind, all revolved round the personality of Mrs Leidner. Until I knew *exactly what kind of a woman Mrs Leidner was* I should not be able to know why she was murdered and who murdered her.

'That, then, was my starting point — the personality of Mrs Leidner.

'There was also one other psychological point of interest — the curious state of tension described as existing amongst the members of the expedition. This was attested to by several different witnesses — some of them outsiders — and I made a note that although hardly a starting point, it should nevertheless be borne in mind during my investigations.

'The accepted idea seemed to be that it was directly the result of Mrs Leidner's influence on the members of the expedition, but for reasons which I will outline to you later this did not seem to me entirely acceptable.

'To start with, as I say, I concentrated solely and entirely on the personality of Mrs Leidner. I had various means of assessing that personality. There were the reactions she produced in a number of people, all varying widely in character and temperament, and there was what I could glean by my own observation. The scope of the latter was naturally limited. But I *did* learn certain facts.

'Mrs Leidner's tastes were simple and even on the austere side. She was clearly not a luxurious woman. On the other hand, some embroidery she had been doing was of an extreme fineness and beauty. That indicated a woman of fastidious and artistic taste. From the observation of the books in her bedroom I formed a further estimate. She had brains, and I also fancied that she was, essentially, an egoist.

'It had been suggested to me that Mrs Leidner was a woman whose main preoccupation was to attract the opposite sex — that she was, in fact, a sensual woman. This I did not believe to be the case.

'In her bedroom I noticed the following books on a shelf: *Who were the Greeks?*, *Introduction to Relativity*, *Life of Lady Hester Stanhope*, *Back to Methuselah*, *Linda Condon*, *Crewe Train*.

'She had, to begin with, an interest in culture and in modern science — that is, a distinct intellectual side. Of the novels, *Linda Condon*, and in a lesser degree *Crewe Train*, seemed to show that Mrs Leidner had a sympathy and interest in the independent woman — unencumbered or entrapped by man. She was also obviously interested by the personality of Lady Hester Stanhope. *Linda Condon* is an exquisite study of the worship of her own beauty by a woman. *Crewe Train* is a study of a passionate individualist, *Back to Methuselah* is in sympathy with the intellectual rather than the emotional attitude to life. I felt that I was beginning to understand the dead woman.

'I next studied the reactions of those who had formed Mrs Leidner's immediate circle — and my picture of the dead woman grew more and more complete.

'It was quite clear to me from the accounts of Dr Reilly and others that Mrs Leidner was one of those women who are endowed by Nature not only with beauty but with the kind of calamitous magic which sometimes accompanies beauty and can, indeed, exist independently of it. Such women usually leave a trail of violent happenings behind them. They bring disaster — sometimes on others — sometimes on themselves.

'I was convinced that Mrs Leidner was a woman who essentially worshipped *herself* and who enjoyed more than anything else the sense of *power*. Wherever she was, she *must* be the centre of the universe. And everyone round her, man or woman, had got to acknowledge her sway. With some people that was easy. Nurse Leatheran, for instance, a generous-natured woman with a romantic imagination, was captured instantly and gave in ungrudging manner full appreciation. But there was a second way in which Mrs Leidner exercised her sway — the way of fear. Where conquest was too easy she indulged a more cruel side to her nature — but I wish to reiterate emphatically that it was not what you might call *conscious* cruelty. It was as natural and unthinking as is the conduct of a cat with a mouse. Where consciousness came in, she was essentially kind and would often go out of her way to do kind and thoughtful actions for other people.

'Now of course the first and most important problem to solve was the problem of the anonymous letters. Who had written them and why? I asked myself: Had Mrs Leidner written them *herself*?

'To answer this problem it was necessary to go back a long way — to go back, in fact, to the date of Mrs Leidner's first marriage. It is here we start on our journey proper. The journey of Mrs Leidner's life.

'First of all we must realize that the Louise Leidner of all those years ago is essentially the same Louise Leidner of the present time.

'She was young then, of remarkable beauty — that same haunting beauty that affects a

298

man's spirit and senses as no mere material beauty can — and she was already essentially an egoist.

'Such women naturally revolt from the idea of marriage. They may be attracted by men, but they prefer to belong to themselves. They are truly *La Belle Dame sans Merci* of the legend. Nevertheless Mrs Leidner *did* marry — and we can assume, I think, that her husband must have been a man of a certain force of character.

'Then the revelation of his traitorous activities occurs and Mrs Leidner acts in the way she told Nurse Leidner. She gave information to the Government.

'Now I submit that there was a psychological significance in her action. She told Nurse Leatheran that she was a very patriotic idealistic girl and that that feeling was the cause of her action. But it is a well-known fact that we all tend to deceive ourselves as to the motives for our own actions. Instinctively we select the best-sounding motive! Mrs Leidner may have believed herself that it was patriotism that inspired her action, but I believe myself that it was really the outcome of an unacknowledged desire to get rid of her husband! She disliked domination — she disliked the feeling of belonging to someone else — in fact she disliked playing second fiddle. She took a patriotic way of regaining her freedom.

'But underneath her consciousness was a gnawing sense of guilt which was to play its part in her future destiny.

'We now come directly to the question of the letters. Mrs Leidner was highly attractive to the male sex. On several occasions she was attracted by them — but in each case a threatening letter played its part and the affair came to nothing.

'Who wrote those letters? Frederick Bosner or his brother William or *Mrs Leidner herself?*

'There is a perfectly good case for either theory. It seems clear to me that Mrs Leidner was one of those women who do inspire devouring devotions in men, the type of devotion which can become an obsession. I find it quite possible to believe in a Frederick Bosner to whom Louise, his wife, mattered more than anything in the world! She had betrayed him once and he dared not approach her openly, but he was determined at least that she should be his or no one's. He preferred her death to her belonging to another man.

'On the other hand, if Mrs Leidner had, deep down, a dislike of entering into the marriage bond, it is possible that she took this way of extricating herself from difficult positions. She was a huntress who, the prey once attained, had no further use for it! Craving drama in her life, she invented a highly satisfactory drama — a resurrected husband forbidding the banns! It satisfied her deepest instincts. It made her a romantic figure, a tragic heroine, and it enabled her not to marry again.

'This state of affairs continued over a number of years. Every time there was any likelihood of marriage — a threatening letter arrived.

'*But now we come to a really interesting point.* Dr Leidner came upon the scene — and no forbidding letter arrived! Nothing stood in the way of her becoming Mrs Leidner. Not until *after* her marriage did a letter arrive.

'At once we ask ourselves — why?

'Let us take each theory in turn.

. . . '*If* Mrs Leidner wrote the letters herself the problem is easily explained. Mrs Leidner really *wanted* to marry Dr Leidner. And so she *did* marry him. But in that case, *why did she write herself a letter afterwards?* Was her craving for drama too strong to be suppressed? And why only those two letters? After that no other letter was received until a year and a half later.

'Now take the other theory, that the letters were written by her first husband, Frederick Bosner (or his brother). Why did the threatening letter arrive *after* the marriage? Presumably Frederick could not have *wanted* her to marry Leidner. Why, then, did he not stop the marriage? He had done so successfully on former occasions. And why, *having waited till the marriage had taken place*, did he then resume his threats?

'The answer, an unsatisfactory one, is that he was somehow or other unable to protest sooner. He may have been in prison or he may have been abroad.

'There is next the attempted gas poisoning to consider. It seems extremely unlikely that it was brought about by an outside agency. The likely persons to have staged it were Dr and Mrs Leidner themselves. There seems no conceivable reason why *Dr* Leidner should do such a thing, so we are brought to the conclusion that *Mrs* Leidner planned and carried it out herself.

'Why? More drama?

'After that Dr and Mrs Leidner go abroad and for eighteen months they lead a happy, peaceful life with no threats of death to disturb it. They put that down to having successfully covered their traces, but such an explanation is quite absurd. In these days going abroad is quite inadequate for that purpose. And especially was that so in the case of the Leidners. He was the director of a museum expedition. By inquiry at the museum, Frederick Bosner could at once have obtained his correct address. Even granting that he was in too reduced circumstances to pursue the couple himself there would be no bar to his continuing his threatening letters. And it seems to me that a man with his obsession would certainly have done so.

'Instead nothing is heard of him until nearly two years later when the letters are resumed.

'*Why* were the letters resumed?

'A very difficult question — most easily answered by saying that Mrs Leidner was bored and wanted more drama. But I was not quite satisfied with that. This particular form of drama seemed to me a shade too vulgar and too crude to accord well with her fastidious personality.

'The only thing to do was to keep an open mind on the question.

'There were three definite possibilities: (1) the letters were written by Mrs Leidner herself; (2) they were written by Frederick Bosner (or young William Bosner); (3) they might have been written *originally* by either

Mrs Leidner or her first husband, but they were now *forgeries* — that is, they were being written by a *third* person who was aware of the earlier letters.

'I now come to direct consideration of Mrs Leidner's entourage.

'I examined first the actual opportunities that each member of the staff had had for committing the murder.

'Roughly, on the face of it, *anyone* might have committed it (as far as opportunity went), with the exception of three persons.

'Dr Leidner, by overwhelming testimony, had never left the roof. Mr Carey was on duty at the mound. Mr Coleman was in Hassanieh.

'But those alibis, my friends, were not *quite* as good as they looked. I except Dr Leidner's. There is absolutely no doubt that he was on the roof all the time and did not come down until quite an hour and a quarter after the murder had happened.

'But was it *quite* certain that Mr Carey was on the mound all the time?

'And had Mr Coleman *actually been in* Hassanieh at the time the murder took place?'

Bill Coleman reddened, opened his mouth, shut it and looked round uneasily.

Mr Carey's expression did not change.

Poirot went on smoothly.

'I also considered one other person who, I satisfied myself, would be perfectly capable of committing murder *if she felt strongly enough*. Miss Reilly has courage and brains and a certain quality of ruthlessness. When Miss Reilly was speaking to me on the subject of the dead woman, I said to her, jokingly, that I hoped she had an alibi. I think Miss Reilly was conscious then that she had had in her heart the desire, at least, to kill. At any rate she immediately uttered a very silly and purposeless lie. She said she had been playing tennis on that afternoon. The next day I learned from a casual conversation with Miss Johnson that far from playing tennis, Miss Reilly *had actually been near this house at the time of the murder*. It occurred to me that Miss Reilly, if not guilty of the crime, might be able to tell me something useful.'

He stopped and then said quietly: 'Will you tell us, Miss Reilly, what you did *see* that afternoon?'

The girl did not answer at once. She still looked out of the window without turning her head, and when she spoke it was in a detached and measured voice.

'I rode out to the dig after lunch. It must have been about a quarter to two when I got there.'

'Did you find any of your friends on the dig?'

'No, there seemed to be no one there but the Arab foreman.'

'You did not see Mr Carey?'

'No.'

'Curious,' said Poirot. 'No more did M. Verrier when he went there that same afternoon.'

He looked invitingly at Carey, but the latter neither moved nor spoke.

'Have you any explanation, Mr Carey?'

'I went for a walk. There was nothing of interest turning up.'

'In which direction did you go for a walk?'

'Down by the river.'

'Not back towards the house?'

'No.'

'I suppose,' said Miss Reilly, 'that you were waiting for someone who didn't come.'

He looked at her but didn't answer.

Poirot did not press the point. He spoke once more to the girl.

'Did you see anything else, mademoiselle?'

'Yes. I was not far from the expedition house when I noticed the expedition lorry drawn up in a wadi. I thought it was rather queer. Then I saw Mr Coleman. He was walking along with his head down as though he were searching for something.'

'Look here,' burst out Mr Coleman, 'I — '

Poirot stopped him with an authoritative gesture.

'Wait. Did you speak to him, Miss Reilly?'

'No. I didn't.'

'Why?'

The girl said slowly: 'Because, from time to time, he started and looked round with an extraordinary furtive look. It — gave me an unpleasant feeling. I turned my horse's head and rode away. I don't think he saw me. I was not very near and he was absorbed in what he was doing.'

'Look here,' Mr Coleman was not to be hushed any longer. 'I've got a perfectly good explanation for what — I admit — looks a bit fishy. As a matter of fact, the day before I had slipped a jolly fine cylinder seal into my coat pocket instead of putting it in the antika-room — forgot all about it. And then I discovered I'd been and lost it out of my pocket — dropped it somewhere. I didn't want to get into a row about it so I decided I'd have a jolly good search on the quiet. I was pretty sure I'd dropped it on the way to or from the dig. I rushed over my business in Hassanieh. Sent a walad to do some of the shopping and got back early. I stuck the bus where it wouldn't show and had a jolly good hunt for over an hour. And didn't find the damned thing at that! Then I got into the bus and drove on to the house. Naturally, everyone thought I'd just got back.'

'And you did not undeceive them?' asked Poirot sweetly.

'Well, that was pretty natural under the circumstances, don't you think?'

'I hardly agree,' said Poirot.

'Oh, come now — don't go looking for trouble — that's *my* motto! But you can't fasten anything on me. I never went into the courtyard, and you can't find anyone who'll say I did.'

'That, of course, has been the difficulty,' said Poirot. 'The evidence of the servants that *no one entered the courtyard from outside*. But it occurred to me, upon reflection, that that was really *not* what they had said. They had sworn that *no stranger* had entered the premises. They had not been asked *if a member of the expedition* had done so.'

'Well, you ask them,' said Coleman. 'I'll eat my hat if they saw me or Carey either.'

'Ah! but that raises rather an interesting question. They would notice *a stranger* undoubtedly — but would they have even *noticed* a member of the expedition? The members of the staff are passing in and out all day. The servants would hardly notice their going and coming. It is possible, I think, that either Mr Carey or Mr Coleman *might* have entered and the servants' minds would have no remembrance of such an event.'

'Bunkum!' said Mr Coleman.

Poirot went on calmly: 'Of the two, I think Mr Carey was the least likely to be noticed going or coming. Mr Coleman had started to Hassanieh in the car that morning and he would be expected to return in it. His arrival on foot would therefore be noticeable.'

'Of course it would!' said Coleman.

Richard Carey raised his head. His deep-blue eyes looked straight at Poirot.

'Are you accusing me of murder, M. Poirot?' he asked.

His manner was quite quiet but his voice had a dangerous undertone.

Poirot bowed to him.

'As yet I am only taking you all on a journey — my journey towards the truth. I had now established one fact — that all the members of the expedition staff, and also Nurse Leatheran, could in actual *fact* have committed the murder. That there was very little likelihood of some of them having committed it was a secondary matter.

'I had examined *means* and *opportunity*. I next passed to *motive*. I discovered that *one and all of you could be credited with a motive*!'

'Oh! M. Poirot,' I cried. 'Not *me*! Why, I was a stranger. I'd only just come.'

'*Eh bien, ma soeur*, and was not that *just what Mrs Leidner had been fearing*? A stranger from *outside*?'

'But — but — Why, Dr Reilly knew all about me! He suggested my coming!'

'How much did he really know about you? *Mostly what you yourself had told him*. Imposters have passed themselves off as hospital nurses before now.'

'You can write to St. Christopher's,' I began.

'For the moment will you silence yourself. Impossible to proceed while you conduct this argument. I do not say I suspect you *now*. All I say is that, keeping the open mind, you might quite easily be someone other than you pretended to be. There are many successful female impersonators, you know. Young William Bosner might be something of that kind.'

I was about to give him a further piece of my mind. Female impersonator indeed! But he raised his voice and hurried on with such an air of determination that I thought better of it.

'I am going now to be frank — brutally so. It is necessary. I am going to lay bare the underlying structure of this place.'

'I examined and considered every single

soul here. To begin with Dr Leidner, I soon convinced myself that his love for his wife was the mainspring of his existence. He was a man torn and ravaged with grief. Nurse Leatheran I have already mentioned. If she were a female impersonator she was a most amazingly successful one, and I inclined to the belief that she was exactly what she said she was — a thoroughly competent hospital nurse.'

'Thank you for nothing,' I interposed.

'My attention was immediately attracted towards Mr and Mrs Mercado, who were both of them clearly in a state of great agitation and unrest. I considered first Mrs Mercado. Was she capable of murder, and if so for what reasons?

'Mrs Mercado's physique was frail. At first sight it did not seem possible that she could have had the physical strength to strike down a woman like Mrs Leidner with a heavy stone implement. If, however, Mrs Leidner had been on her knees at the time, the thing would at least be *physically possible*. There are ways in which one woman can induce another to go down on her knees. Oh! not emotional ways! For instance, a woman might be turning up the hem of a skirt and ask another woman to put in the pins for her. The second woman would kneel on the ground quite unsuspectingly.

'But the motive? Nurse Leatheran had told me of the angry glances she had seen Mrs Mercado direct at Mrs Leidner. Mr Mercado had evidently succumbed easily to Mrs Leidner's spell. But I did not think the solution was to be found in mere jealousy. I was sure Mrs Leidner was not in the least interested really in Mr Mercado — and doubtless Mrs Mercado was aware of the fact. She might be furious with her for the moment, but for *murder* there would have to be greater provocation. But Mrs Mercado was essentially a fiercely maternal type. From the way she looked at her husband I realized, not only that she loved him, but that she would fight for him tooth and nail — and more than that — *that she envisaged the possibility of having to do so.* She was constantly on her guard and uneasy. The uneasiness was for him — not for herself. And when I studied Mr Mercado I could make a fairly easy guess at what the trouble was. I took means to assure myself of the truth of my guess. Mr Mercado was a drug addict — in an advanced stage of the craving.

'Now I need probably not tell you all that the taking of drugs over a long period has the result of considerably blunting the moral sense.

'Under the influence of drugs a man commits actions that he would not have dreamed of committing a few years earlier before he began the practice. In some cases a man has committed murder — and it has been difficult to say whether he was wholly responsible for his actions or not. The law of different countries varies slightly on that point. The chief characteristic of the drug-fiend criminal is overweening confidence in his own cleverness.

'I thought it possible that there was some discreditable incident, perhaps a criminal incident, in Mr Mercado's past which his wife had somehow or other succeeded in hushing up. Nevertheless his career hung on a thread. If anything of this past incident were bruited about, Mr Mercado would be ruined. His wife was always on the watch. But there was Mrs Leidner to be reckoned with. She had a sharp intelligence and a love of power. She might even induce the wretched man to confide in her. It would just have suited her peculiar temperament to feel she knew a secret which she could reveal at any minute with disastrous effects.

'Here, then, was a possible motive for murder on the part of the Mercados. To protect her mate, Mrs Mercado, I felt sure, would stick at nothing! Both she and her husband had had the opportunity — during that ten minutes when the courtyard was empty.'

Mrs Mercado cried out, 'It's not *true!*'

Poirot paid no attention.

'I next considered Miss Johnson. Was *she* capable of murder?

'I thought she was. She was a person of strong will and iron self-control. Such people are constantly repressing themselves — and one day the dam bursts! But if Miss Johnson had committed the crime it could only be for some reason connected with Dr Leidner. If in any way she felt convinced that Mrs Leidner was spoiling her husband's life, then the deep unacknowledged jealousy far down in her would leap at the chance of a plausible motive and give itself full rein.

'Yes, Miss Johnson was distinctly a possibility.

'Then there were the three young men.

'First Carl Reiter. If, by any chance, one of the expedition staff was William Bosner, then Reiter was by far the most likely person. But if he *was* William Bosner, then he was certainly a most accomplished actor! If he were merely *himself*, had he any reason for murder?

'Regarded from Mrs Leidner's point of view, Carl Reiter was far too easy a victim for good sport. He was prepared to fall on his face and worship immediately. Mrs Leidner despised undiscriminating adoration — and the door-mat attitude nearly always brings out the worst side of a woman. In her treatment of Carl Reiter Mrs Leidner displayed really deliberate cruelty. She inserted a gibe here — a prick there. She made the poor young man's life a hell to him.'

Poirot broke off suddenly and addressed the young man in a personal, highly confidential manner.

'*Mon ami*, let this be a lesson to you. You are a *man*. Behave, then, like a *man*! It is against Nature for a man to grovel. Women and Nature have almost exactly the same reactions! Remember it is better to take the largest plate within reach and fling it at a woman's head than it is to wriggle like a worm whenever she looks at you!'

He dropped his private manner and reverted to his lecture style.

'Could Carl Reiter have been goaded to such a pitch of torment that he turned on his tormentor and killed her? Suffering does queer things to a man. I could not be *sure* that it was *not* so!

'Next William Coleman. His behaviour, as reported by Miss Reilly, is certainly suspicious. If he was the criminal it could only be because his cheerful personality concealed the hidden one of William Bosner. I do not think William Coleman, as William Coleman, has the temperament of a murderer. His faults might lie in another direction. Ah! perhaps Nurse Leatheran can guess what they would be?'

How *did* the man do it? I'm sure I didn't look as though I was thinking anything at all.

'It's nothing really,' I said, hesitating. 'Only if it's to be all truth, Mr Coleman *did* say once himself that he would have made a good forger.'

'A good point,' said Poirot. 'Therefore if he had come across some of the old threatening letters, he could have copied them without difficulty.'

'Oy, oy, oy!' called out Mr Coleman. 'This is what they call a frame-up.'

Poirot swept on.

'As to his being or not being William Bosner, such a matter is difficult of verification. But Mr Coleman has spoken of a *guardian* — not of a father — and there is nothing definitely to veto the idea.'

'Tommyrot,' said Mr Coleman. 'Why all of you listen to this chap beats me.'

'Of the three young men there remains Mr Emmott,' went on Poirot. 'He again might be a possible shield for the identity of William

Bosner. Whatever *personal reasons* he might have for the removal of Mrs Leidner I soon realized that I should have no means of learning them from him. He could keep his own counsel remarkably well, and there was not the least chance of provoking him nor of tricking him into betraying himself on any point. Of all the expedition he seemed to be the best and most dispassionate judge of Mrs Leidner's personality. I think that he always knew her for exactly what she was — but what impression her personality made on him I was unable to discover. I fancy that Mrs Leidner herself must have been provoked and angered by his attitude.

'I may say that of all the expedition, *as far as character and capacity were concerned,* Mr Emmott seemed to me the most fitted to bring a clever and well-timed crime off satisfactorily.'

For the first time, Mr Emmott raised his eyes from the toes of his boots.

'Thank you,' he said.

There seemed to be just a trace of amusement in his voice.

'The last two people on my list were Richard Carey and Father Lavigny.

'According to the testimony of Nurse Leatheran and others, Mr Carey and Mrs Leidner disliked each other. They were both civil with an effort. Another person, Miss Reilly, propounded a totally different theory to account for their attitude of frigid politeness.

'I soon had very little doubt that Miss Reilly's explanation was the correct one. I acquired my certitude by the simple expedient of provoking Mr Carey into reckless and unguarded speech. It was not difficult. As I soon saw, he was in a state of high nervous tension. In fact he was — and is — very near a complete nervous breakdown. A man who is suffering up to the limit of his capacity can seldom put up much of a fight.

'Mr Carey's barriers came down almost immediately. He told me, with a sincerity that I did not for a moment doubt, that he hated Mrs Leidner.

'And he was undoubtedly speaking the truth. He *did* hate Mrs Leidner. But *why* did he hate her?

'I have spoken of women who have a calamitous magic. But men have that magic too. There are men who are able without the least effort to attract women. What they call in these days *le sex appeal*! Mr Carey had this quality very strongly. He was to begin with devoted to his friend and employer, and indifferent to his employer's wife. That did not suit Mrs Leidner. She *must* dominate —

and she set herself out to capture Richard Carey. But here, I believe, something entirely unforeseen took place. She herself for perhaps the first time in her life, fell a victim to an overmastering passion. She fell in love — really in love — with Richard Carey.

'And he — was unable to resist her. Here is the truth of the terrible state of nervous tension that he has been enduring. He has been a man torn by two opposing passions. He loved Louise Leidner — yes, but he also hated her. He hated her for undermining his loyalty to his friend. There is no hatred so great as that of a man who has been made to love a woman against his will.

'I had here all the motive that I needed. I was convinced that *at certain moments* the most natural thing for Richard Carey to do would have been to strike with all the force of his arm at the beautiful face that had cast a spell over him.

'All along I had felt sure that the murder of Louise Leidner was a *crime passionnel*. In Mr Carey I had found an ideal murderer for that type of crime.

'There remains one other candidate for the title of murderer — Father Lavigny. My attention was attracted to the good Father straightaway by a certain discrepancy between his description of the strange man who had been seen peering in at the window and the one given by Nurse Leatheran. In all accounts given by different witnesses there is usually *some* discrepancy, but this was absolutely glaring. Moreover, Father Lavigny insisted on a certain characteristic — a squint — which ought to make identification much easier.

'But very soon it became apparent that *while Nurse Leatheran's description was substantially accurate*, Father Lavigny's was *nothing of the kind*. It looked almost as though Father Lavigny was deliberately misleading us — as though he did *not want the man caught*.

'But in that case *he must know something about this curious person*. He had been seen talking to the man but we had only his word for what they had been talking about.

'What had the Iraqi been doing when Nurse Leatheran and Mrs Leidner saw him? Trying to peer through the window — Mrs Leidner's window, so they thought, but I realized when I went and stood where they had been, that it might equally have been the *antika-room window*.

'The night after that an alarm was given. Someone was in the antika-room. Nothing proved to have been taken, however. The interesting point to me is that when Dr Leidner got there he found *Father Lavigny there before him*. Father Lavigny tells his story of seeing a light. *But again we have only his word for it.*

'I begin to get curious about Father Lavigny. The other day when I make the suggestion that Father Lavigny may be Frederick Bosner, Dr Leidner pooh-poohs the suggestion. He says Father Lavigny is a well-known man. I advance the supposition that Frederick Bosner, who has had nearly twenty years to make a career for himself, under a new name, may very possibly *be* a well-known man by this time! All the same, I do not think that he has spent the intervening time in a religious community. A very much simpler solution presents itself.

'Did anyone at the expedition know Father Lavigny by sight before he came? Apparently not. Why then should not it be *someone impersonating the good Father*? I found out that a telegram had been sent to Carthage on the sudden illness of Dr Byrd, who was to have accompanied the expedition. To intercept a telegram, what could be easier? As to the work, there was no other epigraphist attached to the expedition. With a smattering of knowledge a clever man *might* bluff his way through. There had been very few tablets and inscriptions so far, and already I gathered that Father Lavigny's pronouncements had

321

been felt to be somewhat unusual.

'It looked very much as though Father Lavigny were an *imposter*.

'But was he Frederick Bosner?

'Somehow, affairs did not seem to be shaping themselves that way. The truth seemed likely to lie in quite a different direction.

'I had a lengthy conversation with Father Lavigny. I am a practising Catholic and I know many priests and members of religious communities. Father Lavigny struck me as not ringing quite true to his role. But he struck me, on the other hand, as familiar in quite a different capacity. I *had* met men of his type quite frequently — but they were not members of a religious community. Far from it!

'I began to send off telegrams.

'And then, unwittingly, Nurse Leatheran gave me a valuable clue. We were examining the gold ornaments in the antika-room and she mentioned a trace of wax having been found adhering to a gold cup. Me, I say, 'Wax?' and Father Lavigny, he said 'Wax?' and his tone was enough! I knew in a flash exactly what he was doing here.'

Poirot paused and addressed himself directly to Dr Leidner.

'I regret to tell you, monsieur, that the gold

cup in the antika-room, the gold dagger, the hair ornaments and several other things *are not the genuine articles found by you.* They are very clever electrotypes. Father Lavigny, I have just learned by this last answer to my telegrams, is none other than Raoul Menier, one of the cleverest thieves known to the French police. He specializes in thefts from museums of *objets d'art* and such like. Associated with him is Ali Yusuf, a semi-Turk, who is a first-class working jeweller. Our first knowledge of Menier was when certain objects in the Louvre were found not to be genuine — in every case it was discovered that a distinguished archaeologist *not known previously by sight to the director* had recently had the handling of the spurious articles when paying a visit to the Louvre. On inquiry all these distinguished gentlemen denied having paid a visit to the Louvre at the times stated!

'I have learned that Menier was in Tunis preparing the way for a theft from the Holy Fathers when your telegram arrived. Father Lavigny, who was in ill-health, was forced to refuse, but Menier managed to get hold of the telegram and substitute one of acceptance. He was quite safe in doing so. Even if the monks should read in some paper (in itself an unlikely thing) that Father Lavigny was in Iraq they would only think that the newspapers had got hold of a half-truth as so often happens.

'Menier and his accomplice arrived. The latter is seen when he is reconnoitring the antika-room from outside. The plan is for Father Lavigny to take wax impressions. Ali then makes clever duplicates. There are always certain collectors who are willing to pay a good price for genuine antiques and will ask no embarrassing questions. Father Lavigny will effect the substitution of the fake for the genuine article — preferably at night.

'And that is doubtless what he was doing when Mrs Leidner heard him and gave the alarm. What can he do? He hurriedly makes up a story of having seen a light in the antika-room.

'That 'went down', as you say, very well. But Mrs Leidner was no fool. She may have remembered the trace of wax she had noticed and then put two and two together. And if she did, what will she do then? Would it not be *dans son caractère* to do nothing at once, but enjoy herself by letting hints slip to the discomfiture of Father Lavigny? She will let him see that she suspects — but not that she *knows*. It is, perhaps, a dangerous game, but she enjoys a dangerous game.

'And perhaps she plays that game too long. Father Lavigny sees the truth, and strikes before she realizes what he means to do.

'Father Lavigny is Raoul Menier — a thief. Is he also — a *murderer*?'

Poirot paced the room. He took out a handkerchief, wiped his forehead and went on: 'That was my position this morning. There were eight distinct possibilities and I did not know which of these possibilities was the right one. I still did not know *who was the murderer*.

'But murder is a habit. The man or woman who kills once will kill again.

'And by the second murder, the murderer was delivered into my hands.

'All along it was ever present in the back of my mind that some one of these people might have knowledge that they had kept back — knowledge incriminating the murderer.

'If so, that person would be in danger.

'My solicitude was mainly on account of Nurse Leatheran. She had an energetic personality and a brisk inquisitive mind. I was terrified of her finding out more than it was safe for her to know.

'As you all know, a second murder did take place. But the victim was not Nurse Leatheran — it was Miss Johnson.

'I like to think that I should have reached

the correct solution anyway by pure reasoning, but it is certain that Miss Johnson's murder helped me to it much quicker.

'To begin with, one suspect was eliminated — Miss Johnson herself — for I did not for a moment entertain the theory of suicide.

'Let us examine now the facts of this second murder.

'Fact One: On Sunday evening Nurse Leatheran finds Miss Johnson in tears, and that same evening Miss Johnson burns a fragment of a letter which nurse believes to be in the same handwriting as that of the anonymous letters.

'Fact Two: The evening before her death Miss Johnson is found by Nurse Leatheran standing on the roof in a state that nurse describes as one of incredulous horror. When nurse questions her she says, 'I've seen how someone could come in from outside — and no one would ever guess.' She won't say any more. Father Lavigny is crossing the courtyard and Mr Reiter is at the door of the photographic-room.

'Fact Three: Miss Johnson is found dying. The only words she can manage to articulate are 'the window — the window — '

'Those are the facts, and these are the problems with which we are faced:

'What is the truth of the letters?

'What did Miss Johnson see from the roof?

'What did she mean by 'the window — the window'?

'*Eh bien*, let us take the second problem first as the easiest of solution. I went up with Nurse Leatheran and I stood where Miss Johnson had stood. From there she could see the courtyard and the archway and the north side of the building and two members of the staff. Had her words anything to do with either Mr Reiter or Father Lavigny?

'Almost at once a possible explanation leaped to my brain. If a stranger came in from *outside* he could only do so in *disguise*. And there was only *one* person whose general appearance lent itself to such an impersonation. Father Lavigny! With a sun helmet, sun glasses, black beard and a monk's long woollen robe, a stranger could pass in without the servants *realising* that a stranger had entered.

'Was *that* Miss Johnson's meaning? Or had she gone further? Did she realize that Father Lavigny's whole *personality* was a disguise? That he was someone other than he pretended to be?

'Knowing what I did know about Father Lavigny, I was inclined to call the mystery solved. Raoul Menier was the murderer. He had killed Mrs Leidner to silence her before she could give him away. Now *another person lets him see that she has penetrated his secret*. She, too, must be removed.

'And so everything is explained! The second murder. Father Lavigny's flight — minus robe and beard. (He and his friend are doubtless careering through Syria with excellent passports as two commercial travellers.) His action in placing the blood-stained quern under Miss Johnson's bed.

'As I say, I was almost satisfied — but not quite. For the perfect solution must explain *everything* — and this does not do so.

'It does not explain, for instance, why Miss Johnson should say 'the window', as she was dying. It does not explain her fit of weeping over the letter. It does not explain her mental attitude on the roof — her incredulous horror and her refusal to tell Nurse Leatheran what it was that *she now suspected or knew*.

'It was a solution that fitted the *outer* facts, but it did not satisfy the *psychological* requirements.

'And then, as I stood on the roof, going over in my mind those three points: the letters, the roof, the window, I *saw* — just as Miss Johnson had seen!

'*And this time what I saw explained everything!*'

28

Journey's End

Poirot looked round. Every eye was now fixed upon him. There had been a certain relaxation — a slackening of tension. Now the tension suddenly returned.

There was something coming . . . something . . .

Poirot's voice, quiet and unimpassioned, went on: 'The letters, the roof, 'the window' . . . Yes, everything was explained — everything fell into place.

'I said just now that three men had alibis for the time of the crime. Two of those alibis I have shown to be worthless. I saw now my great — my amazing mistake. The third alibi was worthless too. Not only *could* Dr Leidner have committed the murder — but I was convinced that he *had* committed it.'

There was a silence, a bewildered, uncomprehending silence. Dr Leidner said nothing. He seemed lost in his far-away world still. David Emmott, however, stirred uneasily and spoke.

'I don't know what you mean to imply, M.

Poirot. I told you that Dr Leidner never left the roof until at least a quarter to three. That is the absolute truth. I swear it solemnly. I am not lying. And it would have been quite impossible for him to have done so without my seeing him.'

Poirot nodded.

'Oh, I believe you. *Dr Leidner did not leave the roof.* That is an undisputed fact. But what I saw — and what Miss Johnson had seen — was *that Dr Leidner could murder his wife from the roof without leaving it.*'

We all stared.

'The *window*,' cried Poirot. '*Her* window! That is what I realized — just as Miss Johnson realized it. Her window was directly underneath, on the side away from the courtyard. And Dr Leidner was alone up there with no one to witness his actions. And those heavy stone querns and grinders were up there all ready to his hand. So simple, so very simple, granted one thing — *that the murderer had the opportunity to move the body before anyone else saw it* . . . Oh, it is beautiful — of an unbelievable simplicity!

'Listen — it went like this:

'Dr Leidner is on the roof working with the pottery. He calls you up, Mr Emmott, and while he holds you in talk he notices that, as

330

usually happens, the small boy takes advantage of your absence to leave his work and go outside the courtyard. He keeps you with him ten minutes, then he lets you go and as soon as you are down below shouting to the boy he sets his plan in operation.

'He takes from his pocket the plasticine-smeared mask with which he has already scared his wife on a former occasion and dangles it over the edge of the parapet till it taps on his wife's window.

'That, remember, is the window giving on the countryside facing the opposite direction to the courtyard.

'Mrs Leidner is lying on her bed half asleep. She is peaceful and happy. Suddenly the mask begins tapping on the window and attracts her attention. But it is not dusk now — it is broad daylight — there is nothing terrifying about it. She recognizes it for what it is — a crude form of trickery! She is not frightened but indignant. She does what any other woman would do in her place. Jumps off the bed, opens the window, passes her head through the bars and turns her face upward to see who is playing the trick on her.

'Dr Leidner is waiting. He has in his hands, poised and ready, a heavy quern. At the psychological moment *he drops it* . . .

'With a faint cry (heard by Miss Johnson)

331

Mrs Leidner collapses on the rug underneath the window.

'Now there is a hole in this quern, and through that Dr Leidner had previously passed a cord. He has now only to haul in the cord and bring up the quern. He replaces the latter neatly, bloodstained side down, amongst the other objects of that kind on the roof.

'Then he continues his work for an hour or more till he judges the moment has come for the second act. He descends the stairs, speaks to Mr Emmott and Nurse Leatheran, crosses the courtyard and enters his wife's room. This is the explanation he himself gives of his movements there:

'"*I saw my wife's body in a heap by the bed. For a moment or two I felt paralysed as though I couldn't move. Then at last I went and knelt down by her and lifted up her head. I saw she was dead . . . At last I got up. I felt dazed and as though I were drunk. I managed to get to the door and call out.*'

'A perfectly possible account of the actions of a grief-dazed man. Now listen to what I believe to be the truth. Dr Leidner enters the room, hurries to the window, and, having pulled on a pair of gloves, closes and fastens it, then picks up his wife's body and transports it to a position between the bed and the door. Then he notices a slight stain on the window-side rug. He cannot change it with the other rug, they are a different size, but he does the next best thing. He puts the stained rug in front of the washstand and the rug from the washstand under the window. If the stain is noticed, it will be connected with the *washstand* — not with the *window* — a very important point. There must be no suggestion that the window played any part in the business. Then he comes to the door and acts the part of the overcome husband, and that, I imagine, is not difficult. For he *did* love his wife.'

'My good man,' cried Dr Reilly impatiently, 'if he loved her, why did he kill her? Where's the motive? Can't you speak, Leidner? Tell him he's mad.'

Dr Leidner neither spoke nor moved.

Poirot said: 'Did I not tell you all along that this was a *crime passionnel*? Why did her first husband, Frederick Bosner, threaten to kill her? Because he loved her . . . And in the end, you see, he made his boast good . . .

'*Mais oui — mais oui — once I realize that it is Dr Leidner who did the killing,* everything falls into place . . .

'For the second time, I recommence my journey from the beginning — Mrs Leidner's first marriage — the threatening letters — her second marriage. The letters prevented her marrying any other man — but they did not prevent her marrying Dr Leidner. How simple that is — *if Dr Leidner is actually Frederick Bosner.*

'Once more let us start our journey — from the point of view this time of young Frederick Bosner.

'To begin with, he loves his wife Louise with an overpowering passion such as only a woman of her kind can evoke. She betrays him. He is sentenced to death. He escapes. He is involved in a railway accident but he manages to emerge with a second personality — *that of a young Swedish archaeologist, Eric Leidner*, whose body is badly disfigured and who will be conveniently buried as Frederick Bosner.

'What is the new Eric Leidner's attitude to the woman who was willing to send him to his death? First and most important, *he still loves her*. He sets to work to build up his new life. He is a man of great ability, his profession is congenial to him and he makes a success of it. *But he never forgets the ruling passion of his life*. He keeps himself informed of his wife's movements. Of one thing he is cold-bloodedly determined (remember Mrs Leidner's own description of him to Nurse Leatheran — gentle and kind but ruthless), *she shall belong to no other man*. Whenever he judges it necessary he despatches a letter. He imitates some of the peculiarities of her handwriting in case she should think of taking his letters to the police. Women who write sensational anonymous letters to themselves are such a common phenomenon that the police will be sure to jump to that solution given the likeness of the handwriting. At the same time he leaves her in doubt as to whether he is really alive or not.

'At last, after many years, he judges that the time has arrived; he re-enters her life. All goes well. His wife never dreams of his real identity. He is a well-known man. The upstanding, good-looking young fellow is now a middle-aged man with a beard and stooping shoulders. And so we see history repeating itself. As before, Frederick is able to dominate Louise. For the second time she consents to marry him. *And no letter comes to forbid the banns*.

'But *afterwards* a letter *does* come. Why?

'I think that Dr Leidner was taking no chances. The intimacy of marriage *might* awaken a memory. He wishes to impress on his wife, once and for all, *that Eric Leidner and Frederick Bosner are two different people*. So much so that a threatening letter comes from the former on account of the latter. The rather puerile gas poisoning business follows — arranged by Dr Leidner, of course. Still with the same object in view.

'After that he is satisfied. No more letters need come. They can settle down to happy married life together.

'And then, after nearly two years, *the letters recommence.*

'*Why? Eh bien,* I think I know. *Because the threat underlying the letters was always a genuine threat.* (That is why Mrs Leidner has always been frightened. She *knew* her Frederick's gentle but ruthless nature.) *If she belongs to any other man but him he would kill her. And she has given herself to Richard Carey.*

'And so, having discovered this, cold-bloodedly, calmly, Dr Leidner prepares the scene for murder.

'You see now the important part played by Nurse Leatheran? Dr Leidner's rather curious conduct (it puzzled me at the very first) in securing her services for his wife is explained. It was vital that a reliable professional witness should be able to state incontrovertibly that Mrs Leidner had been dead *over an hour* when her body was found — that is, that she had been killed at a time when *everybody could swear her husband was on the roof.* A suspicion *might* have arisen that he had killed her when he entered the room and found the body — but that was out of the question when a trained hospital nurse would assert positively that she had already been dead an hour.

'Another thing that is explained is the curious state of tension and strain that had come over the expedition this year. I never from the first thought that that could be attributed solely to *Mrs* Leidner's influence. For several years this particular expedition had had a reputation for happy good-fellowship. In my opinion, the state of mind of a community is always directly due to the influence of the man at the top. Dr Leidner, quiet though he was, was a man of great personality. It was due to his tact, to his judgment, to his sympathetic manipulation of human beings that the atmosphere had always been such a happy one.

'If there was a change, therefore, the change must be due to the man at the top — in other words, to Dr Leidner. It was *Dr* Leidner, not Mrs Leidner, who was responsible for the tension and uneasiness. No wonder the staff felt the change without understanding it. The kindly, genial Dr Leidner, outwardly the same, was only playing the part of himself. The real man was an obsessed fanatic plotting to kill.

337

'And now we will pass on to the second murder — that of Miss Johnson. In tidying up Dr Leidner's papers in the office (a job she took on herself unasked, craving for something to do) she must have come on some unfinished draft of one of the anonymous letters.

'It must have been both incomprehensible and extremely upsetting to her! Dr Leidner has been deliberately terrorizing his wife! She cannot understand it — but it upsets her badly. It is in this mood that Nurse Leatheran discovers her crying.

'I do not think at the moment that she suspected Dr Leidner of being the murderer, but my experiments with sounds in Mrs Leidner's and Father Lavigny's rooms are not lost upon her. She realizes that if it *was* Mrs Leidner's cry she heard, *the window in her room must have been open, not shut.* At the moment that conveys nothing vital to her, *but she remembers it.*

'Her mind goes on working — ferreting its way towards the truth. Perhaps she makes some reference to the letters which Dr Leidner understands and his manner changes. She may see that he is, suddenly, afraid.

'But Dr Leidner *cannot* have killed his wife! He was on the *roof* all the time.

'And then, one evening, as she herself is on

the roof puzzling about it, the truth comes to her in a flash. Mrs Leidner has been killed from up *here*, through the open window.

'It was at that minute that Nurse Leatheran found her.

'And immediately, her old affection reasserting itself, she puts up a quick camouflage. Nurse Leatheran must not guess the horrifying discovery she has just made.

'She looks deliberately in the opposite direction (towards the courtyard) and makes a remark suggested to her by Father Lavigny's appearance as he crosses the courtyard.

'She refuses to say more. She has got to 'think things out'.

'And Dr Leidner, who has been watching her anxiously, *realizes that she knows the truth*. She is not the kind of woman to conceal her horror and distress from him.

'It is true that as yet she has not given him away — but how long can he depend upon her?

'Murder is a habit. That night he substitutes a glass of acid for her glass of water. There is just a chance she may be believed to have deliberately poisoned herself. There is even a chance she may be considered to have done the first murder and has now been overcome with remorse. To strengthen the latter idea he takes the quern from the roof and puts it under her bed.

'No wonder that poor Miss Johnson, in her death agony, could only try desperately to impart her hard-won information. Through 'the window,' *that* is how Mrs Leidner was killed, *not* through the door — through the *window* . . .

'And so thus, everything is explained, everything falls into place . . . Psychologically perfect.

'But there is no proof . . . No proof at all . . . '

★   ★   ★

None of us spoke. We were lost in a sea of horror . . . Yes, and not only horror. Pity, too.

Dr Leidner had neither moved nor spoken. He sat just as he had done all along. A tired, worn elderly man.

At last he stirred slightly and looked at Poirot with gentle, tired eyes.

'No,' he said, 'there is no proof. But that does not matter. You knew that I would not deny truth . . . I have never denied truth . . . I think — really — I am rather glad . . . I'm so tired . . . '

Then he said simply: 'I'm sorry about Anne. That was bad — senseless — it wasn't *me!* And she suffered, too, poor soul. Yes, that wasn't me. It was fear . . . '

A little smile just hovered on his pain-twisted lips.

'You would have made a good archaeologist, M. Poirot. You have the gift of re-creating the past.

'It was all very much as you said.

'I loved Louise and I killed her . . . if you'd known Louise you'd have understood . . . No, I think you understand anyway . . . '

29

L'Envoi

There isn't really any more to say about things.

They got 'Father' Lavigny and the other man just as they were going to board a steamer at Beyrouth.

Sheila Reilly married young Emmott. I think that will be good for her. He's no door-mat — he'll keep her in her place. She'd have ridden roughshod over poor Bill Coleman.

I nursed him, by the way, when he had appendicitis a year ago. I got quite fond of him. His people were sending him out to farm in South Africa.

I've never been out East again. It's funny — sometimes I wish I could. I think of the noise the water-wheel made and the women washing, and that queer haughty look that camels give you — and I get quite a homesick feeling. After all, perhaps dirt isn't really so unhealthy as one is brought up to believe!

Dr Reilly usually looks me up when he's in England, and as I said, it's he who's got me into this. 'Take it or leave it,' I said to him. 'I know the grammar's all wrong and it's not properly written or anything like that — but there it is.'

And he took it. Made no bones about it. It will give me a queer feeling if it's ever printed.

M. Poirot went back to Syria and about a week later he went home on the Orient Express and got himself mixed up in another murder. He was clever, I don't deny it, but I shan't forgive him in a hurry for pulling my leg the way he did. Pretending to think I might be mixed up in the crime and not a real hospital nurse at all!

Doctors are like that sometimes. Will have their joke, some of them will, and never think of *your* feelings!

I've thought and thought about Mrs Leidner and what she was really like . . . Sometimes it seems to me she was just a terrible woman — and other times I remember how nice she was to me and how soft her voice was — and her lovely fair hair and everything — and I feel that perhaps, after all, she was more to be pitied than blamed . . .

And I can't help but pity Dr Leidner. I know he was a murderer twice over, but it doesn't seem to make any difference. He was so dreadfully fond of her. It's awful to be fond of anyone like that.

Somehow, the more I get older, and the more I see of people and sadness and illness and everything, the sorrier I get for everyone. Sometimes, I declare, I don't know what's becoming of the good, strict principles my aunt brought me up with. A very religious woman she was, and most particular. There wasn't one of our neighbours whose faults she didn't know backwards and forwards . . .

Oh, dear, it's quite true what Dr Reilly said. How does one stop writing? If I could find a really good telling phrase.

I must ask Dr Reilly for some Arab one.

Like the one M. Poirot used.

In the name of Allah, the Merciful, the Compassionate . . .

Something like that.

We do hope that you have enjoyed reading this large print book.

Did you know that all of our titles are available for purchase?

We publish a wide range of high quality large print books including:
Romances, Mysteries, Classics
General Fiction
Non Fiction and Westerns

Special interest titles available in large print are:
The Little Oxford Dictionary
Music Book
Song Book
Hymn Book
Service Book

Also available from us courtesy of Oxford University Press:
Young Readers' Dictionary
(large print edition)
Young Readers' Thesaurus
(large print edition)

For further information or a free brochure, please contact us at:
Ulverscroft Large Print Books Ltd.,
The Green, Bradgate Road, Anstey,
Leicester, LE7 7FU, England.
Tel: (00 44) 0116 236 4325
Fax: (00 44) 0116 234 0205